The Golden Hour

Chains of Darkness
~Book 1~

C.C. Harwood

The Golden Hour
Chains of Darkness – Book 1

© 2015 by C.C. Harwood

Published by D. Monroe Press
San Jose, CA.

ISBN: 9781310170515
ISBN-13: 978-0692700150

Library of Congress Cataloging-in-Publication Data is on file at the Library of Congress, Washington, DC.

This book is a work of fiction. Names, characters, places, incidents, and dialogues are either products of the author's imagination or used fictitiously. Any similarity to actual people, organizations, and/or events is purely coincidental

Cover Design by Dineen Miller
Editor: Susan Lohrer

D. Monroe Press

DEDICATION

This book is dedicated to my mom. I could never have written this novel without her support, encouragement and guidance.

PROLOGUE

The hazy glow of dawn fought its way into the black void of Jada's mind. She sucked in a deep breath, but choked it back out when freezing, damp air shocked her lungs. Where was she? Leaves rustled above her, dotting the back of her neck with icy water. She lifted her head and pain sliced up her skull. That's when it came back to her. The angry fist striking her in the head. The wire made especially for her, tying her to a tree far from everything and everyone she knew. As she opened her eyes, the unbearable truth hit her; she was going to die.

She twisted her hands, and quickly regretted it. The wire cut into her wrists, and a familiar coppery smell stung her nose. Her warm blood ran down her hands and dripped off her fingertips.

Reluctantly, she looked around, already knowing who was there. The hate in his eyes made her tremble. Did she really deserve to die for what she'd done? A heavy knot burrowed into her stomach as the memories of the past few weeks ran through her mind. Her head started to spin, and her knees jerked into lifeless worms. When her torso flung forward, Jada cried out in agony as another wire caught her flailing body. He stomped over and she gritted her teeth as he tightened the wire, cinching her to the tree. An eerie silence settled in the small clearing around her. The worst of it, she would never see him again. The only guy she had ever loved.

The last thing she heard was the strike of a match, and the crackling of flames at her feet.

CHAPTER 1

Beep! Beep! Beep! Beep! Jada blindly reached toward her nightstand, searching for the source of the invading noise. After tapping the snooze button, she fell back on her pillow, her heavy limbs begging her to stay in bed. She blew out a long breath. Senior year. It had finally come. Apprehension stirred in her belly, and she flipped onto her stomach, covering her head with her comforter. She'd expected high school to get easier as the years passed, but today she felt more nervous than ever. As her thoughts jumped into gear, she groaned, realizing she wouldn't be able to go back to sleep. She rubbed her heavy eyelids and pried them open. The only bright side was that in nine months, she would never have to go back to Union High School again. She stretched her arms over her head, picturing the moment, picturing walking out of her last final. What she would do after high school, she had no idea. During the summer she'd heard her mom say *college* more than once while talking to her friends on the phone. Countless adults had told her that college was different from high school, but she wasn't sure she believed it.

There wasn't a good college in Bishop anyway, and she

could never leave the place where she was born. She had certainly thought about it, but there was something keeping her here. She had felt it since she was a little girl. When she wandered deep in the forest surrounding the city, it was almost as if the trees were calling her. Her friends thought she was crazy, so she had stopped telling them about it years ago.

Forcing in a deep breath, she pushed her feet out into the cold morning air and hoisted herself up to a sitting position. Soft yellow light crept through a crack in her door. She stared at her reflection in her vanity mirror. Yesterday her mom had taken her to the salon to get her hair highlighted for the first time. She finger combed her now chestnut stained brown hair over her shoulders, letting it drape down to her waist. The burnt orange specs scattered in her brown eyes glowed next to the highlights.

She rubbed the goose bumps on her ivory skin, wrapping her fingers almost completely around her slim arm. Would she ever fill out? She had stopped growing at sixteen, and at five foot seven with absolutely no curves, she looked like a stick figure.

"Get up, Jada," she said to herself. Before the alarm could blare again, she switched it off and dragged herself to her vanity, stumbling over piles of clothes and books on the way. With half-open lids, she plopped down in the chair and dabbed on a little foundation and stroked her eyelashes with mascara.

After wiggling into her skinny jeans, favorite black UGGS, and V-neck thermal sweater, she threw a blank notepad and some pens into her backpack and wandered out to the kitchen. When she stepped out of her room, the rich smell of bacon tickled her nose, and her mom's soft humming contrasted with the syncopated sounds of clanking pots.

"Morning, Mom. Breakfast?" Jada raised an eyebrow. "What's the occasion?"

"It's your first day of senior year! I thought I would make you something special." Jada's mom reached to give her a hug. Jada pulled back slightly but then relaxed under her mom's tight grip. She loved her mom, but their relationship was strained. Lilah had a lot of opinions about how Jada should run her life, and sometimes it wore her out.

"That's nice of you Mom, but I don't have much of an appetite."

Lilah turned, her plump lips forming a slight frown. "What's the matter?"

"I didn't sleep much last night." Jada stepped up onto the bar stool at the kitchen island.

"Is something bothering you?"

Jada shrugged. "I guess . . . I'm just not sure what."

The pan full of scrambled eggs popped, drawing back Lilah's attention.

With her chin resting in her palm, Jada examined her mom as she flipped bacon onto a plate. To this day it still surprised her how Lilah was always perfectly put together; she never had a hair out of place or a smudge in her makeup. It almost seemed she woke up that way. She, on the other hand, always had her hair in a ponytail and never wore more than her usual foundation and mascara.

"You'll be fine, sweetie. Here you go. Try and eat a little at least." Lilah smiled as she set the full plate of bacon, eggs, and fried potatoes in front of Jada.

"Thanks. Hopefully this will put a little weight on me."

Lilah chuckled. "Honey, don't worry. You have the rest of your life to gain weight. Besides, I thought it was fashionable to be rail thin?"

"I don't think it looks good."

"Well sweetie before you know it you'll have to watch what you eat. Just appreciate what you have now."

Jada feigned a smile and stuck a small bite of eggs into her mouth.

"Don't look so glum. It's your senior year, and soon you'll be eighteen." Worry lines briefly creased her mom's face, and then they were gone. What now? Jada ignored her and went back to her breakfast. Jada huffed. "Yes, college, I know. *Very* exciting."

Lilah's lips tightened. Jada could tell she was growing weary of her avoiding the subject. In the next few months she was supposed to decide what she wanted to do for the rest of her life. The idea terrified her. She might as well throw a dart at a list of degrees and pick whichever one it landed on.

"Do you have any ideas about what you might want to major in?"

Growing anxious, Jada pushed the food around her plate with her fork. It was way too early in the morning to have this conversation. She wanted to put off this decision as long as possible, but her mom was making that very difficult.

"Well, sweetie, you're going to have to start thinking about it. In order to get into a good school, you'll need to start applying soon."

Jada lost what little appetite she had and forced down the bite of bacon she'd been chewing on. She set her fork down and rubbed her forehead. Lilah gave her a sympathetic smile. "We can talk about it later. I have to go to work. Let me walk you out."

She kissed Jada on the forehead, and they walked outside together. "I hope you have a wonderful first day. I might be a little late tonight. I have to make a delivery to a client at five."

An icy wind greeted them and danced Lilah's blonde hair around her face, making her appear even more angelic. She wrapped her coat tighter and crossed her shivering arms over her chest.

"Okay, Mom." Jada gave her a side hug and hurried to her car. When she grabbed the door handle, shards of ice broke off, dripping freezing water down her fingers. After wiping her hand on her jeans, she turned the defrost on full blast and waited for it to heat up. She let her gaze fall to the snow tipped mountains in her rearview mirror. Bishop was a small town known for its scenery and outdoor activities. It was always packed with tourists from photographers to extreme sports fanatics. The Sierra Mountains protected it from harsh winters, although it didn't feel like it this year. Jada cupped her hands and breathed into them. But she still liked the winter. Something about the fog and gray sky always comforted her. She waved once more to her mom before pulling out of the driveway.

She drove slowly to school, hoping along the way time would somehow stop. For some reason she was dreading this year, but she couldn't figure out why. At a stop sign she idled and let her gaze fall on the green Hwy 395 sign. Her grip stiffened on the wheel, pulling it slightly to the right, where the freeway on-ramp stared back at her. A nervous energy rose from her stomach. What would happen if she just got on the freeway and drove? Drove anywhere but here? Jada stretched her fingers out and looked straight ahead, then right, then straight again. A horn behind her brought her back to her senses. She shook her head. What was she thinking? Even if she wanted to, she could never break the umbilical cord holding her here. That much she knew. Her foot reluctantly pressed down on the pedal, pushing her car forward.

She pulled up to campus ten minutes early, as usual. She was always in a hurry, yet she was never late. *Still a bad judge of time.* Sitting in her car, she looked at the main building, where she had spent the last three years of her life. It looked more like a college than a high school with its Spanish-style stucco walls and brick-red tile roof. Surrounded by trees, it was peaceful and welcoming. But it did nothing for her today—today it felt like a prison. The same faces she had seen since kindergarten made their way up to the main entrance. Jada examined each of them as they laughed and talked about their summers. She knew their names, but didn't really know any of them. In junior high, practically overnight she'd become invisible to boys and girls alike. Even if she sprouted neon pink wings, no one would have noticed. She never did figure out why. In

11

the end, she just accepted it. She knew she would always have her friends, Samantha and Jen, and she had been happy with that.

She willed her hand to reach for the door handle, but it wouldn't budge. What was going on with her today? Pulling the lever on the seat, she pushed it into a reclining position and let out a long sigh. A mixture of emotions stirred in her chest.

For the first time in her life, she wanted to be someone else. She was tired of being ignored. She wanted to be noticed, to be treated like a human being, like she existed. *Even just for one day. Is that too much to ask?*

After rubbing her forehead with what little energy she had, she forced herself out of the car.

The heavy doors clicked closed behind her. She adjusted her backpack, and with her head held high, she joined the flurry of students. She hoped something would be different today, but everything and everybody looked the same. As the familiar faces passed her without so much as a glance in her direction, her usual indifference was replaced by annoyance. She was trying to shake the feeling when the co-captain of the lacrosse team, Derek, bumped into her shoulder. He didn't even slow his hurried pace.

"Hey, watch it!" she yelled after him. He didn't look back and didn't stop until he reached his friends at the end of the hall.

This day is not starting out well.

As she walked into her first class, she caught herself cowering from students passing by and straightened her posture before scanning the room for a familiar face.

In the back row she spotted Samantha talking to two boys sitting on either side of her. Sam waved and pointed at the desk next to her, occupied by one of the guys. As Jada weaved between desks, she noticed that Sam looked better than ever. Somehow she seemed to get prettier every day. She had long natural honey-ash-blonde hair that she curled every morning and vivid green eyes. She was tall like Jada, but curvier, which Jada envied.

When she reached the back of the room, no one made any move to acknowledge her. Sam was telling them about her so-called brush with death over the summer. Jada had heard about it from Jen, her and Sam's other childhood friend, who was with her. They were on their way to L.A. and were hit from behind. According to Jen it was more like a tap, but Sam liked to make it sound like she'd nearly died. Sam was popular, although she didn't hang out with the popular girls. Because their moms were friends, they had grown up together and become inseparable. Jada didn't know what she would do without her and Jen. After a few minutes, Jada crossed her arms over her chest and cleared her throat.

"Oh Jada, sorry." Sam winked at her before turning back to the guys. "Well, I'll have to continue later."

"All right." They groaned and got up and left without a look in Jada's direction. Jada wrapped her backpack around the back of the seat and plopped onto the hard wood. "Your story will be the highlight of week." She lifted a sarcastic smile.

"Well, yeah, I almost died."

Jada couldn't tell if Sam actually believed that or if she

13

was just still caught up in the hype of telling the story.

"What's up with you? You seem a little . . . irritated?" Sam eyed her.

"Sorry. Yeah, something has gotten into me today."

The chatter in the room suddenly died down to a soft murmur. At the front of the room, two unfamiliar guys had just walked in with the teacher, Mrs. Jackson. They had similar features yet one towered over the other.

"Okay, everyone, we have some new students. Please welcome Nathan and Seth Aron," Mrs. Jackson said, pointing at Nathan, the taller one, and then Seth. Nathan didn't look up with the introduction, and Seth perused each student with cool intense eyes.

Under a moss green bomber jacket, Nathan's broad shoulders seemed to fill the entire room. His dark blond hair hung an inch past his ears and a faint layer of stubble covered his jaw. Seth, although significantly shorter, still commanded attention beside his brother. A faded blue shirt clung to his finely sculpted muscles in a blatant display of brawn. He ran his hand through his short, blond highlighted hair and let out an impatient sigh.

Although they were attractive, they didn't seem friendly, and they sure didn't look like they belonged in high school. They thudded into their seats, obviously not happy to be here. Samantha turned to Jada wide-eyed with a devilish grin on her face. *Here we go.* Jada released a soft laugh and shook her head. Sam was definitely boy crazy, although she only stuck to one for a few months until she got bored. Then she was on to the next, leaving a trail of broken hearts in her wake.

Jada leaned back in her chair and gazed at the brothers again. She almost felt bad for them; they had no idea what they were in for. Sam would be busy making them miserable all year.

Mrs. Jackson dove right into her lecture, directing the class to the chapter on the Civil War. Through glassy eyes, Jada watched Mrs. Jackson's wild gestures but mostly tuned her out. She learned better by reading the text book, which she would do later. She looked over at Sam, who was more obvious about not listening, not even looking in Mrs. Jackson's direction. Sam could half listen to the lecture and get straight As, while Jada had to study really hard to get Bs. In freshman year, Sam's teachers noticed that she didn't seem to be listening, so they used to call on her to try to humiliate her. To their dismay, she always knew the answer, so eventually they gave up.

"Does anyone know when the Civil War started?" Mrs. Jackson scanned the room. No one moved.

Apathetically, Seth raised his hand. "1861."

"Correct." Mrs. Jackson smiled.

A pencil clattered to the floor, echoing in the still room. Every student's eyes were on Seth. He seemed annoyed, as though the question was too easy and the answer should be obvious to everyone. The rest of the class passed in the same way. Seth answered nearly every question like he had taken the class a hundred times.

Sam leaned over to Jada and whispered, "Smart and hot."

Jada rolled her eyes.

When class ended, Jada slipped into her backpack and

started to head out, but Sam grabbed her arm, pulling her back. "Let's follow them so we can get a better look!"

Jada didn't even try to hide her annoyed sigh. "Okay, but just for a few minutes."

Sam rubbed her hands together, her eyes wild.

After they'd followed Nathan and Seth for a few minutes, it suddenly dawned on Jada that this was something *she* would do. Watch a guy from a distance. So why was Sam discreetly following them? She was the prettiest girl in school. In less than a week, they would know who she was and would have asked her out. She grumbled to herself, realizing that if Sam was caught following a guy, it would somehow be cute, but if Jada was, it would be pathetic.

"I feel like a creepy stalker," she said.

"Shh. I'm trying to hear what they're saying." Samantha waved her hand dismissively.

Students crowded the halls, darting here and there, some stopping to talk, others hurrying to their next class. Even with Sam's graceful maneuvering, they still couldn't keep up with Nathan's long strides. Ahead Jada could see people parting to let him pass. He hadn't said one word, and he was already a celebrity. Seth was nowhere to be seen, and if Nathan hadn't been so tall, they would have lost sight of him too.

When a clearing appeared, Sam rushed forward, pulling Jada with her. In the sudden confusion, Jada didn't see that Nathan had stopped at his locker. Quick-footed, Sam sidestepped around him, but Jada wasn't so deft, slamming into him at full force.

She fumbled as she tried to untangle herself from his massive arms. "Oh! I'm s-sorry." When she had gained her footing, she cursed Sam under her breath, listening to her giggle behind her. She bent down to pick up the books that Nathan had dropped, but he beat her to it.

"I got it. Are you all right?" His deep voice sent a chill down her body.

"Y-yes." She stood frozen with embarrassment, looking around at the laughing eyes of practically the entire student body. Fidgeting with the hem of her shirt, she tried to think of something clever to say, but nothing came. *Say something! You look stupid.* When the heat reached her face, she'd had enough.

Nathan opened his mouth to speak, but she stormed away before he could get a word out.

"Jada, wait!" Sam ran after her. She clamped onto Jada's arm, but Jada tugged it away. "Hey, what's the big deal?" Sam huffed.

"What's the big deal?" Jada stopped and turned to Samantha. "You just threw me into him!"

"What is your problem today? You have major attitude." Sam fisted her hand on the curve of her hip. They stared at each other for a few seconds before a smile crept up on Sam's face. "C'mon, Jada, that *was* funny!"

"Funny for you!" Jada shot back. "I just bumped into the new guy like an idiot in front of everyone!"

"Hey, you're the one who got to feel his arms! So . . . how were they?"

Looking at Sam's wide grin, Jada couldn't help but let out a small laugh. Sam always had a positive way of looking at any situation, however ridiculous. She pulled her hands through her ponytail and took a few deep breaths, trying to shake off the humiliation.

"They were . . . nice." Jada allowed herself another chuckle as Sam wrapped their arms together and led her to their next class. Sadly, Jada knew that was as close as she'd ever get to Nathan. No doubt he and his brother would ignore her like everyone else. Jada squared her shoulders as she entered the classroom and glanced over the students, some of whom looked up to acknowledge Sam.

What had she done to deserve this? Yes, she wasn't the most beautiful girl in school, but she was funny and smart and pretty. Why had she been labeled a nobody? As she made her way to her seat, determination rose within her. This year would be different. Somehow she would make her senior year different. If only she could stand out somehow, be different from everyone else in this town. That would get people to notice her, to treat her with respect. If only something extraordinary would happen to her.

C.C. Harwood

CHAPTER 2

When her morning classes had ended, Jada lugged herself into the cafeteria, eager to put down her heavy backpack at her, Sam, and Jen's usual table. Leaning back in her chair, Jen cradled her phone, her thumbs tapping rigorously on the screen.

"Hey," Jen said, not looking up. She was shorter with straight auburn hair that rested against her chin. She had flawless honey toned skin courtesy of her Italian father.

Jada twisted her lips into a frown. Hopefully, Jen could tear herself away from texting her boyfriend long enough to give Jada her full attention.

"What did your mom cook for you today?"

Jen's mom, Alex, was a writer at the local news station and had done one too many reports on high school cafeteria food, so she made Jen's lunch every day. Sam and Jada teased her but were secretly jealous because Jen's lunch always looked more appetizing than what they called food in the cafeteria.

"A vegetable stir-fry. Looks good, doesn't it?" Jen lifted her dish so Jada could see. Jada nodded and stood to get her lunch, her appetite waning as she thought about what she would have to eat. In the hot food line, the smell of grease and meat wafted over her, making her nose wrinkle. Reluctantly, she grabbed a chimichanga and headed back.

Holding a mini pizza, Samantha sauntered up to their table.

"Have you heard?" Jen blurted out. "We have two new guys, brothers, I saw them registering in the Administration Office."

Jada scowled at Sam, whose eyes were sparkling with mischief. "Yes, we know about them," Sam replied, taking a bite of her pizza. "They're in our history class."

"And . . ." Jada kicked Sam under the table and folded her arms over her chest.

"And I sort of . . . accidently . . . pushed Jada into the taller one in the hall."

"Are you serious?" Jen lifted her hand to her mouth to hide the smile twitching on the corners of her lips.

"It's fine. Go ahead and laugh. Sam already has." Jada waved her hands in the air in defeat. They looked between one another broke into a chuckle.

"Oh! There they are." Jen signaled with her eyes. Trying to be subtle, Jada and Sam peeked over their shoulders in Nathan and Seth's direction. They were sitting together away from the other students, not talking, focusing on their lunch.

"They seem kinda . . . serious." Jada turned back to their table.

"I know. That's what makes them hot. They are *so* mysterious." Smirking, Sam gazed openly at them.

Slinking back in her chair, Jada lazily scanned the cafeteria. Nearly everyone was looking at Nathan and Seth.

Apparently boys and girls alike were fascinated with the new additions to Union High. When she looked back at them, they were still silently concentrating on their lunches. They didn't seem to notice or care that they were the center of attention.

"What else do you know about them, Jen," Sam asked. "Did they just move here?"

"No, that's the weird part. Apparently they've lived in Bishop all their lives, they've just lived in the mountains and been going to Palisade Glacier High."

"Hmm, I wonder why they changed schools senior year." Jada couldn't think of anything worse. Who would transfer to a school where they didn't know anyone their senior year?

"Who cares? At least we have some excitement around here." Sam wrapped a blonde curl around her finger.

Although Jada agreed this was the most exciting thing that had happened in Bishop lately, having more guys in town didn't hold much interest for her. They wouldn't notice her anyway.

"Okay, on to more important things. Now that we're all here, we can plan Jada's birthday party!" Wide eyed, Sam rubbed her hands together.

Jada's stomach shrank. "What do you mean *party*?"

"I was thinking instead of just the three of us, like we usually do, since it's your eighteenth, we should have a party. I'll plan it,"

"Who would come?" Jada raised a skeptical eyebrow.

Sam shrugged. "I don't know. The senior class?"

Leaning her elbows on the table, Jada looked around the

cafeteria. She had to admit the idea of a party just for her sounded nice. She *had* decided she wanted her senior year to be different. This was her chance.

Behind Sam the double glass doors leading outside flew open, and in walked three players from the lacrosse team. Derek, the one who'd bumped into her earlier, let out a loud laugh as another player whispered something in his ear. Crossing her arms over her chest, she watched them through narrowed eyes until they sat at a table in the far corner. Her palms suddenly got hot. What if her birthday party wasn't any different from school?

"Since your birthday is on Monday, we should have a party on Saturday. My parents are out of town, so we can have it at my house. What do you think?" Sam said.

Jada rubbed her palms on her jeans and looked around at Sam and Jen and the lacrosse team, then let out a quick breath. "Okay. Why not?"

"Yay!" Sam clapped her hands. As they ate their lunches, Sam decided on everything from the decorations to the music list. By the time Jada finished her chimichanga, her heart rate had doubled. Her party was growing into a huge event rather than a small gathering.

As she tossed her napkin onto her empty plate, she saw motion from the corner of her eye. Involuntarily she glanced that way and watched as Nathan and Seth rose from their seats and gathered their things. They spoke quietly without looking at each other while making their way to the exit, still oblivious to the fact that everyone in the cafeteria was staring at them. When they reached the door, she started to turn back toward her table, but Nathan stopped suddenly and turned around. His eyes locked directly on her. She stiffened. But when she met his stare, he quickly averted his face and strode out. Jada tapped her fork on her plate as she stared at the empty doorway. Had Nathan been looking at her or did she imagine it? She turned around to see if anyone was behind her, but the table was empty. Then she remembered. He must have been getting a good look at the clumsy girl who ran into him this morning so that he could avoid her. *That has to be it.* Tuning back into Sam and Jen's conversation, she forced the embarrassing replay out of her head.

"What's your next class?" Sam asked Jada.

"Economics. What about you?"

"Ugh. English. It's too bad we don't have more classes together."

Jada stood and picked up her backpack. "Well, I gotta go. Talk to you later?"

"Yeah," Sam and Jen responded in chorus as the bell rang, ending the lunch period.

Nathan was in her econ class, but he didn't even so much as casually look her way. She avoided looking at him too. After the humiliation of running into him had worn off, she was left with the sensation of his solid arms wrapped around her. It made her stomach feel warm and anxious at the same time.

When her last class ended, she left immediately for home. Five minutes later, she pulled into the empty driveway of her quaint cottage-style house and killed the engine. The weeping willow in the front yard hissed as the leaves glided over the wind. She was born in this house;

she loved the little place. It was the perfect size for her and her mom. She didn't even feel the vestige of her father anymore. Jada's mom never told her why her dad left when she was seven, and frankly, she didn't want to know. He had left, and that was that. Nothing to mourn about. The only time she saw her mom upset about it was the night he left. She went out without saying a word and returned at dawn. Jada was terrified, but when she returned, she just picked up her usual mom duties and never said another word about it. It occurred to Jada how strong her mom really was; becoming an instant single parent must have been really hard.

The clanking of the front door lock echoed in the house, and accompanied by a gust of chilled air and leaves, Jada stepped over the threshold and dropped her heavy backpack on the floor. She stretched and rubbed her aching neck, breathing in the familiar smell of lavender and firewood. The house was dim and quiet. Her mom wouldn't get home from work until 5:30 p.m.

"I should make dinner," she said decisively, flipping on the lights on her way to the kitchen.

Opening the refrigerator, she took inventory. From the far back, she pulled out a pound of ground beef and two artichokes and set them on the kitchen island. In the pantry she found spaghetti sauce and pasta, both on the top shelf. She plopped the two artichokes into a pot of water and set it on the stove on medium high. *That will take about an hour*, she reminded herself as she headed out of the kitchen, mentally calculating when she should return and start the spaghetti.

Back in her room, she collapsed onto her bed, exhausted from her first day of school.

Scattered haphazardly on the ceiling were a few glow-in-the-dark star stickers, remnants of her childhood. The next thirty minutes were a blur as she wavered in and out of sleep. Finally, her mental clock prompted her to wake up. She let out a long breath and propped herself up against the headboard. *Time to start homework.* She kicked off her UGGS and headed back out to the kitchen.

What I wouldn't give for textbooks on e-book. Jada grunted, straining under the weight of her backpack as she heaved it onto the kitchen table. She pulled out *Jazz* by Toni Morrison. English was her favorite subject, so she would start there to ease herself back into the swing of studying. Opening the book, she flipped the pages and buried her nose in the crease. She breathed in the scent and let her eye lids flutter close. The smell of the old library book delighted her senses, seeming to release endorphins in her brain. "So good." She sighed. "Okay, maybe just math and econ on e-book."

Strolling into the living room, she tugged open the hutch drawer where her mom kept all of the bills. She sifted through the stacks of paper until she found what she was looking for. As she pulled the bookmark out, the corner of what looked like an old photo caught her eye. She grabbed it and the bottom tore off. Sucking in air through her teeth, she gently lifted the papers on top of it and slid it out. Holding it on her palm, she stared at a black and white portrait of a young woman with long dark hair. When she met her eyes, a shiver ran through her body. At first the eyes looked sad, but then a wickedness washed over them. The picture suddenly felt alive, and Jada dropped it on the top of the hutch. She went back into the kitchen. Who could that be? And why does mom have her picture in the hutch? She shook her head and picked up *Jazz*, trying to shrug off the foreboding that crawled over her.

Forty-five minutes later, she was lost in *Jazz* when a hissing sound startled her. On the stove, water from the pot of artichokes was jumping everywhere, evaporating into steam as it landed on the orange coils. She leaped up and turned down the heat. Moving to the frying pan, she flipped over a chunk of ground beef. She saw the charred surface and gasped. *Maybe this wasn't such a good idea.* She chuckled under her breath. After getting everything under control, she returned to the kitchen island and looked at the time on the oven before going back to her book. Lilah should be home any minute.

The front door opened and closed. After turning off all the burners, Jada grabbed two potholders and slowly lifted the pot of boiling spaghetti.

Her mom appeared in the entryway of the kitchen as Jada was shaking the pot over the sink, trying to get the last few strands of spaghetti into the strainer.

"That is so sweet of you to make dinner," Lilah cooed, setting her purse and jacket down on the dining room table.

"Yeah, I thought it would be nice." Jada returned the strained noodles to the stove and stepped to the side, motioning for her mom to serve herself. As was customary for them since Jada's father left, they set their plates down to eat at the kitchen island. Jada reached for the artichokes.

"Ouch!" she shrieked, yanking her hand from the steaming pot.

Lilah looked like she was fighting back a grin before she stood and hurried Jada to the sink. "Usually those are hot when you pull them out of boiling water."

"Thanks for the tip," Jada replied dryly, running her hand under the tap. She got a slotted spoon and transferred the artichokes to the plates. "So how was work?"

Lilah ran the only flower shop in town. She'd been a stay-at-home mom until Jada's dad left, and then she was forced to work. Old Mrs. Cushing owned the shop and gave her a job helping customers and running the cash register. Mom learned all she could about the flower business, and when Mrs. Cushing passed away, she left the shop to her. Jada thought in some ways, her mom was much happier working.

"Can never be bad when you're surrounded by flowers all day." Lilah smiled. "How was school?"

"Fine." Jada tore off a leaf of the artichoke dipped it in butter and bit down on the tip. "Sam's planning a birthday party for me at her house. Her parents are out of town."

"That will be fun!"

Jada replied with a weak grin, and then silence settled between them in the faintly lit kitchen.

"That's it?" Lilah brought a forkful of spaghetti to her mouth.

"Yeah."

"What's wrong? You usually have more to say. What about Samantha?"

"Sam's the same as she always is."

"What does that mean? Did you guys have a fight?"

"No. No, Mom. Nothing like that." She shouldn't even bother, and she could tell her mom was about to give up, but it was on the tip of her tongue and it wouldn't go away.

"There are two new guys at school."

"Oh!" Lilah's face lit up. "That's exciting!" Lilah wasn't like most moms; she loved to hear high school gossip and who was dating whom. She set down her fork and faced Jada, her eyes glittering with anticipation. "So, what are they like?"

"They're brothers. One is tall and athletic and the other is a little shorter, but very muscular."

Lilah giggled, making her look like she was Jada's age. "What are their names?"

"Nathan is the taller one, and Seth is the shorter one. Aron, I think, is their last name." Bending down, she scooped a heap of spaghetti into her mouth. In her peripheral vision she saw her mom's body tense. When Jada raised her head, Lilah was as frozen as a statue except for the veins throbbing in her neck. Jada gulped down the spaghetti. "What? What is it? Do you know them?"

Lilah was suddenly a million miles away, a grim expression covering her face. Several seconds passed.

"Mom!" Jada yelled.

"Um." Lilah blinked rapidly. "No. I've never *met* them." Her head sank to her chest and her posture deflated.

"You're acting really weird," Jada said, returning to her dinner. "Anyway, who's that woman in the picture in the hutch? It looks like it's a hundred years old."

"What?" Lilah's head snapped up. She peered around

the corner into the living room and stared at the picture lying on the hutch. When she turned back, her eyes were wide and a hot energy screamed behind them.

Jada slowly scooted away, a prickle of fear stabbing her chest. "Mom, what is wrong with you?"

Lilah locked eyes with her, and the air in the room suddenly felt thin. What looked like heat waves flowed over Lilah's arms. Jada's neck tingled.

Lilah's voice was quiet, almost a whisper. "It's your great-great grandmother."

More seconds passed and Jada's heart thumped wildly in her ears. Lilah finally shook her head, and the tension in room vanished. In a flash, her eyes went back to normal. "Why are you snooping in the hutch?"

Jada threw her hand up. "I didn't realize that's where you kept secret family photos. Jeez."

Lilah opened her mouth, but Jada cut her off. "That photo gives me the creeps. What's wrong with her?"

"Nothing. I mean, stop changing the subject." Lilah snapped. "Back to the Aron boys. I want you to stay away from them."

Jada didn't look at her mom. "Why?"

"Just because."

"Oh, you're going to give me 'because I said so'? That's not fair." Jada threw her fork on her plate, the loud clink magnifying in the stillness of the room. "I'm almost eighteen. Whatever it is, I can handle it. Besides, you just said you didn't know them."

"I didn't say I didn't know them. I said I'd never met them." Lilah sighed and crossed her arms over her chest.

She softened her voice. "I need you to trust me on this one. Just this once, do what I say without asking any questions, okay?"

Jada groaned. "Ugh. Okay, whatever. I don't have any interest in them anyway, so no loss."

"Good." Lilah replied, returning to her spaghetti. But she didn't say another word for the rest of dinner. Jada knew something was seriously wrong. She'd never seen her mom this upset before.

CHAPTER 3

A faint orange light danced under Jada's door. *She must have candles lit. Hopefully she fell asleep.* Lilah tapped on the door. No sound came out. She crept in and inched her way through the darkness, feeling with her toes. Something hard stabbed her foot, and she yelped and fell against the dresser, hopping on one foot. She slapped her hand over her mouth and looked over at her daughter's still form. Luckily, Jada slept like the dead and didn't even flinch. After blowing out the candles, Lilah clicked the door shut and made her way into the kitchen. The glowing red numbers on the stove clock read 10:33 p.m. She took a deep breath and grabbed the portable phone. After robotically dialing the familiar number she leaned against the counter, anxiously counting the rings.

Stephanie's half asleep mumble greeted her.

"Sorry for the late call. I just need to talk to you."

"Sure. What is it?" Stephanie's voice sobered.

"Did Samantha mention that the Aron brothers started Union High today?"

"No. She's been in her room all night."

"It's too much of a coincidence that they transferred a week before Jada turns eighteen." Lilah chewed her bottom lip. "They're planning something."

"You don't think Jada could be . . . ?"

"I don't know Steph. I've been trying not to think about it. Not Jada, not my girl."

"You know it's possible, Lilah. Have you told her yet?"

Lilah rubbed her eyelids, fighting a headache. "No. I'm procrastinating."

"Well, you'd better do it soon. The situation just became dangerous."

"I know. I guess I'm going to have to wait until Sunday. I don't want to do it right before her party."

"Oh, yeah." Stephanie groaned. "Thirty teenagers are going to be in my house on Saturday night. I was trying to forg—"

"What are we going to do about the Arons?" Lilah shouted, pacing the kitchen.

"Nothing yet. Let's wait until Jada's birthday."

Lilah slammed her fist down on the counter, rattling the windows. "I can't believe this is happening!" When she lifted her fist, shards of broken tile crashed to the floor.

"It will be all right." Stephanie's voice was calm, reassuring.

Lilah let out a weary breath. "OK. I'll let you know when I tell her. It will probably be Sunday. I'm sure she'll run and tell Sam and Jen right away."

"Thanks for calling and letting me know."

Lilah hung up the phone and turned on the faucet. Filling her hands with cold water, she doused her face and neck. For eighteen years she'd dreaded this would happen. One day *she'd* be back, and Lilah simply couldn't accept that *she'd* choose Jada.

Nathan grabbed the splintered handrail and heaved himself up from the steep wood steps on the back porch. He stomped up, taking two steps at a time, and pulled open the sliding glass door. Inside, Seth sat on the couch with the lights off. His brother could be so dramatic sometimes. Nathan thought about turning on a lamp, but Seth was enough of a pain when nobody antagonized him.

"What are you doing in the dark?"

"Thinking."

Nathan sighed and sank into a deep leather chair at the other end of the room. "Where's Dad?" He looked at Seth's unmoving profile, barely lit by the light glowing from the kitchen.

"He went to the store. Should be back any moment," he replied, not looking up. A few seconds of tense silence passed. "You could have blown it today."

"What are you talking about?"

"The eldest one noticed when you looked at her, and you were following her around like a dog between classes. You need to be more subtle."

"She didn't see me in the hall."

"Well, she saw you in the cafeteria, and she *could* have seen you in the hall."

"What makes you think they don't already know about us anyway? Maybe their moms told them." Nathan glared at his brother, willing him to meet his eyes.

"Obviously they haven't. The blonde one was smiling and checking us out. Do you really think she'd do that if she knew who we were?" Seth finally looked up, his eyes hard.

Nathan didn't respond. Seth thought that was bad? If he knew about Jada bumping into him at his locker, he'd erupt like a volcano.

Down the hall, the front door slammed open. Moments later, Nathan's dad Holdan burst into the room carrying ten bags of food at once. Nathan didn't bother asking him if he needed help. He always said no, determined to prove he was still as strong as he was when he was Nathan's and Seth's ages.

"What are you guys doing in the dark?" His gruff voice broke through the tension.

"Talking," Seth replied dryly.

"What happened today? Did you get a better look at the girls?" Holdan grabbed a beer from one of the grocery bags, tore off the cap with his bare hands, and emptied the bottle in three gulps. He stood at the edge of the room, scratching his neatly trimmed gray goatee, and eyed them suspiciously.

"Yes." Seth crossed his arms over his chest and scowled at Nathan. "But Nathan watched the older one too much. He could have given us away."

"I didn't give anything away." Nathan's voice took on a sharp edge.

"Now you be careful," Holdan growled. "They're tricky little bitches, and you don't know what they're capable of, 'specially that eldest one."

"Yeah, I know, Dad. I remember Grandpa's prophecy." Nathan stood and headed out of the room, but Holdan blocked him. Nathan kept his head down, refusing to look into his dad's disapproving eyes. The tart smell of beer flowed over him.

"Don't mess this up, Nathan. I mean it."

Nathan's lips formed a tight line. "I know."

"What happened to the counter?" Holding a piece of broken tile, Jada arched one eyebrow at her mom.

"Oh. I, uh, dropped a hammer on it." Lilah furiously scrubbed the dirty dishes from last night's dinner.

"Dropped a hammer on it," Jada repeated, a hint of sarcasm in her voice.

"Yeah, I was hanging a picture, and I dropped the hammer."

Jada looked around. No new pictures adorned the walls, but she decided to let it go. Whatever was going on with her mom since she mentioned Nathan and Seth last night, she didn't have the energy to figure out now.

"If you say so," she replied. But in the back of her mind she wondered what could possibly be so bad about the Aron brothers for her mom to forbid her to be friends with them. She obviously knew something she wasn't telling her.

Jada snuck a peek over her shoulder at the hutch. The picture was gone. That was another thing she didn't have time to figure out. Why had that picture spooked her, and why didn't her mom want to talk about her great-great grandmother? Lilah never told her anything about her family history. It would be nice to know something, anything about where she came from.

Lilah set a plate on the dish rack and turned to face her.

"Are you excited about your birthday party?"

"Yeah, I think so." Jada grabbed the milk from the fridge, and with two hands, tried to maneuver it over her cereal bowl. The large jug wobbled, splashing a little over the edge. She set the milk down with a thud and shoved spoonfuls of cereal into her mouth, keeping her eye on the clock.

"Well, I think it will be fun, and turning eighteen is a big deal."

There is was again, that strained look on Lilah's face when she mentioned Jada's turning eighteen. Maybe she was sad that Jada was growing up and would leave someday? She hurried to finish her cereal.

A deafening motor pulled up to the front of the house and stopped with a loud hiss. Lilah waved to the garbage man through the window as the mechanical arms hoisted the trash bins.

"All right, mom, I gotta go to school." She needed to get out of the house. Lilah's strange mood was stressing her out. Jada set her bowl in the sink and was out the door before her mom could reply.

Glacial air greeted her. She tightened her scarf and blew out a long breath watching it turn into a dancing mist. Beyond the perimeter of the yard, a layer of hovering white fog crept toward her. She hoped it would rain. She loved the way it made the air smell cool and fresh.

After parking her car in the student area of Union High's parking lot, she trudged up to school, rubbing her hands together to stay warm. When she walked into History, two empty chairs stared straight at her. Nathan and Seth weren't there. Making her way to Sam, she sidled between crammed desks and backpacks. Had they gone back to their old high school? Had they switched classes? She shook her head. Why did she care, anyway?

"They aren't here," Sam said sullenly, her chin resting on her hand.

"Who?" Jada feigned ignorance.

"Nathan and Seth. They switched classes."

"Oh, well, they're still at the school, right?" She bit down on her lip, scolding herself for the hope that laced her words.

"Yeah, but this was the only class I had with them. Now I'm going to have to find another way to meet them."

Jada chuckled and turned toward the front. "I'm sure you will find a way."

Sam sat up and grinned. "Yes, a challenge. That is exactly what I need!"

A loud *clunk* drew their attention to the front. Mrs. Jackson had marched in and dumped her briefcase on her desk. "Class, today is going to be a self-study day. Please pull out your books and read chapter one. If you have any questions, I will be at my desk."

Jada could really use this time to read chapter one but knew Sam would want to talk. Before Jada had her book out of her backpack, Sam had already started throwing out ideas about how to meet Nathan. Leaning back in her chair, Jada listened, shaking her head and laughing at Sam's outlandish ideas. She had no fear. After an hour, Sam finally settled on staging her own "bumping" into him, but with less awkwardness and more flair, as she put it.

Thankfully, lunch came quickly, and the cafeteria was serving the only edible meal they provided, a turkey club sandwich. Jada hurried to get in line to beat the crowd. Sandwich and bottled water in hand, she arrived at the table at the same time as Jen. Samantha greeted them with a sassy smile.

"So who do you want to go to homecoming with, Sam?" Jen asked.

"Well, in art today, Jesse told me she overhead Ryan and Andrew from the football team betting which one of them I would say yes to. And I have a feeling that Josh—you know, the captain of the chess club—is going to ask me too. Over the summer I kept running into him "mysteriously," and he always found a way to bring up homecoming every time I saw him. He's kinda cute, in a nerdy sort of way, don't you think?"

"Yeah, he's one of those smart guys that works out too." Jen slurped up her noodle soup.

Sam puckered her lips and glanced over at Nathan and Seth's table. "But, you know, after yesterday I have my sights set on someone new."

Jen laughed. "Well, I'm sure you'll have no trouble."

"Which one?" Jada asked.

"Nathan, definitely. They're both cute, but you know how I like tall guys." Sam cupped her hands together and gazed up at the ceiling. "Just imagine him in a tux and me in a strapless black-and-white baby-doll dress twirling around the dance floor. We'd be the best-looking couple there."

"Wow, you got it all mapped out, and you only met him

yesterday." Jen giggled.

"Saw, not met," Jada corrected.

"Very funny." Sam narrowed her eyes.

"So it sounds like you already have your dress picked out?" Jen asked.

"Not yet. Baby-doll is just my best silhouette, and I want to look *amazing* for homecoming. So when are we going shopping?"

Jada pulled out her phone and pretended to check her text messages. She didn't want to talk about homecoming. For the past three years, Sam and Jen had forced her to go to every dance either with someone who was obviously going with her out of pity or by herself. Frankly, she had had enough. This year she would only go if someone *she* liked asked her. But she couldn't tell Sam and Jen that yet. If she didn't find a date, they would hound her for months to go with one of their charity cases.

"As soon as possible!" Jen cooed. "So all the good dresses aren't taken."

Jen straightened her torso and surveyed the cafeteria. Her eyes stopped on her boyfriend, Logan, and they exchanged an affectionate smile. Jen had been with Logan Masters since sophomore year. He was tall with black hair and equally dark eyes. He was the first to turn eighteen in their group and had already gotten a few tattoos on his forearms. No doubt he would be voted most stylish in their senior class. Today he wore a white collared shirt hanging loosely open at the top, skinny jeans, and some Italian looking black boots. He was a little too thin for Jada, but he had a smile to die for. His dad owned a bar called Rusty's

Saloon, and he let Logan and his friends hang out there before 10:00 p.m. It was the best hangout in town, a pool table for the boys and dancing for the girls.

"Oh, there's Becca. I'm going to go over and see who's in the running for homecoming queen." Sam jumped up and bounced over to the cheerleaders' table.

When Sam left, Jen leaned forward and pulled a necklace out of her shirt. "Look what Logan bought me." It was a white gold heart with white crystals lining the edges. "It's from Swarovski."

"Beautiful. What's the occasion?" Jada welcomed the change of subject.

"No occasion."

The rest of lunch they talked quietly, mostly about Logan. Jen relentlessly declared that he was perfect. He called her every night, and he always remembered her birthday and their anniversary. Like today, he surprised her with little gifts for no reason, and he always told her how pretty she was. Jada thought they did seem happy, but she had a hard time believing he was perfect. No guy was perfect, and more often than not, they let you down.

After gulping down the last bit of her sandwich, Jada left lunch a few minutes early to secure a seat in the back of her econ class. Digging through her purse and dodging other students, she zigzagged toward class. When she found her phone, she clicked the volume button three times until she felt the phone rattle indicating it was on vibrate. She looked up just as she arrived in class. Only two students were there: Eddie Ramirez, a kid who had moved to Bishop a few years ago. He hung out with the lacrosse players. And

Emily Roberts, a Goth girl who was even more ignored than Jada. Brushing past both of them, Jada chose a seat in the far back corner and pulled out her econ book.

Casually, she stretched her neck and looked between her textbook and the students pouring in. This class was going to be hard. She'd have to study a lot. She was reading about opportunity cost when she felt rather than saw Nathan come in the room. His presence was unmistakable: severe and strong. What was it about him? She couldn't help but look up. Somehow, he was even bigger today, like a statue of Thor. He stopped to let other students pass and then gazed around the classroom. Today he seemed to look at every single person but her. Jada was surprised when disappointment pricked at her heart. She shielded her eyes with her hand and buried the feeling. She should be used to being invisible to guys by now. He sat down in the only seat left, two rows in front of her to the right.

Mr. Harris popped in and informed the class he'd be a few minutes late because he had to speak to the principal. The second he disappeared, the class erupted in chatter. Jada didn't know anyone in this class, so she people watched. After she ruled out a few uninteresting conversations, her eyes fell on Nathan. He was looking straight ahead, talking to no one.

On each side of him was a girl coyly trying to get his attention. Pathetic. Jada scoffed. Finally the one on the right got tired of waiting and leaned toward him, blatantly displaying her low-cut tank top. Jada couldn't hear what she said, but it must have been a question because Nathan gave a one-word answer and went right back to looking straight ahead. The girl pouted and opened her econ book in defeat. Jada let out a satisfied giggle. The other one was about to take her turn at Nathan when Mr. Harris burst in mid-sentence.

Jada tried to focus on the lecture, but she kept being drawn to Nathan's broad back and outstretched thigh. It was like he and she were opposite ends of a magnet. Well, for her anyway. What was going on? She hadn't liked anyone in a long time, and she barely knew Nathan. It must be a result of her bumping into him yesterday. She had to admit the brief moment of having his body close to hers had stirred in her feelings she hadn't known she was capable of.

She looked at him again. He was good looking. There was no doubt about it. He was taller than her by more a foot, and when he smiled his top lip curled up slightly. He stretched his neck in a slow circle and Jada watched the way his dirty blond hair grazed his collar. She sat up and shook her head. *What am I doing?* She laughed out loud, drawing a few side glances. *This is like a cheesy romantic comedy.*

She couldn't let his good looks get to her. She'd enjoyed watching him ignore those girls, and that was a bad sign that she was starting to like him. She had to focus.

Maybe he could like her.

She scolded herself immediately. *Don't waste your time. Sam likes him, and what Sam wants, Sam gets. Besides, she's prettier than you.* With difficulty, Jada steered her mind away from Nathan and resolved to stay as far away from him as possible.

CHAPTER 4

After her last class, she walked outside to find Sam and Jen waiting for her at her car.

"Becca said Ella Luna is having a sale on dresses today only!" Sam squealed. "We'd better go now before it gets packed."

"Shotgun," Jen yelled as she skipped around the car.

"Oh, come on. I hate sitting in the back." Sam stomped her foot.

"Too slow." Jen tugged on the handle. "Jada, unlock the door."

Jada took her time finding her keys. She hadn't expected to have to go dress shopping so soon. If no one asked her to homecoming, she wouldn't be going at all. Then what would she do with the dress? Going through the motions, she let a pouty Sam into the back and slid into her seat, contemplating what to do.

As her engine rumbled to life, a spark of excitement ran through her. Maybe it was Sam's and Jen's infectious giggling, or maybe it was because she hadn't bought herself a new dress in a long time. But suddenly, she really wanted to go to homecoming. There has to be one guy in this town she'd want to go with. With a grin twitching the corners of her lips, she pulled her car out of the parking lot.

From school to the dress shop parking lot, Jen and Sam gabbed about the dance without taking a breath. Apparently, the other cheerleaders had told Sam that she and Becca were neck and neck for homecoming queen, which put Sam in an uproar. She simply *had* to win. Even Jada was getting into it, devising plans to get Sam more votes.

Thankfully, word about the sale hadn't spread yet, so the dress shop was empty except for an older lady in a neon-teal dress that was way too tight. She paid for her purchase then hurried past Jada, leaving a trail of cheap perfume in her wake. Like two Tasmanian devils, Sam and Jen tore through the place, grabbing dresses left and right.

Jada shifted her weight and tugged on a stray strand of hair as she scanned the blur of colors and fabrics. The chaos was overwhelming. Turning to the closest rack, she wedged her hand between the tightly packed dresses and pried them open. A pink puffy-sleeved empire gown stared back at her. "Uh . . . no."

A saleslady with beehive hair and coral painted lips approached Jada, cupping her hands together. "Miss, you look like a deer in headlights. Let me help you. How about this one? It's a *big* seller."

With her inch-long red fingernails, she pulled out a yellow mermaid gown with a big bow on the bust.

Is she joking? I'd look like a giant banana in that.

"Uh, n-no thanks. I'm just browsing." Jada took a few steps back. With a look of determination on her face, the lady went around the shop, grabbing more dresses just as ridiculous. Jada rubbed her forehead. This was going to be a long night.

Jen suddenly shrieked so loud, Jada had to cover her ears.

"Logan!" She ran past Jada and jumped up and wrapped her legs around Logan's waist.

Standing next to him were Ryan and Andrew from the football team. "Hey, Sam," they said, two goofy half-grins on their faces.

Sam strode up, shifting the dresses she had grabbed behind her back. "Now what are you guys doing here? It's bad luck to see a girl's dress before homecoming."

Jada was impressed with Sam's seduction skills. She knew the exact way to sway her hips and the perfect decibel to speak in.

They both huffed, apparently tongue-tied.

Smart too. Jada rolled her eyes.

"Sam's right!" Jen slid off of Logan and tapped his chest with her finger. "You can't see my dress. Now get going."

"So, Sam, has anyone asked you to homecoming yet?" Ryan asked.

"Not yet, but I know of a few guys who are going to." Sam's lips formed a pout.

Ryan and Andrew eyed each other. The rivalry was obvious.

"We'll leave you girls to do your shopping." Logan flashed his perfect smile and bent down to give Jen a kiss before dragging a reluctant Ryan and Andrew from the store with him.

"Can't see the dress before homecoming, huh? Are you getting married?" Jada gave Sam a snarky look. Sam puckered her lips at her before returning her attention to the racks of gowns.

Before the saleslady could come back, Jada scurried around and snatched the simplest dresses she could find that were dark colors. She followed Sam and Jen to the dressing room.

"I don't exactly have the right bra and underwear to try on a dress," she yelled over the wall.

"Just go braless," Sam yelled back.

"Easy for you to say. You have a full C cup." Jada begrudgingly stripped to her underwear and slipped on the first dress. The deep indigo blue reminded her of the ocean on a stormy day, and when the cool satin hugged her body as she zipped it up, she shivered. After pressing some wrinkles out of the waist, she slowly raised her eyes to the mirror and let out a quiet whimper. The dress was the most beautiful thing she had ever seen. She turned and swirled, looking at it from every angle. It fit almost perfectly; if only she was a little more filled out. She'd have to get it altered. She rubbed the fabric between her fingers. It felt like a rose petal.

Closing her eyes, she pictured herself walking up to the dance, the dress snug against her skin and fluttering behind her. Sam and Jen were there, smiling and waving at her. A warm feeling filled her chest. She was almost at the door when a hand slid under her elbow. It must be her date. She arched her neck and gazed up at . . . *Luke*.

Noooo!

A squeeze of dread clamped her chest. She fell back on the solid wood seat and cringed as she was plunged back into the eighth grade. She'd had a crush on Luke for months. Then one day Sam had had enough of her incessant talking about him, so she convinced her to ask him out. Jada should've known better than to listen to Sam. She was the prettiest girl in school. Every guy wanted to go out with her. But that was not true for Jada.

The events of that awful day played out in her mind like a horror movie. He was at his locker, talking with a friend. Jada wanted to ask him when he was alone, but Sam insisted she do it right then. She walked up to him and tapped her trembling fingers on his shoulder. When he turned around, his face was friendly, revealing nothing that was to come. After she fumbled out the words, his eyebrows pushed together, forming a deep crease. Then a mocking smirk lit up his face. Moments later, he belted out the most obnoxious laugh Jada had ever heard. The hall became silent, every student looking at her. Her chest felt as if it had caved in, crushing her heart. The skin on her face and neck felt as hot as burning coals. It was worse than being invisible.

Utterly humiliated, Jada ran all the way home and cried herself to sleep. For weeks, he and his friends had made fun of her. After that day, she swore he'd be the last guy she'd ever let herself like.

No one is going to ask you to homecoming. What are you doing here?

A loud rapping at the door brought Jada back to the dressing room.

"Come out. Let's see what you look like," Sam said.

Jada fought back tears as she tore off the dress. "No! I'm not coming out."

"What's the matter?"

Jada didn't answer. She tried to temper the pain that rushed in as she pulled on her clothes and burst out the door and out of the shop. She ignored her friends' concerned calls and kept running until she reached her car. Once inside, she texted Sam that they'd have to find another way home and then took off, her tires screeching in the parking lot.

When she pulled into her driveway, she yanked the e-brake and tore the keys out of the ignition, enveloping herself in darkness. The flowers in her front yard, normally full of life and vibrant, were lifeless and brown, mirroring what she felt inside. A flood of tears erupted, shaking her whole frame. Angrily wiping her wet cheeks on her sleeves, she stomped through the door and headed straight to her room.

"I need to be alone," she said to her mom, who was reading a magazine in the living room. She slammed her door and fell against it before Lilah could reply. Thankfully, she didn't come and check on her. She didn't need anyone else seeing her like this.

Buried in her pillow, she'd finally passed out from exhaustion when her phone sang a familiar tune. She pulled it out of her pocket and hesitated before accepting the call. "Hey, Sam."

"Hey, Jada, are you all right? What happened back there?"

Jada released her hair from the ponytail and fell back on her bed. "I'm all right. I just . . . freaked out, I guess."

"About what?"

Jada didn't want to tell Sam about her flashback. She probably had completely forgotten about the long-ago incident. Even if she remembered, she'd think it was no big deal. She wouldn't understand.

"Are you worried you won't have anyone to go to homecoming with? Because you know I'll find someone."

The anger and pain she'd just buried over the last hour came back with a vengeance. "No," she snapped as she paced her room. "I *don't* want to go with some random guy who is just going with me out of pity."

"Jeez, Jada, calm down. All I've ever tried to do is help you. So . . . *who* are you going to go with?"

The sarcasm in Sam's voice stung like a swarm of bees. Her own best friend didn't believe that anyone would ask her to homecoming.

"I gotta go, Sam," she choked out.

After hanging up her phone, she flipped off her lights and threw herself on the bed. The streetlamp switched on, piercing the darkness with a dingy yellow light. The shadows seemed to be laughing at her, saying what she was already thinking. What if Sam was right?

CHAPTER 5

The next day, Jada told Sam and Jen that she had to work on a project in the library at lunch. The truth was, she didn't want to face more interrogation about who she was going to homecoming with.

Mid-lunch she received a text from Jen to meet her and Sam at Jada's locker because she had some news that couldn't wait until the next day. Jada groaned, closed her book with a thud, and strode out of the library. This had better not be a ploy to introduce her to some guy. Trudging through the empty hall, she turned the corner and saw that Sam and Jen were alone. She breathed a sigh of relief. Sam saw her and waved her over, clearly wanting her to rush. When Jada arrived, Sam blurted out, "Okay I can't wait any longer. What is it?"

"I think Logan is going to ask me to marry him!" Jen squealed and jumped up and down.

"Oh, my god!" Sam grabbed her hands and started jumping with her.

"I know. I can't believe it!" Jen released a set of high-pitched giggles.

"Wait." Jada grabbed their arms. "How do you know?"

"I was at his house last night, and I was using his

computer. In the history I saw that last Friday he searched for 'Tiffany's diamond engagement ring.'" Jen cooed the last line and swayed from side to side.

Jada's jaw dropped. She couldn't hide the disapproval in her face.

Jen's forehead wrinkled. "You don't seem happy for me."

Jada paused, unsure what to say. "I-I guess I'm not, Jen. We are too young to get married." Jada knew that would devastate Jen, but she couldn't be happy for anyone, especially one of her closest friends, getting married at eighteen. Jen's smile died, and her eyes pooled with moisture.

"Jen, I'm sorr—"

"Oh, don't listen to her, she's just negative about relationships. You know that." Sam gave Jada a stern look before wrapping Jen in a hug. Jada let her body fall against her locker, defeated, and half-listened to Sam and Jen gush about dresses and colors and bouquets.

What is she thinking? If she's married at eighteen, she'll be bored by twenty-one.

Jada shook her head. She couldn't listen to this anymore. Lunch was nearly over anyway, so she needed to head to class. She reached to tap on Sam's shoulder to tell her she was going to leave, but her stomach suddenly bubbled with unease, and she stopped. The hair spiked on her arms, neck, then down her back. Someone was watching her. She jerked her head left and right, peeking through and over crowds of people, but saw no one.

Eager to get away, she pulled her econ and English book

from her locker, stuffed them in her backpack, and slung it over her shoulder.

Then she spotted them: two predatory eyes staring straight at her from across the hall. She squinted for a better look, but a janitor blocked her view. Jada huffed. *Great timing.* She shifted her head from side to side trying to see past the janitor until he finally rolled his garbage bin away.

Nathan.

When she met his stare, he broke eye contact and gazed curiously at Sam and then Jen before coming back to her again. He looked like he had the weight of the world on his shoulders.

She felt herself blushing under his stare but couldn't pull herself away. A touch on her arm turned her attention to Sam's wide eyes. "He's looking at you!"

"I know, and I don't know why. Don't make a scene, Sam."

Sam ignored her and twisted her torso toward Nathan, grinning. He turned away and started a heated discussion with Seth, who stood next to him. Then, with a loud *bang*, he slammed his locker and stormed down the hall.

"That was weird." Jen's left eyebrow arched.

Sam laughed. "What did you do to him, Jada?"

"I didn't do anything. I've never even spoken to him."

"If you say so," she replied before turning back to Jen.

Jada stood frozen, feeling like her heart had been sucked into a black hole. It was happening again. Another guy was out to humiliate her. Nathan reminded her a lot of Luke—unnaturally good-looking, pensive, intense. Was he mad about her bumping into him? Did he know her? She was certain she'd never seen him before he started Union High. She would've remembered.

"Jada, hello, Jada?" A faint voice suddenly became loud in her head. She snapped out of her thoughts. "Sorry, were you talking to me?"

"Try not to piss him off, okay? I don't need to start off with him already hating my best friend." Sam crossed her arms over her chest.

Jada nodded, and without saying good-bye, walked off into the bathroom to collect herself. She ran cool water over her hands and dabbed her neck, letting it run down her back. The bell rang, and she groaned under her breath. She grabbed her backpack and headed to class. Her shoes squeaked on the linoleum floor as she walked in.

"Nice of you to grace us with your presence, Miss Bell." Mr. Harris had a flare for mockery.

"Sorry, Mr. Harris. It won't happen again." Jada softened her voice, trying to sound apologetic.

"There is one seat in the back. Take it, please, and pull out your econ book."

Jada made her way to the open seat but jolted to a stop halfway to the back. The only seat left was right next to Thor himself. Her breath caught in her chest, choking her. When he started to lift his head, she sat down quickly, keeping her eyes on her desk. She could feel him glaring at her.

Thankfully, Mr. Harris started talking. "Quiet, everyone, and if you have your books open, turn them to page ten."

Jada felt rather than saw Nathan look away and focus on the board. With trembling fingers, she opened her book as

Mr. Harris started talking about supply and demand. She decided she was going to have to leave lunch a little early so she could get a seat away from Nathan. She had no idea what she could have done to make him mad, and she didn't want to know. Even when he wasn't looking at her, his presence unnerved her. All she could hear was her heartbeat thumping wildly in her ears.

As the minutes passed, Jada's leg jumped faster and faster. Nathan too, kept shifting in his seat.

She was forming an excuse to leave class early when Mr. Harris threw his chalk down and pulled out a stack of papers. "Okay, class, it's time for a pop quiz," he declared as he walked down the first row, passing out the single sheets of paper.

The class groaned. "How can we have a quiz on the third day?" an unidentifiable voice challenged from the other end of the room. Several other students grumbled in agreement.

"The interesting thing about economics is a lot of it is common sense, so I just want you to see what you already know. Don't worry about it. Out of the ten quizzes this year, you can drop one, so if you fail, no harm done."

He set the last sheet of paper face down on Jada's desk. "All right, class, you have ten minutes."

After each student's paper was flipped over with a *swoosh*, the room settled into silence except for the faint ticking of the second hand on the clock.

"Excuse me." A husky voice rose to Jada's ears. It took her a few seconds to realize Nathan was talking to her. "Do you have an extra pen?"

She stared at him for what felt like an hour. He was even more attractive up close. His dark blond hair shimmered a honey color in the sunlight, and his steel-gray eyes were intense yet held a hint of softness.

"It's only the third day of school, and you forgot a pen?" She froze, surprised at how sarcastic she sounded.

He narrowed his eyes, and then his flawless lips slowly curved into a smirk. "Wow, got a live one. Well, shame on me."

A smile tugged on her mouth as she dug in her backpack and pulled out a pen. Maybe he was nice after all. Maybe not all guys were like Luke.

With her eyes fixed on her desk, she handed him the pen. He grabbed it and let his fingers graze hers. She gasped and met his eyes, nervously fidgeting with her hair.

"Thanks." He returned a half-grin that made her stomach flip. Her cheeks suddenly burst with heat, and she turned away.

After forcing two deep breaths, she put her hand next to her eye to block him from her view and tried to focus on the quiz. She had to read the first question three times before she could retain it.

If demand rises for butter, what will that do to the price?

As she read through the questions, she tapped her pencil on the desk. Nathan's touch had put her already frayed nerves on overdrive. She finished just as Mr. Harris put the answers up on an overhead machine and ordered everyone to switch papers with another person. Jada's heart palpated as she felt Nathan's massive frame turn toward her again. "Will you grade mine?"

"Sure." She tried to sound nonchalant and traded her paper with his. Seconds felt like minutes next to him, and she found herself acutely aware of every move and sound he made. His rough voice broke her thoughts and filled her ears again.

"A hundred percent." He sounded surprised.

"You too." She scribbled his grade on the top of his paper.

"Good job." He held her quiz in midair.

She snatched it and started talking a mile a minute. "Yeah, well, my mom majored in econ in college, so I'd better do well." Jada laughed internally at herself. She was supposed to be trying to avoid him, not the other way around. Her mom had warned her to stay away from him, and Sam liked him. But . . . she didn't want to stop talking to him. It felt good.

"That's a good degree. What does she do?" He crossed his foot over his knee and watched her curiously. Whatever was bothering him when he slammed his locker closed a few minutes ago seemed to have disappeared.

"Actually, she just owns a flower shop. She never used her degree. She was a stay home—i-it's a long story." Jada waved her hand dismissively.

Nathan nodded and continued to peruse her.

"Why did you transfer to Union High?" She blurted out abruptly. This wasn't the most graceful conversation she'd ever had.

He chuckled and opened his mouth like he was going to answer, but Mr. Harris started talking again. They didn't speak the rest of the class, and Jada scurried out when the bell rang.

Nathan followed Jada out of class, keeping a safe distance behind her. She was practically running, obviously from him. He could tell he made her uncomfortable. On some level, she probably sensed that he wasn't good news. *Not good.* The thought burned in his stomach like an ulcer. Was he really a bad person? He was only doing what his father had taught him was right. He stretched out his jaw and snuffed the guilty feeling in his gut. As he watched Jada's bouncy pony tail he pictured her soft brown eyes. She seemed. . . innocent and sweet. She looked hurt when he stormed out of the hall earlier, clearly thinking it was directed at her. It wasn't though; it was at Seth. His brother's constant criticism about how he was handling the situation was really starting to annoy him.

Jada turned her head slightly when she pushed open the heavy door to the parking lot. Nathan ducked behind a group of student and pretended to text on his phone. Jada was smart, scoring a hundred on her econ quiz, and feisty too. He liked girls with spirit.

When she was out of his sight, Nathan navigated through the crowd to the door and peeked out. Jada's back was toward him, and she was nervously shifting her backpack. Why wasn't she going to her car? He looked past her and saw that annoying chick, Lori, talking to that Goth girl, Emily, from his econ class. He had already had the unfortunate pleasure of meeting Lori when she shamelessly flirted with him at lunch today. He pushed the door open an inch with his foot.

"What do think you are, a vampire or something?" Lori set her hands on her hips. "You know black lipstick went out like two years ago."

Emily stared up at Lori, her eyes pained and defeated.

"Cat got your tongue?" Lori chuckled.

Suddenly, Jada strode over to them, her gait hesitant yet determined at the same time. "Don't, Lori," she said through pursed lips.

Nathan narrowed his eyes.

Lori scoffed. "And what are you going to do about it?"

Jada glared at Lori for a few seconds before grabbing Emily's arm and pulling her toward the parking lot. Lori laughed again and yelled a few more rude comments before heading to her own car.

After wedging his foot out from the door, Nathan scrubbed the stubble on his chin, confusion now prickling his mind. She wasn't at all what he expected.

Zooming down the neighborhood streets, Jada mumbled under her breath. Lori was such a—. She slammed her hand on the steering wheel. Seeing Lori be mean to Emily had brought to the surfaced a deep-seated anger she had been trying to hide.

One day in seventh grade, Lori had decided she hated Jada. Since that day, every chance Lori got, she'd do everything from making fun of what Jada was wearing to scoffing when she spoke. She was the only person Jada actually wished would ignore her. Poor Emily. She'd looked so hurt.

Jada gazed out the window at the orange and brown trees flying by, trying to think about something else. A picture of Nathan came to her mind. She rubbed her finger. It still tingled where he had touched her. It was going to be harder to avoid him than she thought, and going home to her quiet room was not going to help her get him off her mind. Screeching to a stop, she did a three-way turn and headed back the way she'd come. At this time of day the library would be bustling with kids from all the local schools. The action would distract her, and she could get started on her research project for English.

Walking through the automatic double doors, she let the smell of old books fill her nose. They'd been talking about remodeling the library for years, but Jada secretly hoped they wouldn't. The outdated green-and-brick-red carpet reminded her of when her mom used to bring her here for story time as a kid. The peeling old wood bookcases made her feel as if she were in an old library in Rome.

After setting down her backpack at a table in the corner, she meandered through the aisles. She had a paper due next month on Toni Morrison's *Jazz* and wanted to do some research on jazz music, but she also just liked getting lost among the books.

A few minutes later, she found the music section and pulled out a few books. One was on the history of jazz and one was deconstructing the music itself.

Satisfied, she was about to go back to her table when a familiar voice floated down the aisle. She couldn't quite pinpoint who it was, so she followed it. Against the far back wall, she stopped and peered into a small classroom.

When she saw Seth standing at the front of the room, she gulped and stepped out of view. Her gut told her to leave, but curiosity got the best of her. Holding in her breath, she leaned back toward the open door and watched with one eye.

Seth looked like a completely different person. At school he always looked pissed off and intimidating. Here his face was carefree and even . . . *happy*? Whispers drifted toward her, so she flipped around and leaned against the wall, pretending to read one of her jazz books. Something crunched under her shoulder, and she turned around and found a crumpled sign that read, "Physics tutoring today at 3:30 p.m."

Seth is . . . tutoring physics? Jada didn't think they had physics at Union High. When the coast was clear again, she peeked back in and scanned the students. One of them was wearing a Cerro Community College sweatshirt. Seth was tutoring college students. Who was this guy?

Suddenly, Seth locked eyes with her, and his features contorted. His eyes, which seconds ago had a sparkle in them, seemed to fill with black sludge. She jumped back and ran through the aisles toward her table.

"Slow down, miss!" a librarian hissed.

"Sorry," she shot back and slowed to a fast walk.

So much for killing time at the library. In the checkout line, she kept looking over her shoulder, waiting for Seth to come storming after her. While she felt on edge around Nathan, Seth flat-out scared her. Why, every time he saw her, did he have such hate in his eyes? And why was he in high school if he was teaching college classes? It didn't make any sense. She was starting to think her mom was right. Maybe there was something very, very wrong with the Arons.

CHAPTER 6

The cold air bounced off Jada's face as she pushed open the heavy doors of the girls' locker room leading to the back field. PE was exactly what she needed right now. The last few days had put her in an agitated state. Bloated dark gray clouds loomed over the field. Jada hoped Mr. Jameson wouldn't cancel the class. Nothing sounded better than running in the rain.

She waved at Mr. Jameson before stomping onto the gravel path for a warm-up run. He was short and had a belly that looked bigger every day. His blue polo shirt was so tight that she could see his belly button poking out past his stomach. She wondered why he had become a PE teacher. It looked like he hadn't exercised a day in his life.

With each stride, the fine gravel crunched under her feet, and the blood pumping through her veins burned away her stress. When water drops shot down from the sky, she raised her face and closed her eyes. Cool streams ran down her neck, soaking into her shirt. As the rain melted into the track, the gravel became soft, absorbing her every step. She ran harder, enjoying the sharp smell of freshly cut grass. At the end of the track, she was just starting to feel better when she saw Lori standing next to Mr. Jameson. Her shoulders tensed.

"Everyone, Miss Messing just transferred to our class, so please welcome her." Mr. Jameson didn't look up from his clipboard.

Lori gave Jada a dark look before smiling and waving at the rest of the class. Jada swallowed the lump in her throat and kicked up some loose grass. This was the last thing she needed. She didn't have to energy to deal with Lori's abuse.

Mr. Jameson announced that they would be playing soccer for the next six weeks and assigned teams. Lori was on the opposite team. Good. The farther away she was from her, the better.

With everyone in position, Mr. Jameson blew the whistle. Jada and all the other forwards sprinted to the center of the field. In the mass of people, the ball shot out and landed halfway to her team's goal. Jada huffed and meandered back to her position, never taking her eyes off the ball.

"Hey, stupid, think you can run any slower?" Lori's mocking laugh soared over the field. Jada's jaw stiffened. She knew the comment was for her but refused to acknowledge it. She would never give Lori the satisfaction of knowing she'd hurt her. Lori's team scored, sending Jada's team trudging back to center field. Jada bent down to a lunge position, determined to get the ball this time.

The whistle screeched again. In one swift move, Hailey the center forward on Jada's team, hurled the ball down the field. Jada ran as hard as she could, trying to keep up with her in case she passed her the ball. The closer she got to

Lori, the more the muscles in her chest started to squeeze. When she was a few yards from her, Jada could feel the hate rolling off of her. Despite her better judgment, she glanced up.

"Do you ever brush your hair, Jada?" Lori upturned her lips and looked Jada up and down.

Jada jerked around, feeling her strength starting to wane. *What did I ever do to her?*

Forty-five minutes later, Jada stood in the middle of the field, panting and soaked with sweat, her hands resting on her hips. The game was tied 2–2. It seemed like it would never end.

Then the ball came to her, and she dribbled it toward the goal. A new surge of energy filled her limbs, thrusting her forward. The burning in her lungs no longer mattered. If only she could score on Lori, she'd feel a little better. Sidestepping left and right, she blew past three of the other team's players. A smile rose on Jada's face. She was going to score, and Lori, who was supposed to be playing defense, was nowhere in sight.

She pulled back her foot for the shot. A sharp pain cracked through her shin, followed by a blunt elbow slamming into her side. Her scream was all she heard when as she tumbled to the ground. Hands wrapped around her shin, she rocked back and forth as one by one faces of her team mates appeared above her. Finally, Mr. Jameson came over and cleared the girls away. "Lori, what happened?" He lifted his hands to her.

"I don't know, Mr. Jameson. I was going for the ball, I guess I missed and kicked her shin. I was going so fast and accidentally ran into her."

Mr. Jameson turned back to Jada, and she saw Lori's wide, innocent eyes turn to slits and a satisfied smile creep up her face. Jada closed her eyes and imagined she was somewhere else, anywhere. She couldn't believe Lori had gone this far and physically hurt her. Why was she doing this? Tears burned in her eyes, threatening to spill over. Jada chewed on her lip, willing them away. Another face appeared above her but was quickly washed out by the sun.

"Nathan, grab her other arm, let's get her up."

Nathan. No, what is he doing here? Jada kept her gaze down as they pulled her up. She couldn't bear for him to see her like this.

"Now, Lori," the teacher scolded, "you know that kind of contact isn't allowed."

"I know, Mr. Jameson, but it was an accident."

Jada could hear the mockery in her voice, although everyone else seemed to buy her innocent act.

"Bullshit," Nathan snapped.

Jada's and Lori's mouths dropped.

"Young man, watch your mouth," Mr. Jameson started, but Nathan ignored him and stepped toward Lori.

"I saw you. You knew exactly what you were doing."

Lori's skin flushed, and she started nervously looking around at the other students. Her eyes widened in fake disbelief. "How could you say such a thing?" She offered him her most childlike doe eyes and parted lips. When Lori let her hand fall to her chest and gently graze the top of her breasts, Jada thought he would surely fall for it.

"Apologize," he said through gritted teeth.

"What?" The edge jumped back into her voice.

"You heard me." Nathan's hands formed tight fists.

Lori slowly arched toward Jada and gave an apology laced with sarcasm. Jada turned her head to hide the pain in her eyes.

"All right, everyone, go on to the locker room. Class is ending early." Mr. Jameson's chubby fingers released Jada. "Nathan, can you help Jada to the nurse's office?"

"Yes." Nathan turned to her. "Can you walk?"

Wobbling on one leg, Jada tried to put weight on the one Lori had kicked, but pain seized her muscles. Her mouth opened, but nothing came out. She couldn't believe this was happening right now.

Nathan bent down and slid his arms under her knees to pick her up.

"Oh, no, please don't do that," she pleaded. "I'll walk." As if she weren't suffering enough, he wanted to carry her like a baby in front of the whole class.

Nathan sighed and gently placed his hand on her hip and pulled her against him. He was offering his body as a crutch. With his other hand, he wrapped her arm around his waist.

This isn't much better, she thought as she breathed in his delicious scent. She couldn't tell if the heat soaring through her body was from the pain in her leg or being so close to Nathan. As they made their way to the nurse's office, she felt suddenly grateful that he was here. Having someone to walk with lessened the humiliation, if only a little. He didn't say a word the rest of the way. She was learning that he didn't say much, but when he did speak, people listened.

In her peripheral vision she saw thick veins dancing in his neck. Was he mad at her? He didn't seem happy to be here. And what was he doing outside?

Despite his hard face, when they got to the nurse's office, he gently set her on the chair as if she were made of glass.

The smell of rubbing alcohol and plastic was thick in the air. The nurse, a woman almost as thin as Jada, had platinum-blonde hair wrapped in a tight bun at the back of her neck. Looking at her concerned face, Jada felt guilty for all the times she, Sam, and Jen had made fun of her for all the plastic surgery they suspected she'd had. When she bent down to examine Jada's leg, her stiff face strained to form a sympathetic smile. "Well, it doesn't feel broken, but you'll have a nasty bruise in a few hours. Best to go home and ice it. I'll write you a note."

Nathan's shoulders relaxed and he finally looked at her. He bent down to her level and grazed her shin with his thumb. She flinched, not from the pain, but from the way his touch made her skin prickle. For a brief moment all she could think about was the way her stomach burned when she was around him.

"Don't you have class?" Jada asked while the nurse wrapped her leg in a tight bandage.

"I skipped."

The nurse eyed him, clearly wondering why he was admitting cutting class in front of her. As usual, Nathan couldn't care less. He didn't seem to have much fear of authority. Jada wanted to remind him that the PE field was nowhere near the parking lot, where a normal person would go if he was skipping class, but decided against it. Her leg was throbbing, and she just wanted to get home.

"Mr. Aron, can you take Miss Bell home?" The nurse asked while she washed her hands in the sink.

"No. I can drive," Jada protested.

"Oh, yeah? Let's see you walk." Nathan leaned against the wall and crossed one foot over the other.

Gripping the arms of the chair, she pressed herself up on her feet, determined to prove him wrong. She took a step, but her leg faltered, and she stumbled into him.

"You seem to be falling on me a lot lately. If I didn't know better, I might think you were doing it on purpose." His eyes sparkled with mischief.

Jada knew her face was as red as a tomato. She wanted to pull away from him and run as far away as possible, but she couldn't. Her leg was useless.

"All right, stubborn, let's get you home." He picked her up—again—in one swoop.

"Is this really necessary?"

"No, but it's fun." He grinned.

Jada huffed and crossed her arms over her chest as he carried her out to the parking lot.

After making her give him the keys, he set her in the passenger seat and got in the driver's side of Jada's Honda. Jada stifled a laugh as she watched him adjust the seat. At the farthest setting, his knees were still at his chest. He looked like a giant stuffed in a clown car.

"It's a little cramped." He laughed. It was the first time she had heard him laugh, and it was intoxicating. "Stick shift, huh? I'm impressed."

"Why? Girls can't drive a stick shift?" She raised her left eyebrow.

"Usually not." He chuckled again. "So which direction?"

"Oh." It suddenly dawned on Jada that he was taking her to her house. Lilah's warning about Nathan set her nerves reeling. Jada looked at the time on the dashboard clock. Lilah wouldn't be home at this hour, but she would have to get Nathan to leave as soon as possible, just in case. She pointed in front of them. "Take that left, then go straight."

Five minutes later, they were parked in her driveway, and Nathan was rounding the front of the car to get her. When he reached to lift her up again, she threw up her hand. "No more carrying please."

"Yeah, yeah." He held his hand out, and she reluctantly took it. She did need some help, as much as she didn't want to admit it.

After nudging the front door open with his foot, he helped her waddle to the couch. She scooted up and stretched out her leg. It had already started to get red and puffy under the bandage. It was worse than she thought. She sighed, feeling totally helpless.

Nathan examined her leg, his lips in a deep frown. "I'll go get some ice."

"The kitchen is through that door." She pointed and forced a smile.

Moments after he disappeared, the ice machine rumbled and cracked, and she wondered what on earth she was going to talk to him about. She couldn't think of the last time she'd been alone with a boy, especially one who made her this uncomfortable.

"So that Lori, she's got a real problem." He walked in with a bag of ice wrapped in a dish towel. The couch sank when he plopped next to her, pushing her knee into his. She grimaced and pulled her leg back.

"Sorry." He raised his eyebrows and moved away.

His big hand looked like it could wrap twice around her ankle as he lifted her foot and set in on the coffee table. She held her breath when he set the ice on her shin, wanting to appear strong.

"Yeah, she's hated me for years. No idea why," Jada replied.

"Well, who cares what she thinks? She's nothing."

"Nothing? Are you serious? She's one of the prettiest girls at Union High."

Nathan shrugged. "Doesn't do anything for me. I prefer girls who are more subtle." He locked eyes with her when he said the last words.

Jada felt as if her blood had turned to boiling water. His lips twisted when he noticed her discomfort; he obviously was enjoying it. Luckily he changed the subject. "So isn't your birthday coming up?"

"How did you hear about that? No one knows." Under her breath, she added, "Or cares."

"Oh—" He looked down at the floor and rubbed his forehead where tiny beads of sweat were forming. "Someone mentioned it. I can't remember who."

Jada could tell he was lying. But why would he? She gazed at his face freely now, not holding back. He was by far the most mysterious guy she had ever met. Most days he ignored her, others he looked angry, then today he came to her rescue. She looked at the time again. Despite her mom's warning, which was constantly gnawing on the back of her mind, she wanted to be around him.

"Well, I'd better go. Are you going to be all right?" He stood and looked down at her.

"Yes. And thanks for bringing me home."

"No problem. See you tomorrow," he said and then strode out.

Jada's heart skipped a beat. His statement felt more like a promise than a casual pleasantry. Did he really want to see her tomorrow? Despite her pain and the humiliation of the day, Jada couldn't get the smile off her face. She didn't move from the couch. As the sky turned orange and pink and the icy night air started seeping through the windows, she replayed every touch, every look, every smile he'd given her.

She was so deep in thought that a few hours later when her mom burst in the front door and dropped a heavy box on the floor, the sound made her jump.

Lilah's brows puckered as she knelt at Jada's side. She lifted the bag of now lukewarm water and took in a breath between her teeth. "Honey, what happened to your leg?"

"Oh, it happened in PE. I ran into someone." Over the years, her mom didn't exactly believe her that Lori was so mean to her. She suggested that Jada be extra nice to her, and maybe she'd return the sentiment. In eighth grade, Jada tried that. She and her mom had just gotten back from a vacation in San Diego. While browsing in jewelry shop, Jada saw a teal necklace. She remembered that Lori loved teal, so she bought it for her. At school, when she gave it to her, a look of utter disgust came over Lori's face, and she threw the necklace to the ground, shattering it. So from then on Jada had avoided her as much as possible. Apparently that wasn't enough.

"It'll be fine, Mom." Jada shooed her away. Lilah was a worrier and would make a bigger deal out of it than it was.

After eating dinner, Jada limped to her room and opened her history book at her desk. The ice had numbed the pain, but her skin had turned an angry black and green. It would take weeks to go away. Unable to focus, she lit her candles and stared out her bedroom window. Periodically, headlights flooded her room as cars turned down her street and drove past her house. Lori had kicked her on purpose, and she couldn't do anything about it. Defeat settled into her chest. She took in a deep breath of vanilla, forced Lori out of her thoughts, and started to think about Nathan.

He'd stood up to Lori Messing, one of the most popular girls in school, for her. She still couldn't believe it. No one had ever done anything like that for her. Although her face was sore from smiling earlier, her lips curled up again. Then she remembered his words.

I'll see you tomorrow.

Shit. Shit. What am I doing? Nathan tromped down Jada's driveway and yanked the hood of his sweatshirt over his head. As if that would hide all 6'2" of him if his brother was driving around spying on him. Why had he helped her and taken her all the way home? He shook his head. When he saw Lori kick Jada, rage punched through his veins. Just picturing her smug face made his fists clench again.

He shouldn't have touched her. The heat between them was palpable, and it was still penetrating every cell in his body. When he reached school, he spotted his white pickup and crossed the parking lot. He needed to focus, stick to the plan. As he hurdled himself into his truck, slamming the door behind him, he knew that meant he had to keep his distance from Jada.

The only problem was, that was the last thing he wanted to do.

CHAPTER 7

After throwing her backpack in her trunk, Jada rolled her neck and lugged herself into her Honda. Exhaustion nipped at her from every direction. Her leg felt better this morning, but throbbed now from limping around all day. As Jada expected, Lori wasn't punished for kicking her. And as if things couldn't get any worse, Jada was forced to sit on the sidelines during the soccer game and watch Lori prance around in vainglory. She grumbled and started her car. If this week was a preview of how the rest of her school year was going to turn out, her senior year was going to be the worst yet. She desperately needed a pick-me-up. A splash of sun glinted off her windshield as she made a right turn towards the only place where she could leave the world behind.

Within ten minutes, she recognized the obscure spot on the side of the road where her familiar tire tracks lay encased in dried mud. She must've parked here a hundred times. Allowing her wheels to dip into the worn channels, she pulled to a stop. Outside, she set her foot on the front bumper and unraveled the white bandage around her shin. It would be a short hike to her favorite spot, but to hell with the pain. She needed to clear her head.

A large truck rumbled behind her, and she sandwiched herself against her car to let it pass. Examining her bruise again, she didn't register when the truck turned off the side of the road and parked.

"Are you stranded?"

Jada popped her head up just as Nathan strolled into view. What was *he* doing here? How did he find her? Her heartbeat quickened. "No, actually. I was just about to go for a hike."

He examined her leg as he twirled his keys around his index finger. "Doesn't look much better, sure you're up for it?"

She grimaced once more at the green and brown splotch before rolling her pants back down and lowering her foot. "Probably not, but I need to get out." For a moment, they just stared at each other.

"How'd you know I was here?" she asked.

"I didn't. I was on my way home and saw you. Thought your car might have stalled. So . . . can I come along?"

Jada felt her eyes widen with shock and willed her features to relax. "Uh, sure."

Nathan scanned the jumble of untamed trees surrounding their cars, one eyebrow lifted. "Looks a little sketchy. You aren't going to chop me up or anything, are you?"

Jada laughed, feeling the tension leave her body. "I guess it depends on how you behave."

His lips twisted to the side. "I'll keep that in mind."

She ducked under a wayward branch and led him through a maze of overgrown brush. There wasn't an actual trail, but she didn't hear a peep out of Nathan. A quarter mile later, a wall of densely packed trees stood at attention like British Royal Guards. Jada stopped and fisted her hands on her hips. "It's at the top of this hill."

"What is *it*?" He looked up, squinting against the pale winter sun.

"It's just somewhere I go to be alone. I've never taken anyone there before." She suddenly felt sheepish for admitting that. Maybe he would think this was too personal—or stupid.

Instead, he took a long step up. "Let's go."

He climbed with ease as Jada trailed behind him. She knew he was fit, but he looked like he was breathing effortlessly. When they reached the top, she shed her sweatshirt and tied it around her waist. She felt Nathan watching her and turned to see his gaze inch down her neck to her white tank top and then quickly back up. She felt a pull of desire between them and a warm blush tickled her cheeks. "It's just through there," she choked out. He nodded and stepped ahead of her, clearly trying to hide a grin.

"Wow, I see why you like this spot." Nathan circled the small clearing and scanned the expanse of blue sky. Swelling rain clouds darkened the distant mountains, but vibrant yellows and greens illuminated the valley below. A herd of mule deer meandered across the plain, their small black tails flicking nervously.

Jada lowered herself onto a patch of thinned grass and crossed her legs. She instantly felt better just being up here. She felt safe. Nathan thumped down next to her and rested his forearms on his knees. The hem of his shirt rode up, revealing a deep crescent shaped scar.

"Where'd you get that?" She traced her finger over the raised flesh.

A frown pinched his eyebrows together, and he picked a leaf off his shoe. There it was again, that guarded look in his eyes. He was holding something back.

To her surprise he started talking. "My dad was in the military, and when I turned fifteen and Seth fourteen, he put us through a marine style boot camp." Nathan stretched the skin on his arm until he could see the scar. "I remember that day like it was yesterday. It was like five in the morning. I was exhausted, and I snagged my arm on a barbed wire."

"That seems extreme. What were you supposed to be training for?"

He looked up at her, his steely eyes filled with so much emotion that it startled her. Just this once she wished he would tell her what he was thinking. What was behind the wall he had around him? He offered her a forced smile. "Nothing. I mean, Seth had just started playing football, and I was boxing on the weekends."

She knew that wasn't the truth, or whole truth anyway, but decided to drop it. Boot camps and boxing at fifteen. Who was this guy? A far cry from the skinny boys at school who would flip out if a girl accidentally stepped on their designer shoes.

"Do you miss Palisade High?"

He shook his head. "No. Well, just one thing. My wildlife photography class. It was the only time I had off from sports and my dad's rigorous training."

She couldn't picture him trekking around the outskirts of Bishop, sneaking up on wild animals. He was too . . . conspicuous.

"I ran into this bear once but didn't have my camera with me. I got him on my phone though." He handed her his phone, and she tapped the screen to make it larger. The black bear was on its hind legs staring straight at the camera. Nathan had a good eye. The picture could have been in a magazine.

"You look pretty close to him. Were you scared?"

Nathan took his phone back and stuffed it in his jeans pocket. "Nah. Never been afraid of bears."

Before she could stop herself, the words came rushing out. "Do you have a girlfriend at Palisade?"

His eyes held laughter as he looked at her. "Why do you ask?"

She couldn't tell whether he was mocking her or flirting with her. Her shoulders curled toward her chest, but she pushed them back out and forced confidence in her voice. "Just making conversation."

He let a few seconds pass, and Jada thought her mind was going to implode. Finally, he shook his head. "No girlfriend."

A smile fixed on her face, and she stared toward the horizon.

"Enough about me. Tell me about your family."

Boom! A leap, and Nathan was on his feet. Adrenaline rushed through Jada's veins, and she stumbled up. Nathan's piercing stare darted left, and Jada followed his line of sight. Around a sharp bend, a puff of white smoke rose above the trees and faded into the murky clouds. They had been shot at. In a flash, veins spider-webbed down Nathan's neck, and he pushed her aside. He whirled right, but the bullet hit him, and he slammed to the ground.

"Nathan! Oh my god! Are you all right?" Jada doubled over him, scrubbing her hands over his chest and stomach. Where had he been hit? Smoldering black eyes stared up at her, and his skin looked like it was going to tear over his screaming muscles. He jumped up just as an older man came running into the clearing.

"What the *hell* are you doing? You just shot at us!" Nathan snarled like a bull ready to charge.

Terror glistened in the man's eyes as he shifted his camouflage overalls. "Son, I'm sorry, I was aiming for a deer behind you. I didn't know anyone was up here."

Nathan stomped toward him, and the man toppled backward. "We're five minutes from the road. Isn't it illegal to hunt up here?"

"I—I—." The man flipped off his weathered green hat and swiped the back of his hand over his thinning hairline. "There aren't any trails around here. I didn't think anybody came up here."

"I come up here all the time!" Jada limped to Nathan's side and pulled on his T-shirt. A red streak crept across the outside of his sleeve, and she gasped. "You hit him!"

The man's face whitened, and the shotgun started to shake in his meaty hand. His gaze slid down to Nathan's arm, and he sucked in a raspy breath. "Let me call an ambulance."

"I'm fine," Nathan bellowed. "Just get the hell out of here. Now!"

The man jumped at Nathan's booming voice, then wobbled back into the trees. His mumblings slowly faded as he made his way back to wherever he had come from. Nathan ran his hands through his disheveled hair, clearly still trying to calm himself down.

Jada turned to him. "You're bleeding. Let me take a look."

"No it's fine, really." But she already had his sleeve pulled up, and his arm stretched toward her. There was a shallow indention in the middle of his bicep, then a thin red line curving around his arm. Jada blinked and rubbed her eyes. She must be seeing things. When her vision focused again, the same odd markings stared back at her.

"Looks like it just nicked me." Nathan tugged his sleeve down and took a step away. They were only a few feet apart, but they might as well have been on opposite sides of the world. Jada hugged herself, trying to stifle the ache growing in her chest. Just when she was starting to open up to him, he shut down again.

"Let's get out of here," he said.

As they snaked down the hill, Jada's thoughts roared into overdrive. She had never seen anyone move that fast. And that bullet had hit Nathan square in arm. It should've gone straight through, but it didn't. It curved around him like he was made of metal.

Jada could feel Nathan studying her as she shifted the gearshift into first and steered her Honda back toward school. The passenger seat cranked, and Nathan lounged back, stretching out his massive legs. "I'm sorry about what happened back there. I have a bit of a temper."

A bit of a temper was an understatement. He'd looked like he was about to turn into the Hulk. Nathan's head slumped, and he rubbed his forehead. "I—just couldn't stand it if you got hurt."

A warm sensation threaded through Jada, slowly eliminating away any traces of fear. He was protecting *her*. A surge of emotion bubbled up to her throat. She swallowed hard, trying to force it back down. The last time she'd felt protected was when her dad was still at home. No matter what, she'd always known he wouldn't let anything happen to her. Oh, how she missed that feeling.

When she parked next to Nathan's truck in the now empty lot, he turned toward her. "Where are you going now?"

"Home. It's been a long day."

"Guess our little brush with death didn't help."

She shrugged. "It wasn't your fault."

He nodded and got out of the car. Reluctantly, she backed out of the spot and turned toward the exit. As she navigated the lot, she couldn't stop thinking about Nathan's arm. The only possible explanation was that she was going nuts, because no matter how hard she tried, she couldn't think of one logical reason that bullet didn't rip through his flesh.

CHAPTER 8

Nathan didn't sit next to her in econ class for the rest of the week. She was starting to think he had two personalities, sometimes being friendly and even flirty and other times cold and distant.

Lunch was tense because of Jada's disapproval of Jen getting married. Jen talked to her, but she couldn't hide the irritation in her tone. She wasn't her usual bubbly self.

On Friday when class ended, she felt relief but also a sliver of sadness. She wouldn't have to see Nathan for two days, which meant she might actually get some homework done. But she wanted to see him. She wanted to be distracted. She waited for the other students to leave the classroom before heading out. "Have a nice weekend, Miss Bell." Mr. Harris gave her a plastic grin.

"Thanks . . . you too," she mumbled as she shoved her arms into her sweater and walked out. Students scurried throughout the halls, rushing to empty their lockers and start their weekend. She pressed her way through the chaos and let herself outside. After setting her stuff down on a nearby bench, she pulled her hair up into a ponytail and waited a few minutes for the parking lot to empty. There was always some kind of accident when so many cars were fighting to exit on a Friday afternoon, and she didn't want any scratches on her flawless Honda.

Within the crowd she spotted Samantha's long hair bobbing up and down. She was talking to someone, but Jada couldn't see who. She inched her way over, navigating through the circles of talking people. She was nearly there when a group parted and revealed Nathan standing across from Samantha. Jada stopped and watched them through narrowed eyes. Samantha had a huge smile on her face and was playfully wrapping a strand of hair around her finger. To Jada's surprise, Nathan was laughing at whatever Sam was saying.

Hot coals suddenly ignited in her stomach. She forced herself to look away, realizing at that moment how much she liked him. *You knew this would happen. He is just like Luke. What are you so upset about? He never liked you.* She wanted desperately to look back and see that she was mistaken, that it was someone else laughing with Sam. But she kept her eyes averted, knowing she'd be unable to keep herself from bursting into tears if she saw them laughing together again.

Without looking back, she speed-walked toward her car, bumping into a few people and ignoring their curses. A hand suddenly grabbed her shoulder, startling her.

"How's your leg?" In the sunlight, Nathan's eyes look iridescent, and the wind made his hair dance like waves in the ocean. But her pain was stronger than his allure.

"Fine." She turned abruptly and kept walking to her car. With one step, he caught up to her and effortlessly kept up with her hurried pace.

"What's wrong?"

"Nothing. I just have somewhere I need to be."

"I don't believe you." When they reached her car, he put his hand against the driver's door. She furiously tugged on the handle, but it wouldn't budge under his weight.

"You're in my way." She kept her gaze down.

He stepped closer to her, sending a flutter down her spine. She watched his wide chest rise with each breath. The surge of emotions that tore through her was both terrifying and exciting. She wanted to feel this every day. But then the pain of seeing him with Samantha fought its way through and took over.

Nathan shifted his weight. "Not until you tell me what's wrong."

She looked up at him, knowing full well that he'd see the hurt in her eyes. His face softened when she met his gaze. She forced herself not to care.

"Why do you care anyway?" she spat.

Nathan tilted his head slightly and searched her face. When he didn't make any move to respond, she tried again to get him to leave. "It's nothing. I just thought something that wasn't true. That's all. I made a mistake. It doesn't have anything to do with you." The last words came out shaky, giving her away.

His eyes grew sad as he removed his hand from her car and tucked it in his jeans pocket. "Okay. I'll let you go."

She heaved open her door, nearly hitting him, plopped inside, and slammed it behind her. She forced herself to focus on the road even though every cell in her body wanted to look back at him. Tears stung her eyes, but she wiped them away. This wasn't his fault or even Sam's. It was hers. She'd let her guard down against her better judgment. She took a deep breath and willed her feelings away. Tonight she would go home and read *Anna Karenina*, one of her favorite books, because that's what real love was: broken hearts and disappointment.

CHAPTER 9

When Jada arrived home, Lilah's car was parked in the driveway. Jada moaned. Of all days for her mom to be home early, it had to be today. She pulled down her visor mirror and examined her face. Her eyes were bloodshot and pink so she pulled her foundation from her backpack and dabbed a little under them before going into the house. Hopefully her mom wouldn't notice. She was on the front porch fumbling with her keys when the door flew open. The familiar comfort of her mom's smile greeted her.

"What are you doing home?" Jada tossed her keys back into her purse and stepped inside.

"Happy birthday, sweetie!"

Jada forced a smile. "Thanks, Mom, but you're a little early."

"I know, but I thought we could celebrate it tonight. Tomorrow you're having the party with your friends, and Monday is a school night. Can I take you out to a nice restaurant? How about Convict Lake?"

"Isn't that, like, an hour away?"

"So what? It's Friday, and you don't have school tomorrow. And hey, you've been saying you want to try new things. Get out of Bishop."

Jada couldn't argue with that. "Okay, Mom, let's go."

"Great! Now go shower and get dressed."

Jada nodded and went into the bathroom, thankful for the solitude. Her muscles slowly relaxed as the hot water beat down on her neck. But the sight of Nathan laughing with Sam kept pressing its way into her mind. Turning around, she put her face under the showerhead and let the sound of pounding water drown out her thoughts. When the bathroom was thick with steam, she felt the indifference she had relied on for so many years cover her aching heart. She had been a fool this week, but at least it hadn't gone as far as it had with Luke. At least she'd come away with some dignity.

On the way to the restaurant, Jada turned the heater on full blast and opened the window. The mixture of hot and cold air swirled around her. It definitely felt good to get out of Bishop. Her mom stretched her skirt over her knees and pointed both the heater vents directly on her, clearly not enjoying the fresh icy air.

"I wish you'd wear a dress on occasion," Lilah said. "You'd look very pretty."

Jada had put on her nicest jeans, a tunic top, and a scarf. She did secretly have a few dresses but had never worn them. She just felt more comfortable in pants.

"It will be a long time before you see me in a dress." She half grinned.

"Well, a mom can hope."

When they arrived, they were escorted to a dimly lit booth at the far end of the room. Circles of candlelight glimmered on the cherrywood paneling and high ceilings.

Outside it had started to rain, making the restaurant feel even cozier. It smelled like butter and garlic, one of Jada's favorite smells. Her stomach grumbled.

The waiter, a guy in his late twenties with a receding hairline, came to the table flashing a synthetic smile. "Can I start you off with something to drink?" His voice was higher than Jada expected. She picked up the wine menu and looked at her mom, eyebrows lifted.

"No." Lilah chuckled. "You want me to go to jail?"

"Fine, I'll have a water, and I'm ready to order. I'll have the salmon," Jada said.

After Lilah ordered a glass of merlot and the duck, they were alone again. "So how was your first week of senior year?"

Jada scoffed. "Terrible." She kicked herself for blurting that out. She didn't want her mom to know what had happened.

Lilah set her elbows on the table and rested her chin on her palm. "Why? What was so bad about it?"

"Actually, Mom, let's not talk about it. We're out of Bishop, and I just want to forget this week." She ripped off a piece of bread from the loaf the waiter had brought, spread it with butter, and stuck it into her mouth.

Lilah sighed and shook her head. "If that's what you want."

At the next table over, the waiter pulled out the seats for an older couple, who looked to be in their eighties. The older man tenderly held his wife's hand while whispering something to her. The woman released a bashful giggle that lit up her face, making her look twenty years younger.

After the man ordered for her, he resumed caressing her hand and speaking quietly to her. They were obviously still in love. The sight, which would normally make Jada smile, made her body feel like dead weight. Would she ever find someone to love her like that? She tore her stare from them and turned back to her table. She started when she found Lilah's face hard and staring at a table across the room.

"What's wrong, Mom?"

Lilah's body stiffened. "Nothing."

Jada turned to see what her mom was looking at, but a loud crash made her stop. Lilah's hand was frozen in a warped fist over a spray of broken glass. A flash of gray rippled over her fingers.

Jada blinked. "What the—?"

"Oh, oops!" Lilah unwrapped her fist and her skin returned to flesh color. She shook her napkin open and dabbed the pool of water and glass. "I'm so clumsy." After signaling the waiter, she folded her fingers over her palm and examined her nail polish.

Jada slowly waved her hand at her mom. "Hello."

Lilah looked up and shrugged. "What?"

"You just crushed that glass with your hand. And you're not even bleeding."

Lilah dropped her hand in her lap. "Don't be ridiculous. That's impossible."

"There was nothing else near your glass. You're skin too, it looked . . . weird."

"Jada, cut it out! You sound crazy." There was an uncertainty in her voice.

"Just let it go. The glass must have been chipped

already." Lilah gave her a stern look. After the waiter had cleaned their table and replaced Lilah's water, she leaned back in the booth and folded her hands in her lap. "Don't be upset."

Jada chewed on the tip of her thumb. Was she going crazy? She studied her mom's face. Her body language was relaxed, but there was just the slightest hesitation in her smile, and her eyes looked heavy, like they had been holding a secret for decades.

Jada shook her head. "Whatever. At least tell me what you were looking at."

"Fine." Lilah looked down. "Over there—" Her voice came out raspy. She cleared her throat and closed her eyes. "Over there is the woman your father ran off with."

All the blood drained from Jada's face. She set her elbows on the table and rubbed her temples. She opened her mouth, but the waiter shuffled up with their food before she could get a word out. "Here's the salmon and the duck. Can I get you anything else?"

"No," Jada replied curtly. The waiter gave her a smug grin and strode off. Jada jerked her head in the direction of the woman, taking in every inch of her. She was beautiful. Tall and slender with long dark brown hair and big eyes. She looked to be in her forties, but the wrinkles around her eyes didn't diminish her beauty. She was sitting with a man, who was not Jada's father, tracing leisurely circles on the top of his hand. They were obviously a couple.

"Are you sure, Mom?"

"Yes, I'd know her anywhere."

For the first time, Jada saw pain and loss in her mom's

soft features. All these years, she'd been suffering and hadn't said a word.

Suddenly Lilah's eyes grew wide and veins throbbed in her forehead. Jada didn't have to look to know that the woman had spotted them. Seconds later, the brunette towered over them, an unassuming smile on her face.

"Lilah, it's been a long time." Her voice was soft.

A shiny film covered her mom's eyes. "Yes, it has, Karen."

Karen shifted her weight and glanced at Jada. "Listen, I'm sorry to say this in front of your daughter, but I need to get this out. I want you to know I didn't run off with Ethan. I tried to tell you, but you wouldn't return any of my calls. I'm sorry."

Lilah didn't look up at her. "I have a hard time believing that, Karen. If you didn't, then where did he go?"

"He just asked for a ride to L.A. That's all I know. He didn't want to take your only car, so he asked me for a ride." She released a sigh. "Lilah, I'm not going to lie to you. I wanted to be with him. At first we started out as friends, and then I grew to love him. But I didn't want to be with him like that—when he was still married. In the end, he said he didn't feel the same way about me, so he asked me for a ride, and that was it."

Karen was talking so fast, Jada could barely process it all. The beautiful face she'd seen across the room moments ago had completely changed. With each word she spoke, her skin became more strained and pale. Jada realized Karen must have been holding on to this pain for the past eleven years.

Karen dabbed the corners of her eyes. "Honestly, Lilah, he never said why he was unhappy. Whenever we spoke of you, he was always vague."

Lilah's features softened slightly as she scanned Karen's face. When Karen reached out and touched her shoulder, she was as still as a statue. Jada wasn't sure she was still breathing.

"I'm sorry, Lilah," Karen said and then turned and went back to her table.

Jada sat with her mouth agape for a few moments before speaking. "Mom, are you okay?"

Lilah brought a shaky napkin up to her lips. Silent tears wet her cheeks. It was the most emotion Jada had ever seen her mom express about her dad.

Jada had so many questions, she didn't know where to begin. Why hadn't Lilah told her about this woman before? "Do you believe her?"

Lilah shrugged. "I . . . don't know."

"So if he didn't leave for her, why did he leave?"

Lilah patted her napkin under her eyes before looking Jada straight in the eye. "I don't know exactly, but I have my suspicions. It's complicated."

Jada groaned and slid back in her chair. "Were you ever happy together?"

"Yes. In fact, we were madly in love. We couldn't get enough of each other." Lilah dipped her head, but not before Jada saw her quivering lip.

It didn't make any sense. They were in love and then he left suddenly. She suspected her mom knew exactly why he left and wasn't telling her. But whatever the reason, there was no excuse. "Well, it's his loss. We don't need him. Now can we change the subject?" Jada sliced up the salmon and threw a piece of it into her mouth.

"Why don't you want to hear about him?"

"He's gone. He isn't a part of our lives. What is the point in talking about him?" She could feel her jaw tensing as she spoke.

"It isn't that simple, Jada."

"Why not?" Her head began to throb. He'd made his choice; he'd abandoned them; it *was* as simple as that.

"He's still your father."

Jada shrugged, hoping that was the end of the conversation, but her mom's words sank deep into the pit of her stomach. She felt the slightest hint of anger rising up her rib cage, but she quickly shoved it back down.

Before she knew it, it was Saturday afternoon, and she had to start getting ready. This morning, she'd woken up thinking about Nathan. Why couldn't she let him go? She couldn't blame Sam for liking him. And Nathan hadn't asked Jada out, so she had no reason to think he liked her. Her emotions had taken over, and she'd fantasized about something that would never happen.

Her phone sang a familiar song. Jada blew out a breath and picked it up. "I knew you'd call."

"Yes, well, I had to make sure you were still coming and that you were going to dress up," Samantha replied in a smooth voice.

Jada sat at her desk chair and looked outside at the

swelling dark clouds. "Dress up? You're crazy. It's freezing!"

"I don't care. You'll be inside anyway. Wear that gray dress you have. I love gray on you!"

"Dress. Ha, you're funny. When was the last time you saw me in a dress?"

"My point exactly."

"Look, Sam, I let you throw this party for me, and I *am* going to show up, but you need to pick your battles. I'm not wearing a dress." Jada leaned back in the chair, balancing on two legs. A few seconds passed, and she knew Samantha was thinking of a counterargument. Jada hoped she would give up. She was getting tired of bantering with Samantha lately. A grunt came through the line. "Okay, fine, but at least wear a cute top, and no UGGS."

"Deal," Jada agreed. "See you at eight?"

"Yes, and you're going to have a good time!"

"I'm sure I will." Jada hung up and stood, stretching her arms over her head. She hoped she would have fun—and that this would be a changing day for her.

After swinging the closet doors open, she brushed her fingers along the hanging clothes. A stream of grays, blues, and blacks stared back at her, obviously her favorite colors. Nothing interested her in the closet, but then she remembered a white tube top she'd bought a few years ago. She opened her bottom dresser drawer, and a heap of tank tops exploded out. Digging through them, tossing some on the floor, she found what she was looking for. She held it up and nodded in approval, then laughed when she spotted the price tag still hanging from the top. "Well, now's as good a time as any."

Hands on her hips, feet planted in front of her full-length mirror, she evaluated herself in the white tube top, dark blue skinny jeans, and patent leather black flats. "Almost perfect." She draped a long beaded chain around her neckline.

The bedroom door slowly glided open, and her mom leaned in the door frame. "Honey . . . you look great," she said dryly.

Jada turned back to her image, a flicker of pain in her eyes. "Wow, that was convincing, Mom."

"Sweetie, I'm so sorry!" Lilah leaped into the room and was at Jada's side in an instant, tenderly brushing a strand of hair behind her ear. "You look wonderful. I guess I'm just not feeling well."

Jada smoothed out the wrinkles in her top and yanked her hair out of a tie, finger combing it as it unraveled around her chest. "Yeah, I know. You've been acting weird ever since that night I mentioned the Arons." Jada forced her voice to sound casual to see if she could catch her mom off guard and cause her to just spit out whatever was bothering her.

Worry puckered Lilah's brow. Shifting nervously, she anchored her body away until her back was to Jada.

"Oh, Mom." Stealing her gaze from the mirror and half rolling her eyes, she wrapped her mom in a firm hug. "Whatever it is, we'll talk about it tomorrow. I've got to go curl my hair. I'm going to be late."

Jada ducked into the shadowed hall and into the bathroom. She quietly clicked the door closed behind her.

Leaning against it, she heard her mom mumbling as her slippers padded down the hall to her room. Jada sucked at curling her hair and normally would've asked for Lilah's help. She knew her mom would be hurt that she didn't. But Lilah was just in such a dark mood lately.

Half an hour later, standing hesitantly in the bathroom door frame, Jada peeked down each end of the hallway. The house was completely dark except her room, where a single candle glowed. Lilah must have gone to sleep. The brown curls bouncing around her face felt unnatural. More than once she found herself pulling her hair back to put it into a ponytail. One stray curl poked her in the eye as she entered her room. She probably should've asked for Lilah's help after all.

She quickly blew out the candle, grabbed her purse and car keys, and tiptoed down the hall. The old house betrayed her, creaking and groaning with her every step. Finally, she made it out the door. It was already almost dark. She stood on the front step. This was it. There was no turning back. She took in a deep breath and squared her shoulders. It was time for her life to change. With determination stirring in her belly, she jumped in her car and headed to Sam's house.

CHAPTER 10

Muted, indistinguishable chatter erupted into a thunderous noise as Jada cracked open Samantha's front door and slipped inside. Three boys lunged by her, nearly knocking her over. After regaining her balance, she bit her bottom lip and squeezed in between hordes of people, inching her way down the hall.

"Jada!" Samantha shrieked. In the kitchen, she clutched Jada, locking her arms against her body.

"Birthday girl is heeeere!" Samantha's voice sang throughout the house. A roar of cheering exploded, and everyone turned toward Jada, grinning. She felt her skin flush and returned a hesitant glance at the crowd. "Tha-thanks." A jerky, almost inaudible sound came out of her mouth.

As quickly as the attention came, it was gone, and the others went back to their conversations. Jada felt her face return to a normal temperature.

"You look cute!" Samantha cooed as she shoved a drink into Jada's hands.

Jada arched a suspicious eyebrow. "What's this?"

"Oh, nothing. Just punch." Samantha's eyes rolled.

"I can't believe you invited all these people." Jada

leaned on the kitchen counter and sipped her punch. The tart liquid had no traces of alcohol. She was thankful her drink wasn't spiked.

"I didn't. I only invited thirty, but word of mouth, I guess. What can you do?" Samantha shrugged, but a satisfied grin lit up her face as she tore open a bag of chips and dumped them into a bowl. This would be the biggest party of the year. And Sam loved it. The noise doubled when the front door opened and closed, filling the already packed house with more kids. Jada ran her teeth over her bottom lip. Was this really about her?

She shook her head and stood up straight.

"Go mingle; I have to make some more dip." Sam waved Jada away and yanked open the refrigerator.

Before Jada could protest, a group of people shouldered her aside and surrounded Samantha as she dug through the refrigerator. Meandering slowly back down the hall, she scanned over the family photos she'd seen a hundred times. A snicker escaped her lips at the darker squares of paint scattered across the wall. Samantha had taken down photos of herself she deemed unworthy to be viewed by kids from school. Most likely junior high photos. Back at the front door, Jada searched the living room for a friendly face. In the corner, affectionately whispering to each other, were Jen and Logan. Jen rushed over and embraced her, gently swinging her from side to side. Apparently, for her birthday at least, she had forgiven her for not being excited about Logan proposing. Although he hadn't done it yet, which made Jada worry that Jen might get her heart broken.

"I can't believe you're turning eighteen!" Jen released

her, her auburn bob bouncing up and down.

Jada opened her eyes wide and grinned in fake excitement. "I know. I can't believe it either."

"I'm going to start calling you Grandma." Logan rolled his head back and laughed.

Jada tilted her head. "How nice for you that you find yourself so amusing."

"All right." Jen teasingly hit Logan in the chest. "We're going to go get a drink. See you later."

"Yeah . . . definitely." Jada nodded, but they had already disappeared into the mass of people. She sipped her drink and anxiously clicked her cell phone, trying to bring up the clock. The display flashed 8:20 p.m. She let out a quick breath. *It's going to be a long night.*

Without warning, someone rammed into her, sending her head snapping backward. She dove forward, her knees cracking on the hardwood. Her drink tumbled to the floor, splashing the punch straight up like a fountain.

"Oh, Jada, sorry 'bout that. We were just wrestling."

Jada dragged her eyes from her dripping hands to find Jason, the captain of the lacrosse team, wavering above her. Practically every girl in the school was infatuated with him, but Jada didn't see it. He was tall and muscular, yes, but he was a jerk.

"Lemme help you up." His knees trembled as he lowered them down. Jada braced herself, knowing what was coming. As if on cue, he lost his balance and plummeted face-first into the floor. His breath gusted out of him, blowing the stench of alcohol into Jada's face. She grimaced and rolled her eyes.

"Whoops!" He let out a deep chuckle before clamping onto Jada's arm and yanking them both up.

"That hurt!" She pried her arm from his grasp and rubbed the pink indention his thumb had left.

Jason wrapped his arm around her shoulders. "So you're eighteen now, huh? Legal." He gave her a sleazy wink.

Jada gulped down the sting of vomit crawling up her throat. *All right, that's about all I can take.* She peeled his bulky hand from her shoulder and let it fall behind her. Luckily, he had the attention span of a goldfish. He bellowed out an obnoxious laugh at a jumble of arms and legs in the living room. Derek, the co-captain of the lacrosse team, had Eddie Ramirez pinned to the ground in a choke hold. Jada didn't known limbs could bend and twist like pretzels. Eddie tapped out furiously, but Derek just laughed even more and gripped him harder. Finally, Jason ran over and jumped on them both, sending Derek flying into the wall. Rolling on the floor, Eddie grabbed his throat and choked in air, dripping spit onto the carpet. Derek hurled himself up, barely missing a swipe from Jason, and slapped Eddie in the back. "You're fine. Stop being a girl."

"What happened?" Sam's voice startled her. Jada turned to find Sam standing in the entryway, hands on her hips, glowering at the spilled punch.

Jada lifted her hands. "It wasn't my fault. Jason was wrestling and bumped into me."

Sam eyed Jason and let out a playful growl. "Okay, I'll get a towel." She returned a minute later and dropped two towels on the pink liquid and then handed a wet paper towel to Jada. "For your hands." She smiled.

100

Jada rubbed the sticky punch off her fingers. "Thanks."

After wiping up the mess, Sam disappeared into the laundry room, and Jada found herself alone in the corner of the living room. She tugged on her ear nervously as she watched the tightly packed circles of people talk and laugh. Everyone from her senior class was there. She knew all of their names, and yet she didn't know them at all. She'd never had a meaningful conversation with any one of them. Her throat constricted, and tiny beads of sweat formed on her hairline.

Everyone was only here as an excuse to party. She was just as invisible at her own party as she was in school.

Her stomach hollowed as loneliness washed over her. She lowered her head so no one would notice her eyes glistening with moisture and rushed blindly toward the back door. As she tried to push her way through a roadblock of people, their laughter taunted her from every direction. Unease erupted into panic.

A gap formed in the crowd, and she elbowed her way through but tripped on a potted plant and flew into the open space. A white flash filled her vision right before she landed on a hard chest. When a rough grip caught her shoulders, she winced. A rich aroma surrounded her. For a moment, she forgot where she was. Her eyes fluttered closed as a mixture of citrus, fire wood, and soap swirled into her nose, igniting her senses. She filled her lungs with the scent, then realized what it was.

Cologne. Nathan's.

Jada flinched and pulled back. Blinking furiously, she looked up and found Nathan's fierce gray eyes staring down at her.

"Oh," she gasped. A few moments passed before he released her. She wrapped her arms around herself, instantly feeling the loss of his touch. Every inch of her body wanted to dissolve into his and feel his strong arms engulf her again. Then she remembered seeing Sam and Nathan laughing together. She closed her eyes, unable to look at him. Her hand flew to her chest, where she was sure someone had sliced through her heart with a knife.

Fighting the emotions surging through her, she pushed past him, heaved open the sliding glass door and slammed it behind her. The freezing dewy air wasn't able to cool her boiling skin. Moving away from the house, she slumped on the wood fence and stared at the moonlit trees. Crickets performed a symphony all around her. Why is he here? Jada kicked the fence. If she could just not see him, she'd be fine. She took in deep, smooth breaths, trying to regain her composure, when the door ground open behind her. She swung her head around just as Sam strode up to her. "What are you doing out here?"

Jada didn't want to hurt her feelings and tell her she wasn't having a good time, so she lied. "Oh, I'm fine, I just wanted to get a little fresh air. Look how pretty the stars are." She pointed at the sky, trying to get Sam's attention away from her face.

"OK . . . if you say so. Just don't stay out here too long. This is your party!" Sam turned to go back into the house.

Her party. Really?

"Wait," Jada called, not turning around. "You didn't tell me you were inviting Nathan."

Sam scoffed. "Why wouldn't I? He's gorgeous. And of course, it ended up being the perfect excuse to meet him."

Jada rolled her head back so only the dark, star-speckled sky filled her vision.

"Just ignore him if you don't like him, although I really don't understa—" Sam was still talking as she stepped back into the house, her voice disappearing with her.

Jada sighed loudly and twisted her fingers around the string of orange lights Sam had strung through the fence. She wondered why her emotions were coming unraveled. All these years, she had been fine with not being popular. Even preferred it in some ways. But lately, rejection had started to tug at her indifference. She had the feeling it had something to do with Nathan. Every time he smiled at her or talked to her, it put another small crack in the wall she had built around her heart. Somehow she needed to break the spell he had on her; after all, she had been mistaken about him. He liked Samantha.

The door grunted open again and quickly closed.

"I'm almost done—" Expecting Sam, she stopped mid-sentence when she turned and found Nathan instead. He stood quietly, shadows hiding his beautiful face.

"Are you all right?" His voice was low.

"Yeah, I'm fine, I just . . . got a little claustrophobic, I guess." Jada returned her gaze to the backyard, hoping he would take the hint and go back inside. He didn't. The deck creaked as his footsteps grew closer. His large frame appeared in her peripheral vision, but she wouldn't look at him. The fence screeched, straining against the pressure of his forearms.

The bushes rustled, and what looked like a possum scurried across the lawn. Jada hugged herself and grimaced at the rat-like creature.

"You aren't having a good time." It was more of a statement than a question.

Jada rubbed her eyes. Why was he talking to her? Shouldn't he be following Sam around?

"No it's not that. I've just never had a big party like this for myself before. All my past birthdays have been just me, Sam, and Jen, so I didn't really know what I was getting into."

He tilted his head slightly and traced the edge of his jawline with his fingers. "Yeah, I don't really like being the center of attention."

Jada arched her head and eyed him. "C'mon."

"What?" He raised his eyes to meet hers, a slight grin growing on his face.

"You're—" She raised her eyebrows.

"I'm—?" He raised his eyebrows back at her.

"Never mind." She didn't feel like telling him he was gorgeous and could be the most popular guy in school in an instant, if he wanted. "So, why did you start Union High your senior year?"

He looked away from her, his neck and jaw stiffening. A reaction Jada was getting used to every time she asked him about his personal life.

"The drive to Palisade was too long. It was becoming hard for Seth and me."

Jada waited for more but nothing came. "That's it? You changed schools senior year because of the drive?"

Nathan didn't respond. Without thinking, Jada reached her hand out to touch him, but something moved behind them, and she stopped. She turned to see who it was. Samantha was watching them from behind the door, her face blank and unreadable. Even when Jada waved, she didn't smile.

Jada slid away from Nathan. "I think Samantha wants to talk to you." She pressed her lips together, preparing for him to leave her again. He twisted until he faced Samantha. She flashed him her biggest smile and a seductive wave.

He responded with a nod.

"I don't have anything to say to her." He returned his attention to Jada, clearly unfazed by Sam's charm. Jada tried to fight a grin.

His eyes sparkled. "What?"

"Nothing." But she couldn't wipe the smile off her face. She'd been mistaken; he didn't like Sam. That conversation she'd witnessed in the parking lot at school must've been when Sam invited Nathan to her party. And he had come. Come to see *her*. Jada searched his eyes and let the electricity that was penetrating her every cell take over. She was tired of overthinking everything. For the first time in her life, she felt reckless. She wanted to throw herself into Nathan's arms and never look back.

He faced her, leaving one arm on the fence. "You're very hard to read. What are you thinking?"

"Just how interesting life is sometimes."

"That's a bit vague."

"It is. Sorry. I guess it's just hard to explain."

He reached up toward her face and draped a strand of

hair around her ear. Her body shuddered pleasantly at his touch.

"Your hair was sticking up," he said softly.

"Oh . . . thanks." She looked into his eyes again, knowing full well that her face was as pink as a rose. When he treated her to that sexy grin of his, nothing else mattered. In an instant, her heart rate doubled, and he closed the gap between them and covered her lips with his. Time seemed to stop. She could no longer hear the animals and insects of the night. All she could hear was their heavy breaths. His lips were firm and she relished in his masculine smell as he wrapped his large hands around her neck and pulled her deeper into him. She couldn't believe this was happening.

He pulled away and looked down at her, his chest pumping vigorously. It took a minute before the animal look in his eyes faded away. "Jada, I—"

The door suddenly flew open and slammed into the wall. They both jerked apart. This time Seth stood at the threshold. He glared from Nathan to Jada, his eyes like hard black stones.

"Let's go," he hissed. The moon inched behind a dark cloud, hiding Nathan's face, but she didn't have to see his expression to feel the waves of anger radiating off of him. When he looked back at her, he hesitated as though wanting to say something. Instead, he took off through the door, nudging Seth in the shoulder. Moments later he was gone, disappearing into the crowd like he had never existed.

"What are you doing?" Seth felt the skin on his face growing tight. Nathan didn't answer as the car's engine turned over.

"I said—"

Nathan gripped the door handle, his knuckles turning white. "I'm getting close to her, earning her trust."

"That's not what it looked like." The tires screamed as Seth steered the car away from the curb. Sam's house slowly disappeared in the rearview mirror.

"Stay out of it," Nathan growled.

"What are you talking about, stay out of it? You know this concerns both of us."

"I can handle it."

"Dad's not going to like this."

Nathan snarled. "Dad's not going to know about it because you aren't going to tell him."

Seth cleared his throat, rolled down the window, and spat. "You're not in control of the situation, Nathan."

Nathan yanked the emergency brake, bringing the silver Audi to a screeching halt.

"What the hell are you doing?" Seth yelled. "I paid a lot of money for this car."

Nathan grabbed Seth by the shirt and pulled him within inches of his face. "You know, Seth, you are a smart guy. You have a lot going for you."

"What the hell is that supposed to mean?"

"It means you're smart enough to jump to my grade, you're tutoring college kids, and you worked for two years to buy this car. Why don't you do something else with your life?"

Seth stared him down, his fingers clenching into a fist and then releasing. "You know I can't." His voice was thick with bitterness.

Nathan released him with a jerk. "You're ridiculous sometimes, you know that? Someday you should consider making your own decisions and not just following what someone else tells you to do."

This time Seth slowly pulled his car into the street. He opened his window again and let the rough wind soothe his fuming face. Nathan was reckless, getting too close to Jada. Seth was starting to doubt Nathan's loyalty to their family, to their duty. But he would have to let it go for now. Their father said he must follow Nathan's lead because he was the eldest. For now he would. But that wouldn't stop Seth from watching his brother's every move.

CHAPTER 11

Blinding gray light broke through the slits in her eyelids, forcing her out of a deep sleep. Lifting her head, she squinted at the blurry numbers on her alarm clock. Gradually, 1:37 p.m. came into focus. She turned over and buried herself in her pillow. All at once, the events of last night flooded into her mind. After Nathan left, she'd gone back inside to talk with Sam. She knew Sam well enough to know she was mad at her. She was friendly, but there was an edge to her voice, and she seemed to find excuses to talk to other people. A ball of anger churned in Jada's stomach. *Sam can have any guy she wants, and the one time a guy likes me, she's mad.*

Her arms and legs started to tingle. Nathan liked her. A giggle burst out of her. It was time to admit it; she really liked him too. Most of the time, he made her feel on edge, like he was dangerous. Whenever his eyes met hers, her blood ran hot and fast. But there was something behind his hostility, something protective. After that day in PE when he stood up to Lori, she knew he wouldn't let anything happen to her. With a smile glued on her face, she kicked off her blankets, leaped out of bed, and skipped to the kitchen. Lilah was sitting at the island drinking tea.

Jada kissed her on the cheek. "Morning, Mom."

"You're in a good mood. Did you have fun last night?"

"Yeah, I did." When her eyes met Lilah's, she remembered her mom's warning about Nathan, and her heart sank. She couldn't tell her.

"What happened? Who was there?" Lilah's tone was flat, like she wasn't really interested in the answer. Not like her at all.

"There were a lot of people, pretty much everyone from our senior class. Nothing much happened. We just ate and listened to music." Jada plopped down next to her mom, a bowl of cereal in her hand.

Lilah set her tea down and started fidgeting with an empty sugar packet. "So, it's your last day of being seventeen. What are you going to do?"

Jada huffed. "I have a ton of homework to do, since I didn't get any done yesterday."

Lilah nodded, and silence settled in the kitchen, except for the clanking of Jada's spoon at the bottom of her bowl as she scooped up the last bites of cereal. Lilah sat up straight, filling the room with tension. Jada stepped one foot off the stool, feeling the impulse to leave, to go back into the warmth of her memories of the night before. She eyed her mom. Lilah was ripping a sugar packet into little pieces now.

"I need to talk to you." Lilah's voice was grave, and Jada knew whatever it was it couldn't be good. Jada set her spoon down and waited.

"Tomorrow, when you turn eighteen"—her face drained of all color, revealing dark circles under her pink rimmed eyes—"you're going to notice some . . . changes."

Jada jumped up, sending her stool sliding into the wall. "Oh, my god, are you serious, Mom? Like what? My body is going to change? I'm going to become a woman or something? I thought we did this in junior high!" After grabbing her bowl, she stomped to the sink and tossed it in. Crossing her arms over her chest, she looked out the window, keeping her back to Lilah. She didn't need this right now. She was having a good day, dammit.

Lilah let out a long breath. "That's not exactly what I mean."

Jada smacked the heels of her palms on her temples. "Well, I don't want to hear it. I can handle it, okay, Mom?" She bolted out of the kitchen and into her room, slamming the door behind her. With a hard snap, she flipped on her stereo and threw herself onto the bed. The sound of John Frushiante's "Light\Dark" came out of the speakers. It was her favorite song. The melancholic chorus always relaxed her. She couldn't believe her mom was trying to talk to her about *changes*, whatever that meant. She was definitely too old for a mother-daughter talk. Yesterday was the best day of her life, and her mom was ruining it. Well, she wouldn't let that happen. She grunted and then sang along with the lyrics.

A few more songs on the album and her heartbeat had slowed to a steady rhythm. She lifted her head and scanned the mound of textbooks scattered on the floor. Without getting out of bed, she leaned over and grabbed the first one she could reach. "Econ it is."

An image of Nathan flashed through her mind, making

her body feel warm. He had his arm around her as they walked down the hall. He was smiling that wicked smile of his and looking down at her. Then Seth's face interrupted her happy vision. What's his problem? Every time she saw him, he was pissed. He obviously didn't want Nathan to be around her—even in her daydreams. Jada blew out a breath and opened her econ book. "I've got to focus. No more thinking about Seth or Sam."

She was reading about game theory when the words started to blur. She needed a quick power nap. After cradling her head in the crook of her elbow on top of the book, she closed her eyes.

Jada's eyes snapped open as a blurry white fog snaked around her room. Her body, moving on its own, slowly sat up and draped her legs over the bed. Her feet gracefully slipped onto a cushion of air and she floated out of her bedroom. In the middle of the living room, white light blinded her from every corner.

"Mom?" Her voice softly echoed through the room.

No answer.

Scanning the familiar surroundings, her eyes stopped on the front window. It was the only dark object in the room. She willed her body toward it. Reaching up, she slid her fingers down the cool glass. Something was on the outside. When a flash of light revealed a dark red liquid, she gasped.

Her hand jerked back, and her breath caught in her chest. *No.* She tried to run back to her room, get as far away as possible, but her legs were paralyzed. The front door beckoned her, as if it were a living, breathing creature. She wrapped her arms around her face. *No, please.* Warm air tickled her arms, and she knew she was moving toward the door. The same force that got her out of bed was pushing her again. Then a bright light and a slap of cold. The door was open. Unable to stop herself, she dropped her arms.

A pile of bodies lay on her porch, and all their faces were looking at her. She knew them. Her knees sank to the floor.

"Everyone," she heard herself say.

Then a set of eyes blinked.

She squinted, trying to see familiarity in the badly slashed face. The mouth opened and a dark red sludge poured out. It was then she recognized her. "Mom? No. Noooo!"

Her own shriek jolted her awake, sending her econ book plummeting to the floor. Her door flew open, and Lilah's worried face hovered in her blurry room. "Honey, are you okay? You were screaming."

Before her mom could reach her, Jada put up her hand. She couldn't look at her. Not after the gruesome vision she just saw.

"I'm fine, Mom. Please . . . just shut the door. I fell asleep for a few minutes, and I must've had a bad dream."

"What was it about?" Lilah shot back.

Jada rubbed her eyes, still trying to get those bloody faces out of her mind. "I don-don't remember." But she did remember. Every detail. "Don't worry, Mom, I've got to get back to homework. I'm fine."

Lilah squeezed her eyes closed and rubbed her head with the back of her hand. Finally, her shoulders slumped and she looked away. "Okay, Jada. You know where I am if you need me."

When she disappeared behind the door, closing it without a sound, Jada slid to the end of her bed and buried her face in her hands. Dread gnawed at her mind. In the dream, every person in the town was dead, and somehow she knew deep down, she was the killer.

Silent tears wet her cheeks and formed small dark circles on her light blue sweat pants. She dried her eyes with her sleeves and slowly walked over to the window. Everything looked normal. What was she expecting? Her lungs ached, reminding her she was holding her breath. *Just a dream.* She hugged herself and released a long sigh.

The muted sound of her phone ringing brought her back to the present. She shuffled around the room, throwing clothes and papers until she found it on her desk under her history book. She answered it, not looking at the caller ID.

"Jada?" A deep voice greeted her.

"Yes." She realized how exasperated her voice sounded and pinched the narrow part of her nose, trying to relieve the pressure that had settled there.

"It's Nathan."

Her ears burned at the sound of his name. "Hi."

"I hope you don't mind. I got your number from Logan. We have PE together."

"Sure, no problem. What's up?" Her cool voice didn't reveal the tornado that was wreaking havoc on her insides.

"Actually, I was hoping I could see you . . . today."

"Oh." She bit her bottom lip, unable to hide the smile in her voice. "Yeah, sure."

"Great. I'll come pick you up?"

"No! I mean, I'll meet you somewhere. I could use the drive anyway. How about City Park?"

"See you there."

Jada stood frozen, looking at her phone in disbelief. Was she still dreaming? No, Nathan had just called her and asked to see her. She tossed her phone onto the bed and ran to the bathroom. Minutes later, the shower head spat out a few cold spurts then a steady stream of hot water. Any residual tension holding her captive broke loose and floated down the drain. Her heart was the only organ that refused to relax, bubbling with excitement at the thought of seeing Nathan. After blow-drying her hair and dabbing on some foundation, she threw on some jeans and a T-shirt and headed out to the kitchen. She scribbled a note for Lilah and dropped it on the counter on her way out.

"Why is every light red when I want to get somewhere?" she said, as she skidded her Honda to yet another stop. It felt like some sinister force was trying to keep her from Nathan. Finally, she pulled into the parking lot, shoved the clutch into first, and turned off the engine. Other than one family having lunch at a picnic table, the place was empty. The pale sunlight peeked through the clouds, casting a hazy glow on the soft green grass. Down the path, a man sat at a bench, head bowed and elbows on his knees.

That must be him. She grabbed her keys from the ignition and stepped outside. Scattered patches of sun warmed her skin as she made her way to him. Her breath quickened as she neared the bench and Nathan's large physique came into focus. Before he saw her, she stopped and watched him for a few moments. He seemed tense, cracking his knuckles and then running his hands through his hair. Although she knew she was falling in love with him, something still nibbled at her mind when she was near him. Something wasn't right. In some ways, that made him more alluring, but it also terrified her. Either way, she found herself marching toward him at full force.

He spotted her, and his weighty expression became friendly. She returned a smile and covered the last few feet of trail between them. He stood when she reached him, forcing her to look up. She still hadn't gotten used to how tall he was. "Hey, thanks for coming."

"Yeah, sure."

A family of ducks squawked by, momentarily distracting her before she braved a glance at him again. Each time she saw him, he looked different and better, if possible. Today his hair seemed darker, which turned his eyes a pale gray, making them stand out even more. Although they still held that pensive look Jada was starting to realize might never go away. He wore a long sleeved white cotton shirt and military green cargo pants.

"Do you want to sit?" He motioned to the bench.

"Yes, thanks." The old wood creaked as they both settled onto it. A light breeze stirred up the sweet smell of wildflowers in their last attempt to hold onto life before the freezing nights rendered them brittle and dead.

"Did you enjoy your party last night?" Nathan asked after a few quiet moments passed. She felt him studying her profile.

Jada shrugged. "Most of it." The only part she'd really

enjoyed was the time she spent with him. She smiled.

He smiled too, seeming to know what she was thinking.

She pulled a strand of hair out of her eye. "You left so suddenly."

"I know. Sorry about that. Seth, he—"

A snort escaped her lips. "He's an intense guy." She gazed out at the lake at a young couple on a paddleboat. Their laughter rode over the smooth, glistening surface like a water ski.

"He hates me, doesn't he?"

Nathan frowned. "He doesn't know you."

Jada let out a nervous laugh. "He doesn't seem to want you around me either."

Nathan arched toward her and pulled her chin up with his finger. "I don't care what he wants." His voice was gentle and firm.

Jada could've sworn her heart had stopped beating. He leaned closer to her and brushed his fingers across her cheek. Goosebumps followed his finger everywhere he touched. She was still in a state of shock. This dangerous, beautiful, mysterious guy liked her. She caught his hand as it fell from her face, sending a charge throughout her body. She bit her bottom lip as he leaned in and grazed her cheek with his smooth lips. The intoxicating smell of his skin sent rolls of heat through her stomach. Then he pulled back and looked at her tenderly.

"I don't care what Seth thinks, or anybody for that matter. I want to be near you."

At that moment Jada's body and mind completely emptied of every thought and worry. She didn't care that her mom or Seth didn't like her and Nathan being together. She knew from this moment on, she wouldn't be able to stay away from him.

She searched his eyes. "How come you didn't come into my life sooner?"

He grabbed her hand and slowly turned the silver ring she wore on her index finger. "I don't know. I guess now was the right time."

The sky slowly turned a grayish pink as they talked about everything and anything. She was surprised at how interested he was in her life. Finally, the sun dipped behind the mountains and the pulsating blue lake stilled into dark glass.

"I'd better go. My mom will start to worry." Jada lifted herself from the bench.

"Okay. Let me walk you to your car." They walked around the trail, brushing hands, reaching Jada's car far too quickly.

Nathan gripped her shoulders. "I want to see you tomorrow, make sure you're all right."

Jada searched his face, confusion plaguing her mind. Even though his fingers dug deeper into her, she couldn't pull herself away. She slid her hand onto his chest. His heartbeat was steady and strong. "What do you mean?"

"Just meet me in front of school before your first class. I want to see you." Having Nathan's lips so close to hers made her forget what he was saying. He apparently felt the same, because his eyes kept shifting from her eyes to her partly open mouth.

She let her eyelids fall. He teased her at first, sweeping

his lips against hers, and then his calloused hands lightly scraped her cheek and pulled her mouth into his. A shock wave ran through her, waking every dormant nerve in her body.

She pressed against him, sliding her hand up his hard chest. His fury slowed to a tender pace, and he playfully chewed on her lip. She smiled and reached her hands up to meet his, letting their foreheads lean onto each other. A tingle danced over her skin like a million little butterfly wings. She had never felt anything like it. Looking down on her now, his eyes held a mixture of pain and tenderness. He licked his lips, and Jada prepared for the crisp taste of him again. Instead he pulled away, leaving her heated skin at the mercy of the icy wind.

"Remember what I said. Meet me in front of school."

She nodded as he backed away. When he turned the corner and was out of sight, she let out a breath. The warm dizziness in her head was slowly dissolving as she unlocked her car and got in. After the engine caught, Jada sat for a few minutes staring at the empty space where he had just been, wishing he would reappear. A grin fixed on her face. She wrapped herself in a hug, trying to recreate the feeling of Nathan's thick body so close to hers. She closed her eyes and pictured his strong jaw and full lips coming toward her.

As she tugged on her seatbelt, about to head for home, a distant memory slammed her heart to the ground. It was Luke's face, in the hall, surrounded by everyone when she'd asked him out. Those mocking eyes, that hateful smirk. A menacing cloud snuck out from behind the trees, covering the park in a hazy shadow. The family that was there quickly packed up its stuff and left just in time to avoid the rain. She hugged herself again, but this time, to steady the tremor in her limbs. *Any minute now, Nathan is going to hurt me. I can't believe I let it go this far!* She looked again at the spot where Nathan was last and pictured his chiseled face. Forming a fist, she slammed it on the steering wheel.

No, I'm not going to let the past ruin my life. He is not going to hurt me. She repeated the last words, trying to convince herself. By the fourth time, she pulled out of the parking lot and almost believed it.

As a blur of houses and trees flew by her, Nathan's words came back to her mind. *I want to make sure you're all right.* What had he meant? Her thoughts whirled into a flurry of chaos. Her mom's strange conversation about changes, Seth's blatant dislike of her. Before she could attempt to answer the unending questions, a wave of exhaustion froze her mind. She decided to deal with it tomorrow. It was her eighteenth birthday, after all. This should be the best time of her life.

CHAPTER 12

Lub-dub, Lub-dub, Lub-dub. Jada fought through the cobwebs in her mind, trying to wake herself up. She slashed from side to side, the heartbeat thumping faster now behind her eyelids. Suddenly her body jolted up and her lungs gulped in air. Sweat dripped down the middle of her back as she scanned her room through half-open lids. An unnatural orange light hovered around her window, forming dim squares on the floor and ceiling. *This must be a dream.* She pushed the covers aside and walked up to the window. Standing at the corner, she pulled the curtain open and peeked outside. The mountains were still black from the night, their silhouette scribbling across a blazing orange sky.

She'd never seen anything like it.

Behind her, her lamp flickered on and off, then the bulb shattered with a loud crash.

Eyes wide she hugged the wall and stared at the dark circle on her lamp shade as the last few sparks died with a hiss. Fear plucked at her nerves.

Suddenly, her stomach folded into a knot. She doubled over, wincing as the pressure exploded into pain and crawled through her body inch by inch. She collapsed to the floor and tried to scream, but nothing came out. Her skin rippled as the pain shot through her arms.

Panic tore through her mind, but then another wave of pain shot through her veins, numbing her thoughts. She feebly tugged on the leg of her bed, trying to pull herself toward the door, but her arms were trembling and her legs were like anvils anchoring her body to the floor.

She thought about her life, how short it had been, and how much more she wanted to do. And her mom. She couldn't leave her mom. Not like this.

A woman's faint voice called her name.

Jada.

She froze and listened, convinced her mind was playing tricks on her. But then the voice called her again. This time louder.

Jada.

An invisible current cracked through the eerie stillness. The birds chirping outside hushed and the old house went silent.

She hadn't imagined the voice. Someone was in her room. She looked around furiously, but her vision was blurred from tears. Jada closed her eyes and tried to breath. When the floor vibrated under her cheek, her mouth went dry.

Footsteps.

Before she could react, a heavy presence pinned her to the floor. Sharp fingernails sliced into her legs and arms, and hot blood trickled down her skin and pooled beneath her. Then, a cool breath prickled her ear. *Jada . . .*

She opened her mouth to scream, but an iron grip folded

over her throat. She flailed her lifeless arms in the air. A thousand needles jabbed her flesh as they thrashed in the empty space above her. Forcing her eyes open, she scanned the light mist swirling around her.

A face formed, two piercing eyes and a sinister smile. It was laughing at her, mocking her. Jada's entire body shook uncontrollably. A flash of white burned her eyes.

Then, as fast as the pain came, it vanished. Her body sunk into the hardwood floor, and her eyelids closed with exhaustion.

The blackness faded as Jada pried opened her eyes to a view of the shadowed clutter under her bed. How long had she been lying there? Lifting herself up, she found the clock. 7:14 a.m. She'd been out for hours. She stumbled up and examined her room. There was no one else in there, and everything was in the same place as it had been. She rubbed her hands over her body. No pain or traces of wounds. In fact—her eyes narrowed in confusion—she felt good. Her body felt lighter and yet stronger somehow. *Maybe I'm still dreaming.* Something moved to her left. She jumped back, holding her palms out to defend herself. But when she turned, she only found her own image staring back at her from the mirror.

She breathed a sigh of relief and arched herself toward her reflection to look for any signs of injury. As her body came into view, her posture stiffened. Her straight hips now curved into a heart shape against her blue sweats, and small fleshy bumps peeked out of her tank top.

When a strand of long black hair fell in front of her face, she blinked and shook her head in disbelief. What was happening? Finally, she met the eyes of a stranger, and her hand flew to her mouth in shock. Her eyes, which used to be a soft brown color, had changed to a bright, almost neon cerulean blue. She leaned closer to the mirror and touched it to make sure it was there.

A loud knock made her jump, and Lilah's voice pressed through the door. "Happy birthday, honey! Are you awake? You're going to be late for school."

"I'm awake, Mom," Jada yelled back. "I'll be out in a minute."

She heard Lilah's steps move toward the kitchen. What was she going to do? She closed her eyes, unable to look at herself again. Then robotically she started moving, not knowing what else to do. She pulled her hair back into a ponytail and dug through her closet, looking for the only sweatshirt she owned, an oversized Union High hoodie. She found it and squirmed into the soft cotton. Then she remembered last year she'd bought some jeans that had stretched out after wearing them a few times. She bet those would fit her now. She found them buried in the back of her closet and rolled back on her bed, stuffing both legs in at once. They fit perfectly and even left a little room, so her new curves wouldn't be too obvious.

"Now what am I going to do about my eyes?" She was still in disbelief at their radiant color.

The only thing she could do was get colored contact lenses, and the only place to get them at this hour was the drugstore. But what about her mom? Jada looked around her room for ideas until she spotted her sunglasses on top of her dresser.

"Well, I'll look a little weird with sunglass on this early in the morning, but I have no choice." She slid them on. After stuffing her books into her backpack, she stepped into the hall and made her way directly to the front door.

"Jada, wait, don't you want breakfast?" Her mom's voice chased after her.

Jada waved dismissively and kept her pace. "No, thanks, Mom. I'm late. I'll pick something up at the cafeteria."

A quick breath escaped her as she shut the door behind her. One obstacle down.

One step away from her house, a cracking sound vibrated her head, like someone was stabbing her eardrums. She dropped her backpack and stuffed her fingers in her ears. Bent over, she searched for the source of the thunderous noise. Her eyes stopped on a squirrel chomping on a nut near the base of the tree in her front yard. No, it couldn't be. Every bite he took magnified in her head and rumbled down her body.

Then a flood of other noises came pouring into her ears. Her eyes darted around, locating each sound. A bird drinking water out of the gutter, a kid singing across the street, her neighbor's mailbox creaking open. The sounds relentlessly beat on her mind, and the ground started to spin. When she heard Lilah walking toward the front of the house, she panicked, grabbed her backpack, and stumbled to her car. Just as the front door opened, Jada pulled out of the driveway and slammed her foot on the gas pedal. The engine revved as high as it could go, screaming for her to shift.

Thoughts refused to form as she sped down the

neighborhood streets. Halfway to the drugstore, she noticed that her sight was impeccable. She struggled to focus on the road as her eyes locked onto every moving object along the way. When a crossing guard jumped in front of her car, waving frantically, she shrieked and smashed her foot on the brakes. She'd almost run a stop sign. After prying her stiff fingers off the steering wheel, she flipped on the AC and rolled her wrists, trying to relax.

Ignoring the angry gestures from the crossing guard, she furiously rummaged through the glove box looking for anything she could use as earplugs. She found a napkin, tore a few pieces off, and stuffed them into her ears. They barely softened the noise.

By the time she parked in front of the drugstore, she was mentally spent. The sounds had become unbearable. Raindrops, conversations, doors opening. Every noise sounded like it was hooked up to an amplifier. And she could see everything, even a trail of ants on the sidewalk. She hurried into the store to get away from a truck driving by but was greeted by a screeching intercom announcement about a sale on makeup. She gritted her teeth, pushing the torn balls of napkin deeper into her ears as she made her way back to the pharmacy.

"Well, if it isn't Miss Bell. What are you doing here at this hour?" Mr. Chase had worked at the pharmacy for as long as Jada could remember. He wore thick glasses that always looked as if they were going to fall off his nose. His hair had gotten so thin, strands of it were always standing straight up.

She grimaced. "Do you mind not talking so loud, Mr.

Chase?"

"Why, I had no idea I was, Miss Bell. I'm sorry."

Her hand shot up. "Anyway, can you show me where the contact lenses are? And earplugs."

"Why, sure, Miss Bell, but I didn't know you wore contacts. In fact, I've never even seen you in glasses." He didn't move, apparently set on getting an answer first.

"I don't." His small town nosy questions were scraping on her nerve endings. "There's a play at school, and I need some colored contacts." She forced a smile.

He smiled back, and the wrinkles on his thick, leathery skin dug deeper in his face. "Oh, I see. Well, they're right over here."

Jada followed close on his heels as he wobbled down the aisles. "Here you go, Miss Bell. Oh, and earplugs are on aisle three." He grinned and pointed at the collection of contact lenses.

"Thanks, Mr. Chase." She turned toward the rows of lenses.

But he didn't leave. Like a wave of earthquakes, Jada felt the phlegm rattling in his throat as he breathed. She looked him up and down. He had his hands shoved in his pockets and was watching her with a childlike look on his face. His sweaty stomach had popped out of the bottom of his shirt. Jada could feel a ball of anger squeezing her gut. "That's all I need, thank you," she said through tight lips.

After a few seconds, he looked down, defeated and walked away mumbling about how teenagers have no respect these days. Jada shook her head and focused on the different packs of contacts. She found brown ones and snatched them up, then grabbed a few packs of earplugs before heading to the front cash register.

There were only a few people in the checkout line, but they were all eyeing her suspiciously. Under her breath, an older woman muttered that Jada must be on drugs to be wearing sunglasses this early in the morning. Jada took off her glasses and glared at the woman. The color in her face drained, and she started to shuffle nervously through the items in her basket. Jada smirked as she pushed sunglasses back on with one finger, casting the store in a muted brown.

What am I doing? I don't bully people! She took in a deep breath and looked away. The line seemed to be going exceptionally slowly. When the cashier rang up her items, Jada didn't look at her and gave one-word answers to her cheerful questions. After paying, she hurried to her car, placing the earplugs in on the way. She could still hear everything, but it was manageable. When she opened the contact lenses, she glanced at the time and grunted. She was going to have to skip history.

As she inserted the delicate lenses, her eyes blinked, trying to dispel the foreign objects. Finally, they gave up the fight, and she examined her face in the visor mirror. It worked. She leaned back in the car seat, relief settling in her chest. What on earth was happening to her? Her hearing and sight—it wasn't possible. Maybe she had died in her room this morning? Maybe she was in some kind of afterlife? The thought weighed on her heart like a ton of bricks. She wasn't ready to die. She hadn't had enough time with Nathan. Rubbing her head, she steered her thoughts in another direction.

She looked down at her body. Not only had she filled out, she felt a power pulsating underneath the surface. She felt the urge to run for miles or jump to the roof of the drugstore.

A few kids on skateboards rolled by, reminding her that she should get to school, so she snapped on her seat belt and pulled out. On the way, she remembered she was supposed to meet Nathan outside of the main building. She drove slower, hoping he would go inside after the first bell rang. He'd want to see her sometime today, but he couldn't. No, she couldn't let him see her like this.

When she reached campus, he wasn't outside. "Thank God," she whispered.

Her phone vibrated. She pulled it out, already knowing what she would find. Five text messages from Nathan. Without reading them, Jada turned off her phone and headed up the parking lot. As much as she wanted—needed—to see, she would have to wait until she figured out what was going on with her. She slipped inside the main hall, trying to act as normal as possible. Luckily, it was minutes before the first class ended, so no one other than her was in the hall.

When she slumped in her seat in her second class, as usual, no one even glanced her way. But today, she was thankful for it. The real test would be lunch with Sam and Jen. They knew her better than anyone and would notice right away that she looked different.

Outside the cafeteria, she took a quick look in her compact mirror to make sure the contacts were still in place. After snapping it shut, she zipped it up in the small front pocket of her backpack and peeked around the door. Sam and Jen were already seated at their table, gabbing away, and Nathan and Seth were nowhere in sight. Her heart ached when she didn't see Nathan, but she convinced herself it was for the best—she wouldn't have to face both him and the girls at the same time.

She gathered what courage she could and walked in. Plopping into a chair next to Samantha, Jada offered them a weak smile and shoved her hands into her sweatshirt pockets.

Right away Sam took in Jada's appearance with a deep frown. "What are you wearing?"

"Clothes," Jada replied, cocking her head.

"Very funny. I mean, why are you wearing such huge jeans and an old sweatshirt? You look like you're going to clean out your garage." She took a bite of fries, not taking her eyes off Jada.

Jada looked down at her sweatshirt and shrugged. "I . . . forgot to do laundry last night. This is all I could find." When Sam didn't reply, she slowly raised her eyes and found both of them staring at her, eyebrows raised.

"Your eyes." Jen leaned over the table and squinted. "They're . . . strange looking. Darker maybe?"

Jada anxiously looked from Sam to Jen. "Look, I'm fine. Lay off, okay? I'm just out of it today." Jada cringed at the harshness of her words. First Mr. Chase, then the lady in line, and now her friends. She had never been a mean person. Where was this coming from?

"Okay, whatever." Sam gave Jen a sidelong glance

before they went back to their lunch. But the conversation was strained after that. They obviously weren't accepting Jada's excuse for the way she looked. Although she'd given up for now, Sam wouldn't relent until she found out the truth. But what was the truth? Jada gulped down the lump in throat. Somehow, she would have to find out.

CHAPTER 13

As Jada pulled out the last book from her locker and shoved it into her backpack, the bell rang for her class to start. She cursed under her breath. She'd gotten so caught up trying to act normal around Sam and Jen, she'd forgot about Nathan. It was good she was late to econ class. He wouldn't be able to talk to her and notice how different she'd become overnight. At the end of the hall, she spotted Emily also strolling in late and skirted in behind her. The only seats left were four rows to the left of Nathan. After giving him a cursory wave, she sat quickly, leaning back so that the students between them blocked her from his view.

Thirty minutes later, as usual, Mr. Harris's voice threatened to put her to sleep. She couldn't tell if he was talking slower or if her heightened senses made it seem that way. The green chalkboard blurred, then went black, then back to blurry again as she fought her heavy eyelids.

She stood in a dense forest. Massive weathered tree trunks and floating sprays of greens and boughs surrounded her. A gust of wind danced tiny droplets of dew across her face. She looked around. There was a lot of forest in Bishop, but this place had a hint of familiarity. Ahead of her, a slight movement flashed through the maze of green.

She squinted. It looked like a person leaning against a tree.

She trudged through the thick mulch, clumps of damp leaves sticking to the bottom of her pants. When she got closer, she picked up her pace.

A woman slumped against ropes that tied her to the tree, her clothes soaked in long streaks of blood. Jada's hand clasped her throat in horror as she searched for the woman's face, but it was hidden beneath a matted ball of wet black hair. She moved closer and her chest squeezed.

She's wearing my clothes.

Her body started to tremble, but she forced herself forward, stopping a foot away from the limp figure. She had to see her face.

Her trembling hand reached up and gently pushed aside the woman's damp hair. Malicious blue eyes snapped open and burrowed into her. She stumbled back, tripping over a fallen branch.

Jada . . . the woman's voice sang as a sardonic smile crept up her face.

Jada jerked awake to her desk rattling under her. She was back in class and everyone was staring at her.

"Miss Bell, I apologize that my lecture is not exciting enough to keep you awake." Mr. Harris stood in front of her, arms crossed over his chest, his chalky hands leaving dusty white smudges on his cheap shirt.

Jada stared at him, unable to speak.

Mr. Harris pointed at her desk. "What happened here? Are you going to pay for that?"

She looked down. A long crack zigzagged across the desk between her white knuckled hands. Her mouth

133

dropped open. Slowly, she unwrapped her stiff fingers from the desk and watched wide-eyed as it split in two and crashed to the floor. Her lunch fizzled in her stomach, threatening to resurface. The sting of vomit rose to her throat, and she grabbed her backpack and ran out. Mr. Harris's voice chased after her, but she kept running. As she neared the bathroom, that pulsating strength she'd felt earlier exploded under her skin. Each step she took thrust her down the hall like a gazelle running for its life. Finally at the bathroom, she threw the door open, slamming it into the wall. The door bounced back and pieces of tile shattered to the floor. A girl meticulously applying a bright red lipstick, flinched, smearing the color down her cheek. Jada tossed her backpack down and bent over the sink, choking in large swallows of air. The girl quickly washed her face and hurried out, walking in a dramatic circle around Jada.

What is happening to me? How did I break the desk?

The hinges on the bathroom door creaked, opening it an inch.

"Jada?" Nathan's husky voice bounced off the bathroom walls. "Are you in there? Are you all right?"

"Ye-yeah, I'm okay." Her voice was muffled with tears.

"Can I come in?"

Her fingers clamped onto the sides of sink. "No, I'm fine. Can we meet later?"

The door creaked closed. She pictured him behind it. Could she trust him and tell him what was happening? She felt dizzy and confused. She twisted the cold water knob and filled her palms with the brownish water. The smell of chlorine and iron penetrated her nose. Her lip upturned. *I can smell everything too?*

After dumping the water into the sink, she assessed her appearance. Her hair was sticking out in several directions, and her contacts had gone askew. Unable to reset the contacts, she popped them out and chucked them in the trash. When she saw her vibrant blue eyes, the vision of the woman's bloody face flashed in her mind. She pinched her eyes shut, trying to get rid of her taunting grin.

That voice. I know that voice.

And then she remembered. It was the same voice she'd heard this morning in her room. Who was she, and why was she in her head? Biting her bottom lip, she knelt and searched her backpack for her brush. After pulling it through her tangled hair, she stood and looked herself over. Her eyes were bloodshot, and her hair looked like she'd just gotten out of bed. It would have to do. Before leaving, she took out her earplugs and stuffed them into her pocket. She had to look as normal as possible if Nathan was still out there.

With sunglasses on, she snuck out the bathroom door. The halls were empty—except for Nathan, who was leaning against a locker, concern consuming his face.

Jada kept her gaze down. "Can we meet later?" she repeated and darted down the hall toward the parking lot. It took everything she had to not look at him, when really all she wanted was for him to comfort her.

He silently fell into step next to her, looking ahead. He must think she was insane. She sighed. That would be her luck. Finally a guy likes her, and she scares him off.

When they reached her car, she pulled her keys out and clicked the unlock button. He grabbed her hand.

"Wait, Jada. Just talk to me for a minute."

Lifting her chin, she braved a look at him. His eyes were severe yet calm, like he knew exactly what he was doing. Did he know what was going on with her?

He touched her cheek. "Jada," he murmured. His rugged voice soothed her like a warm fire in the freezing dead of winter.

Like the flip of a switch, she suddenly wasn't afraid of him seeing her and was overwhelmed with need to be near him. His feral aura comforted her. It felt . . . familiar. She threw her keys back into her purse. To hell with worrying about dents and paint scratches—she jumped backward onto the hood of her car. Wrapping her arms behind her head, she leaned back against the windshield. He leaped onto the car and slid next to her, nudging his upper arm into her shoulder. The windshield screeched under his heavy torso.

"Maybe you should lay off the gym for a while." She gave him a weak smirk and released her arm, letting it dig into his.

He grinned. "Glad to know you still have a sense of humor."

They sat in silence for a few minutes, watching the blue-gray clouds inch their way south. A loud whistle from the PE field behind the school screamed in her ears. She winced, wondering how she was going to figure out what was wrong with her.

Then her mom's words suddenly came into her mind.

You are going to notice some changes.

"Mom," she whispered. Lilah knew what was happening, and she'd tried to tell her last night.

"What did you say?" He raised his head. When his eyes fell on her body, he looked her up and down, clearly noticing for the first time she was wearing clothes that were too big for her.

"Nothing, but I should go." She slid off the car.

"Let me come with you. You're obviously not feeling well."

Jada hugged herself and looked down. "I think I'm just coming down with something. I should go home and rest."

In one swift movement, he was off the car and looking down at her. "You are stubborn." He reached for her face.

"No—" She tried to catch his hand, but he already had her sunglasses off and tucked into his shirt pocket.

He wrapped his hands around her shoulders. "It's okay, Jada."

Jada squeezed her eyelids closed, terrified of him seeing her freakish new eye color. She couldn't lose him, not now when she really needed him. She tried to imagine the look on his face.

"You don't know what you're doing!" She shrieked.

"Yes, I do. Look at me."

She hesitated. *What will he say? How can I explain this?* But a warmth grew in her stomach from being near him. After a few seconds, she couldn't stop herself. She had to see him. She slowly lifted her face and met his eyes, hoping that tenderness she saw moments ago was still there. To her surprise, his face held not even the slightest hint of shock or anger. He picked up a piece of her hair, rubbed it between his fingers, and brought it up to his nose, smiling as he breathed in.

His calm demeanor made Jada feel at ease. Maybe her heightened senses, her super strength, weren't as big a deal as she thought. Maybe they would all go away tomorrow, and things would return to normal.

After releasing her hair, he grabbed her waist and effortlessly lifted her back onto the hood of the car. Liquid fire ignited under her cheeks. He took a step toward her and pressed his leg between her knees. She flashed him a mischievous grin and flexed her thighs, holding her legs together. The wildness in his eyes exploded, and he pressed harder. She released her muscles, and he slid between her thighs, tugging on her knees until her chest was inches from his. Jada's legs burned as his hands slowly inched up. With a tender smile on his face, he ran his fingers through her hair. Jada closed her eyes, focusing on his every touch. His hands slid around her neck and then gently pulled her face upward. The muscles in his legs contracted, sending what felt like an electric spark up her body and out her fingertips.

When his lips met hers, her heart beat faster. He was gentle yet aggressive, sending goose bumps down to her toes. He softly bit down on her tongue before furiously burying his lips in hers again. Before pulling away, he kissed her on the forehead and ran his fingers through her hair once more.

Without any strain, he picked her up again by the waist and set her on the ground. They smiled at each other, and

Jada felt her cheeks grow hot again. Would she ever stop blushing around him?

"I'm going to call you later." He gave her a stern look, like she didn't have a choice.

Reluctantly, she let go of his hands and turned toward her car door, fumbling through her purse for her keys. As she navigated the lot, watching him in her rearview mirror, the slightest bit of unease flickered in her chest. Why hadn't he asked her about her eyes? They were practically glowing blue. But when she signaled to turn the corner and he waved at her and smiled, the feeling disappeared. It didn't matter. She needed him. She was in love with him.

Nathan stood and watched Jada's car become smaller and then disappear. His heart felt like it was sinking into the depths of the ocean, a thousand pounds of water pressing down on it. *She was the one. The prophecy was true.* Ever since the day he saw her in the cafeteria, he'd been hoping his grandfather was suffering from dementia when he made the prophecy. When her soft brown eyes locked with his, a hot vibration exploded out of his stomach and through his body. He hadn't wanted to feel this way about her, had fought it every time he saw her. But he'd finally given in at her birthday party. She was not what he expected at all. She was sarcastic, tough, smart. But also sweet and caring. Not at all like other girls. Not to mention her smooth, pale skin and the way her dark hair lightly brushed her bare shoulders. It made his heart pound against his ribs. He'd wanted to touch her hair since that fateful day in the cafeteria, and today he had. He still felt the silky strands between his fingers.

The bell rang for class to end, and moments later, the school doors opened and voices ripped through the still air like thunder. Kicking up some gravel, he thought about what he was going to have to do. He ground his teeth as he looked down at the spot where Jada's car had been.

Footsteps behind him brought him back to the present. He didn't turn, already knowing who it was. Seth seemed to pop up wherever he was, and it was starting to get on his nerves. Somehow he must know that Nathan cared for Jada, because he was watching him like a hawk. Nathan bit down hard on his cheek, realizing Seth may have seen him kiss Jada. He needed to be more careful.

"Is she the one?" Seth's accusing voice floated on the wind from behind him.

Nathan's shoulders relaxed. Seth hadn't seen him. "Yes," he replied, not facing his brother.

With arms crossed tightly over his chest, Seth stopped in front of Nathan, demanding his attention. "The titanium came in this morning. It's all set."

CHAPTER 14

At a stoplight, Jada shoved her earplugs back in and massaged her temples.

What a day. The mysterious pain that consumed her body, her eyes, the dream, and then kissing Nathan. It was all too much. The light turned green, forcing her car forward as a few raindrops spattered on the windshield. She rolled down her window and stuck her hand out. Cold liquid ran down her arm. The gray clouds had turned black and were joining into a ghoulish ball slowly devouring the light blue sky.

By the time she pulled into the parking lot of her mom's shop, it was pouring. Through the heavy streams of water, she noticed that Lilah's car was nowhere in sight. She grabbed her phone and dialed the shop number.

"Lilah's Blossoms." The shop assistant answered.

"Hi, it's Jada. Is my mom there?"

"Why no, your mom left about a half hour ago. She said it was a family emergency. I assumed it was you. Is everything all right?"

Alarm sat Jada straight up. "Oh . . . yes, everything is fine. I'm fine." What emergency could Lilah be talking

141

about? Her mom didn't have any brothers or sisters, and her parents had been dead for years.

Jada chewed on her thumb. "Well, I'm going home. I'm sure she's there. Thanks."

"Okay. Let me know if there's anything I can do."

"I will. Bye." After disconnecting, Jada jerked the car into reverse, and steered toward home, the mucky gravel crunching under her tires.

A flicker of fear split her mind. What if her dad had come back? What if he was hurt? The cyclone of thoughts made her head feel like it was being crushed like a soda can. She slammed down on the gas pedal, thrusting the car well over the speed limit. Her house was ten minutes away, but she could get there in five.

Turning down her street, she rubbed the condensation that had built on her windshield, trying to get a better look at her house. There were two cars in her driveway and one at the curb directly in front of her house. She frowned. As she got closer, she recognized Lilah's car, Samantha's mom's car, and Jen's car.

She pulled in next to the curb, jumped out, and ran to the front door.

When she walked in, soft conversation led her to the living room. Sam and her mom, Stephanie, were leaning against the entryway door and turned when they heard the front door. Jada pushed between them and lifted her hands to her mom. "What's going on? Are you all right?"

When Lilah saw her, her hand flew to her trembling lips. Before Jada could say a word, Sam twirled her around and studied her through narrowed eyes. "Why are you wearing blue contacts?"

Jada stared back at her, unblinking. Sam leaned closer. Jada could see the blood pumping in Sam's neck. It pumped faster. "Oh, my god, you're not wearing contacts. H-how?" Sam took a step back.

Jada opened her mouth to answer but just released a sigh. She didn't know.

Jen scooted to the end of the chair she was sitting on. "I knew something was different about your eyes.

A throat cleared and Stephanie walked to the front of the room. "Girls, take a seat."

Lilah lowered herself slowly, grabbing the chair arms to steady herself. Sam sat next to Jen's mom, Alex, on the couch, and Jada settled cross-legged into a chair across from Lilah.

"Lilah, Alex, and I have something to tell you girls." Stephanie's hand was steady as she grabbed a glass of water off a side table and took a long drink. "I'm sorry this is going to come as a shock, but I'm just going to get it out. To start, the three of you are related."

Jada suddenly felt cold. It was too much to take in right now. All that happened to her today and now this. The girls stared at each other, searching for any sign of resemblance, confusion covering their faces. All at once, they erupted into a hundred questions, talking and shouting over each other.

"Girls, stop!" Lilah yelled. "Just calm down and let us explain." She wrapped her hands behind her neck and took in a deep breath. "We all have a . . . unique ancestry."

Lilah's words rang in Jada's head. Closing her eyes, she

rubbed the bridge of her nose. Something was starting to click, like a puzzle slowly coming together. She just didn't know what. Lilah's warning her about changes on Sunday, her acute senses, her *unique* ancestry. What did it all mean?

Lilah pushed herself back in her chair and nudged her feet in the cushion. "Our story began over a century ago with your great-great-grandmother Edana . . ."

It was an unusually warm September in 1922. Edana pulled the wood comb through her long black hair and smiled at her reflection in the mirror. She was turning eighteen tonight and was excited about it. She was getting a little old not to be married, but secretly, she liked it that way. She loved her job teaching children at the only school in Bishop and didn't want to be told what to do by a husband. Her parents had died three years ago when an earthquake collapsed their home, but she had survived and was taking care of herself.

Tilting her head as she wrapped her hair in a loose bun, she peeked behind her vanity and out the window. The sun had just slipped behind the mountains. The town was having a small party for her, and she was going to be late. She stood, pinched her cheeks until they turned pink, and stepped out the door.

On her porch, she wrapped her shawl around her shoulders and looked up. The sky was solid black and clear, the moon full and the color of dry bones. Despite the warm air, a shiver ran through her. After surveying the area around her house and finding nothing out of the ordinary, she shrugged off the foreboding feeling and headed to Main Street.

When she pushed open the heavy oak doors, cheering and hugs greeted her. Even Father David had come, likely to the chagrin of his fellow priests. She suspected he wanted to marry her. Every time she saw him, he stood up straight, taking his hat off, and gave her an unrestrained smile. Sometimes she found herself wishing he weren't a priest. He was tall, with a full head of dark brown hair, and was the sweetest man ever to live. But then she would scold herself. She wanted to be the first woman in her family to be independent, to make her own decisions.

The party was a success and lasted till midnight. She even had a little wine warming her tummy when she walked home. Father David had tried to escort her, but she insisted on walking alone. She needed the fresh air, and besides, nothing bad ever happened in Bishop.

When she reached her house, she pulled out her key from a pocket in her dress. But before she could get it in the lock, darkness crawled down her door like thick oil. She shuddered and spun around. The moon had been swallowed up by a long black cloud. Squinting, she let out a shaky breath, feeling that same heavy sensation upon her again. The key clanked against the door as her trembling hand searched for the lock. Finally, the door swung open, and she jumped inside, slamming it behind her.

Her legs suddenly felt heavy as she slipped out of her dress and into her nightgown, gently draping her camisole and bloomers over her chair. After crawling into bed, she pulled her wool blankets up to her neck and curled her feet up to her thighs.

She let out a long breath. "A perfect night."

A deep sleep seized her instantly. The wind picked up outside, rattling her windows, but she didn't stir. It was the most peaceful sleep she ever had, or would ever have again.

Dawn was about to break when a deafening boom ripped through the still air and shook the ground under her. She jerked up in bed, tiny drops of sweat growing on her brow. *An earthquake? Not again, not to me!*

She threw her blankets aside, slid her bare feet onto the cold hardwood floor, and ran to the front door. But by the time she got there, the noise was gone, replaced by a heavy silence. Standing to the side, she cracked open the large door. The rusty hinges screamed, drowning out her fast breathing. She peered through the two-inch gap. A thick fog surrounded her house, slithering in between the fence posts like a snake. She waited, her breathing slowly returning to normal. She must have dreamed about an earthquake. It wouldn't be the first time. She was closing the door when the sound of crunching leaves came through the crack. She stopped.

"Is s-someone there?" Her tiny voice disappeared in the darkness.

No reply.

Suddenly, a blast of wind threw the door open, knocking her to the floor. A dark figure stepped inside, its head nearly brushing the ceiling. She let out a cry and crawled backward until she hit the wall.

Then the most beautiful deep voice she had ever heard filled the room. "Don't be afraid," it sang.

She shrank back. "W-what do you want?"

"I've come for you, my love. I saw you from above. I've

given up everything for you."

He stepped forward and reached out his hand. Ashen moonlight shone through the window, illuminating glistening black eyes in a perfect chiseled face and hair the color of the sun. She knew at that moment that he wasn't human. Her first thought was that he looked godlike and angelic, but his eyes told a different story. The black stones pierced through her flesh and into her bones. Whatever he wanted, it wasn't good.

"My name is Azael. I've come for you. You will be mine," he repeated as he glided toward her.

Be *his?* Tears streamed from her blue eyes, and she tried to run, but he caught her and lifted her in his arms like she weighed as much as a feather. Her body started to tremble. He laid her on the bed and stroked her hair.

"Now you are mine . . ."

When Lilah finished the story, she folded her hands in her lap and looked at the girls.

Samantha huffed and cocked her head. "C'mon, is this really true? It sounds like a movie."

"Yes." Lilah's stern voice echoed in the room. "It is, and it affects us all."

Jen pulled her knees to her chest. "What . . . was he?"

The chair's fabric started to tear under Jada's fingers. She tucked her hands under her arms and rested her head on the back of the chair. It was starting to come together now in her mind, but she didn't want to believe it, couldn't believe it.

"Let me finish the story." Lilah said.

The next morning Edana woke to a throbbing pain

between her legs. Grimacing, she slowly pushed herself up. When she saw Azael lying next to her, she let out a cry but then slapped her hand to her mouth. He was still asleep. His skin was as pure as a newborn's. And his arms were the size of her thighs. Her eyes burned as she watched his large chest rise and fall. Ripping the blanket off her, she shrieked. Tiny pools of blood stained the sheets under her legs. He had taken her. Against her will. Now, even if she wanted to get married, no one would ever have her.

Hot tears now soaked her face as she pulled her robe over her nightgown and stumbled out the door. She ran as hard as she could, her soles somehow impervious to the jagged rocks under her feet. Her lungs burned as she slammed her fists on Father David's small cottage door.

"Edana—What are you doi—you're bleeding!" Father David set down his mug of steaming coffee and pulled Edana inside. He gazed at her bloodstained nightgown and dirty feet. "What's happened?"

Edana broke into a jumble of words and cries. Flailing her hands in the air, she choked out what happened in between sobs. When she got to the part about Azael setting her on the bed, her throat started to tighten, letting out raspy breaths.

Father David froze, a look of horror on his face. "Azael. That's the—the fallen angel who mated with women. He's supposed to be chained in the desert."

Edana's knees shook, and the floor started coming toward her. Father David caught her and gently set her in his reading chair. She rocked back and forth, her eyes bulging and unblinking. "What do I do?"

Just then, Azael appeared in the entryway, fists clenched. Father David jumped in front of Edana and glared up at him. "You can't have her."

Azael let out a sardonic laugh that shook the little cottage. "I already did. Out of my way, pathetic human." He pushed Father David aside and clamped on to Edana's arm. Father David crashed into the stove and slumped to the floor. Azael pulled Edana up to his face, her toes reaching for the ground.

"I told you, you are mine," he spat through clenched teeth and then dragged her home.

Months turned into years, and she gave birth to three daughters. She adored her sweet girls, but enduring her captor's depravity with no respite consumed her with bitterness. One day while Azael was asleep, she was overcome with anger and picked up the dining room table and threw it across the room. She realized then that she had absorbed his powers and decided that she would kill him that night. Before he woke up, she got rid of the pieces of the table and bought a new one. It was easy enough to convince him that she had spilled something on it, ruining it. He didn't care about those things anyway, as long as he got what he wanted.

When the sky was still black, she lay awake in bed next to him, flexing her fingers, feeling the unnatural power flowing through her. No matter what the consequences, the need to be free of his cruelty and to protect her beloved daughters from him outweighed this hellish existence. Wrapping her hands around his neck, she leaned all her weight into him. His eyes shot open and he grabbed her wrists. She gripped tighter and felt his hands start to tremble. For the first time, fear glazed his cerulean blue eyes. When she realized he couldn't fight her, rage that had been repressed for years surged through her body and bore down on him like an avalanche. The force of her clutch doubled, tripled, then in one swift jerk, she shattered his neck.

Jada ran to the kitchen and splashed cold water on her face. She felt like she was going to faint, holding onto the walls as she staggered back in the living room.

"What happened to her?" Jen asked.

Lilah stood to help Jada, but she waved her off and returned to her chair.

Lilah sighed. "Unfortunately, her problems didn't end there. After killing him, she left her house and went into town. She wandered the streets and tore apart trees and ripped through buildings. The people of the town were terrified. A few men tried to stop her, but she tossed them out of the way like they were paper dolls. After about an hour, she finally collapsed in the street from exhaustion and sobbed."

Jen shook her head. "Did anyone help her?"

"No one helped her, and in fact, just the opposite happened. She was alienated from the town, and rumors quickly spread that she was a witch or possessed by a demon."

"But she wasn't, was she?" Jen asked.

"No, she was a Nephilim."

"What's a Nephilim?" Sam crossed her arms over her chest.

Lilah rubbed her neck, "A Nephilim is the offspring of the sons of God and the daughters of man. In other words, the children of angels and humans."

"But—she wasn't an offspring." A sheen came over Jen's eyes.

"No, but apparently we are, genius." Sam snapped.

Jada, Sam and Jen looked between each other as the heavy realization settled in.

Lilah continued. "No she wasn't an offspring, but somehow she became—what we are—half human, half angel. After that day, she did her best to isolate herself, not even letting her girls go out to play. She was terrified they would be taken from her and killed." Lilah bent forward and rested her elbows on her knees.

Jada hugged herself. "Didn't the town people know that Azael had forced her?"

The icy, moist air from the rain was starting to creep through the corners of the windows. Stephanie crossed the room to the fireplace and stacked a pile of wood over the dying embers. "Yes, they knew, but it didn't matter. Azael was a fallen angel, a creature of darkness. And now Edana and her girls were too."

After lighting a piece of newspaper and stuffing it under the wood, Stephanie sat back down. "I don't think she ever recovered from the years she had spent trapped with Azael. Something had snapped in her mind. She and her girls were now totally secluded. No one, not even the people she thought were her closest friends, wanted anything to do with her. On her bad days, she would have fits of anger and would rip through the streets, frightening people. The hysteria didn't take long to spread. It was only a few weeks later when they went to her house, dragged her out . . . and killed her. They tied her to a tree, beat her, then burned her alive."

The woman's bloody face from her dream barged into Jada's mind. Cringing, she bent over her legs and buried her face in her hands.

"What is it, honey?" Lilah leaned forward.

Jada squeezed her eyes shut tighter. "Nothing, I've just been having these dreams, bad dreams."

"There is a reason for that," Lilah said. "What that means for you three—well, and all of us—is that, as her descendants, we all are endowed with some of her powers."

Jada let out an uncontrollable whimper and sat up again. "I'm guessing we all get these powers when we turn eighteen?"

"Yes," her mom replied. "What have you experienced so far?"

Jada's hands formed claws over her ears. "The noise is unbearable. I can hear every little thing."

Stephanie and Lilah shared a knowing glance and Stephanie started again. "We all have the power to self-heal but we also each have a unique power. Lilah can turn herself into stone. I can read people's thoughts, and Alex can breathe under water."

Jada eyed her mom. "The broken counter. That didn't get smashed by a hammer, did it?"

Lilah gave her a shaky smile. "No, I broke it. I was angry and slammed my fist into it. When I get emotional my power tends to have a mind of its own."

"And the water glass at the restaurant?"

"You were right. I shattered it with my hand." Lilah lifted her arm up, and her hand morphed into stone.

Jada scooted to the edge of her seat. "That was the strange gray flesh I saw on your skin."

"There's more, Jada. I think we can say with certainty now that you are different. You see, right before Edana died, she declared to the people of Bishop that she would return one day and kill all of their descendants. Wipe out the whole town."

Jada tried to swallow the lump in her throat, but it wouldn't budge. "What do you mean? What does that have to do with me?"

Lilah pulled on her jittery fingers. "Honey, Edana's spirit has finally come back to take her revenge. . . through you."

Jada couldn't speak. Her throat felt like it was collapsing.

"Jada, look at me." Lilah reached out and touched her leg. "Throughout all the years, only Edana had the acute senses. This explains your hearing. Do you also have better sight and feel stronger?"

Jada nodded.

"You will have the power of nature too, like Edana. You can manipulate trees, rocks, dirt—anything of the earth."

"Also, from what we have learned from our ancestors, the only way you will be able to die is by fire. Apparently, they tried everything else on poor Edana," Stephanie said.

The fire cracked and spat. Jada imagined the flames covering her body, turning her skin to ash. Why was this happening? Why her?

Pressure built inside her chest. A framed photograph toppled from the mantel. The glass shattered on the hearth, a shard disappearing under the couch. Did she do that? She didn't even know. Squeezing her eyes shut, she tried tuning out the unwanted emotions, focusing instead on this room full of people who cared about her.

When she opened her eyes, everyone was staring at her. She rolled her eyes. "Seriously, you guys. Best. Birthday. Ever."

No one laughed at her attempt at a joke. After a minute of tense silence, Lilah leaned closer to Jada. "Edana's desires do not have to be your own. You can fight this."

Jada jumped up and started pacing the living room, running her hands through her hair. "Fight this? I'm a Nephilim, and my great-great-grandmother has possessed me and wants me to slaughter everyone I know."

"Honey, it is manageable." Lilah stood and grabbed her shoulders. "Steph, Alex, and I have never been suspected. It is possible to live a normal life."

Jen got up and backed up against the fire. "Are we really evil, though? I mean, just because Edana did evil things doesn't mean we will?" Her eyes held a flicker of hope.

Alex went to Jen and pulled her into her chest. "Unfortunately, honey, fallen angels are evil. There is a part of you that will want to do bad things, terrible things. A part of you that you will always have to fight."

The room fell silent except for the wood floor creaking under Jada's feet as she paced again.

"Wait." Samantha's fingers became rigid, spreading out

like a fan over her thighs. "If Edana was so powerful, why didn't she just fight the people off when they came to kill her?"

Gazing out the window, Lilah crossed her arms over her chest. "Well, Azael knew that Edana would have to be stopped, so right before he died, he gave one person the power to kill her, the most noble and pure man in the town. Her powers were useless against him. His name was Michael Aron."

CHAPTER 15

Jada froze and stared at her mom's lips in disbelief at what she'd just heard.

Her jaw knotted. "Aron, as in Nathan Aron?"

A deep red color rose up Lilah's neck and face. "Yes. He is the great-great-grandson of Michael Aron. Every generation has been told about Edana and her inevitable return. Since birth, Nathan has been preparing and training to kill you girls, in case Edana came back through one of you." Lilah looked down, the veins throbbing in her neck. "Somehow the Arons knew that it was time, that Jada was the one. That's why Nathan and Seth started Union High this year, to get close to you."

Jada felt like a knife had sliced through her heart. She bit down on her lip and looked away as a sharp pain built behind her eyes. *How could I be so blind? All this time he was deceiving me, trying to gain my trust so he could . . . kill me!* She started to pace again and thought of every moment they had spent together. A tear slid down her face for each touch, each smile.

A ball of anger ignited in her stomach, tightening her fingers into hard fists. Then it erupted, tearing through her body like spewing lava. Tremors rolled down her legs and into the ground, shaking the house to the foundation. The TV screen shattered and crashed onto the floor. The house moaned and shifted as Jada replayed every second of Nathan's deceit.

"Jada!" Lilah rushed to her side and cupped her face. "You have to calm down. You are going to destroy the house." A floor board flipped up, knocking Lilah into the corner.

"Jada, stop!" Alex yelled as she and Jen struggled to keep their balance. The scene seemed far away, like it was part of a movie.

Her mom's screaming stopped suddenly, as though someone had hit the mute button. Jada's rage slowed to a steady simmer and, strangely, soothed her aching heart like a balm. She closed her eyes and pictured Nathan.

He would pay.

Jada!

Lilah's terrified voice vibrated behind her eyes.

I'm hurting my mom. I've got to get out of here!

Prying her eyelids open, she tightened all her muscles and hurled her body towards the door. Her mom reached for her, but she slipped just out of her grasp.

When she stepped out, a flurry of sounds bit at her eardrums like piranhas. It fueled the adrenaline pumping through her, and she ran faster. The icy rain evaporated instantly as it collided with her roasting skin. She didn't know what to do or where to go. All she knew was that she needed to get away from her house, from this madness. She ran to the end of her block and kept going until her neighborhood disappeared behind her. With each step, her anger slowly burned away. She slowed to a stop when her lungs felt as if they were going to ignite, reminding her that she was still part human. Warm tears mixed with the cool rain on her face as she leaned onto her knees and gasped for air. Squinting, she tried to see where she was through the droplets on her eyelashes. A massive cross filled her vision. She'd run all the way to Our Lady Catholic Church.

She took in the grandeur of the huge cross, illuminated by a bright light at its base, before heading up the long grassy walkway. When she reached the door, she wiped the water off her face and looked around. There were only a few cars in the parking lot, and the windows were dark. She grabbed the door handle, but her hand froze.

Am I allowed in here anymore? Her wet shirt clung to her chest, rising and falling with her strained breathing. She exhaled slowly, her breath turning into a stream of delicate vapor as she tried to calm her racing heart. Finally, before she could change her mind, she swung the heavy door open and stepped inside. The pounding of the rain was replaced by silence as the door gently closed behind her. Thankfully, the sanctuary was empty.

The smell of incense and old wood swirled inside of her nose. She took a step into the sanctuary. Pale light filtered through the stained glass windows casting an array of colors over the benches like handfuls of jewels had been strewn over them. Any moment she sure she'd be struck by lightning for being in here. She was, after all, some kind of evil demi-god.

Ne-phi-lim.

Thinking it wasn't helping. It felt surreal. She reached

the last pew and sighed before sliding onto the stiff wood.

Jada scanned the sanctuary. She had lived in Bishop her whole life but had never been inside this building. Lilah was not very religious, and of course now Jada knew why. What place did a half human, half fallen angel have in a church? The crucifix hanging above the pulpit caught her eye. She couldn't tear her gaze from it. There was something soothing yet . . . frightening about it. She took another deep breath and tried to release the tension in her shoulders.

Distant clicking gradually became louder. By the time she realized the clicks were footsteps, it was too late. She stood as a tall, thin, elderly man entered the room and made his way to the front. He was wearing a long-sleeved black cassock, and he held a Bible in his left hand. He stopped unexpectedly, ran his hand through his disheveled, cotton-white hair, and mumbled something unintelligible. He twisted back toward the way he'd come, evidentially forgetting something, and spotted Jada.

"Oh, miss, I didn't see you there." A warm smile lifted his wrinkled cheeks.

"I'm sorry, sir. I mean, Father. The door was unlocked." She didn't know anything about the Catholic Church except what she'd seen in movies. The only thing she could remember was that in *The Exorcist* the priests were called father.

He walked toward her, still smiling. "It's always open. You are welcome here anytime, my dear." He reached out his hand. "I'm Father Steve. And you are?"

She allowed his large warm hand to wrap around hers.

"Jada Bell."

A hint of recognition flashed in his pastel blue eyes. "Miss Bell, yes . . . very nice to meet you."

"Do y-you know me?" What if somehow he already knew about her? He'd certainly make her leave or worse.

"Nope, never laid eyes on you before. Have met your mom though, at the flower shop." His face had a tender expression. There was something about him that made her feel at ease, like she could trust him. There wasn't even the slightest hint of hostility on his face.

"Well, thank you, Father Steve. I could really use a place to escape to right now."

"Is everything all right?" He shifted the Bible to his other hand and scratched the light gray stubble on his jaw.

"Yes. Well, no, actually."

He looked down at the pew. "Let's sit, I'm all ears." They sat down in unison, causing the old wood to groan under their weight. His rhythmic breathing comforted her as he waited patiently for her to start.

After a few seconds of trying to find the words, she huffed. "It's complicated. I thought I knew this guy, but it turns out I was wrong about him." Her heart filled with anger again at the thought of Nathan. "And I'm just . . . going—having—uggh, I'm not making any sense, am I?" She lifted her chin and found his sympathetic eyes.

"You're making fine sense. Don't be so hard on yourself. Sometimes expressing how you feel can be very challenging." He patted her on the shoulder and shifted toward the front.

"What's the guy's name?"

"Nathan."

When he looked at her, his eyes were pensive. "Oh, Mr. Aron?"

Jada nodded and looked away. "He—" She was unable say out loud that Nathan had betrayed her. He had lied to her, pretended to like her. Kissing her, the way he tenderly looked at her, it was all a lie. She felt as if her heart was being slowly shredded with a dull knife.

"Miss Bell, I'm so sorry." Father Steve's voice wafted over her. "But I *know* Mr. Aron, and he is a fine boy."

Jada's skin started to tingle as she looked up into Father Steve's eyes. "Well, you must be mistaken about him." Her voice was curt, and she hoped it would signal to Father Steve that any more talk of Nathan was not welcome. She gazed forward, a few silent tears falling down her face.

Father Steve's posture loosened, and he relaxed again. "Unfortunately, Miss Bell, life can be really difficult sometimes. Some people even spend their whole lives struggling. And people will disappoint and even hurt you. It's a guarantee."

She let out a bitter laugh. If he only knew what was really going on. She wasn't just in a silly fight with her boyfriend. He was trying to kill her.

"What is it?" He matched her smile.

"I thought priests were supposed to say everything will work out." To her relief, he chuckled at her admission.

"Nah, that would be boring, and not necessarily true. Not my style." His eyed sparkled. "Father Jeffrey, on the other hand, he'll tell you everything will be just fine and dandy. Want me to go get him?" A snicker twitched on the corners of his mouth.

"No." She allowed her lips to curve slightly. "I prefer your honesty, however hard it might be to take."

Despite what she was going through, she liked Father Steve. He was humble and sincere and had a sweet face. And he was right. Life wasn't always going to be easy. But the upsetting part about that was she already knew it. This was her fault. She'd known Nathan would hurt her, but she went against her better judgment and let herself get swept away by his good looks and smooth words. She shook her head. *Never again.*

The sanctuary door opened, and a few people walked in. She watched them dip their fingers in a large bowl of water and touch their foreheads, chests, and shoulders.

"Well, Miss Bell, I need to go prepare for the evening mass. You're welcome to stay if you like."

"Thank you, Father Steve, and please call me Jada."

"Will do. And Jada, consider giving Nathan a second chance. He's a good guy."

Jada dug her fingernails into her palm. Father Steve couldn't be more wrong about Nathan. She gave him a strained smile, turned quickly and walked out. Her mouth threatened to spew venom, but she controlled herself. She wouldn't take it out on an innocent priest.

Lilah hugged herself as she watched her daughter run down the lawn and out of sight.

She turned from the window and faced her guests. "That went well."

Stephanie scoffed and looked around the living room. Lamps, pictures, and plants littered the floor, and the furniture had been thrown in every direction. "It wasn't ideal, yes, but at least she knows now."

"I can't believe how powerful she is," Alex said. "If she'd stayed any longer, she could have demolished your house."

Lilah dragged a chair back to its place and plopped down in it. "I just don't understand why she was so mad."

"I know why." Jen rubbed her finger over her bottom lip. "She likes Nathan. I saw her with him at her birthday party."

Lilah threw up her hands. "I told her to stay away from him. Why couldn't she just listen to me?"

Stephanie turned to her daughter. "Are you all right?"

"Yes, I'm fine," Sam replied, lips twisting.

"What is that smirk on your face?" Stephanie crossed her arms over her chest.

"Nothing, Mom." Sam widened her eyes in mockery. "I'm just taking it all in."

Stephanie pursed her lips. "You're enjoying this? I should have known you would react this way. You are just like your father. Well, you listen to me." She grabbed Sam's chin. "This is not a joke. When you turn eighteen, you will not flaunt your powers. What happened to Edana could just as easily happen to us today. You could get us all killed."

Samantha jerked her chin away. "Okay, calm down."

Stephanie turned toward Lilah. "You need to tell Jada that they will only kill her if she abuses her powers."

Lilah rubbed her eyelids and nodded. Although that was true, it wasn't all that comforting. Why did this have to happen to her daughter?

Sam lifted herself off the couch, and sauntered toward the door. "I just have one more question. What happed to Edana's daughters? They obviously escaped, since we are all here."

Stephanie picked a picture off the floor and set it on the side table. "Edana had a maidservant who took them to her family's country home before the people of the town came back. She loved them and raised them as if they were her own daughters. When the first one turned eighteen and transformed, she told them all the story of their mother. She also taught them that it was wrong to use their powers to hurt people. After thirty years had passed, they returned to Bishop and lived here the rest of their lives."

With her hand on her hip, Sam cocked her head. "No one ever suspected them?"

"No, because they hid their abilities. They controlled themselves, like *you* are going to do." Stephanie replied.

Sam let out an exaggerated sigh and met her mom's stare. "Are you reading my thoughts?"

"Should I be?" Stephanie shot back.

"All right, you two, let's not fight. Today has been stressful enough." Lilah marched to her room, returning with jeans and tennis shoes on. "I'm going to go look for Jada."

"Lilah, why don't you just wait here? She'll be back. And besides she's more powerful than you are. She can take care of herself," Stephanie said.

"I can't just sit here, Steph. What if the Arons are out there? She's still vulnerable." Picking her rain coat off the floor, she pulled it on and stuffed her keys into the pocket. Stephanie crossed the living room. "Okay, Lilah, then why don't we come with you?"

"No." She shook her head, opening the front door. Rain drops jumped in like an army of tiny frogs and pooled at her feet. "Just go home, I'll be fine."

CHAPTER 16

Outside the church Jada leaned against the stucco wall. The rain hitting the pavement sounded more like someone beating on a set of drums. Somehow she had to learn to manage her new senses. She focused beyond the rain, staring into the bland gray sky. After a few minutes she was able to tune out the individual drops, hearing now only a soft patter.

Cool.

A white pickup truck rolled by, reminding her of Nathan. *Give him another chance? I will not! He's a liar.* She rubbed her clenched jaw, trying to get her muscles to relax.

With difficulty, she pushed Nathan out of her mind. She wasn't ready to go home yet, but she couldn't stay here. Umbrellas were popping out of car doors as people arrived for Father Steve's service.

She took off down the church lawn, grimacing as the rain soaked her clothes again. Each step sank into the soggy grass, flipping mud up behind her. When a burst of lightning lit up the gray sky, followed by the sharp rumbling of thunder, she flinched but kept running.

166

Then she got an idea and swung a hard right. As she passed cars, she heard people saying she'd gone mad, running in the rain as she was. When she reached the familiar row of trees, she sprinted up the hill. That energy she felt brimming under the surface of her skin at the pharmacy was now hurling her body up. Each step felt like she was leaping off a trampoline. At the top, she darted through a maze of scattered trees, the heavy brush scratching her arms as she went.

Finally, the trees opened up to the circular dirt platform. When she saw the small patch of grass in front of her, the image of her and Nathan sitting on it just a week ago plowed into her mind. She winced and looked down. She had forgotten she'd brought him here. Now her favorite spot was tainted with his memory. Taking a deep breath, she wiped back a strand of wet hair that was sticking to her forehead, and skirted around the grassy mound. She stopped at the cliff and leaned her hand against a large tree. The green below was lush from the rain, and the mule deer were huddled under a fan of boughs hiding from the downpour.

A tickle of pain stung her arms, and she looked down.

Red-tinted rainwater rolled out of little cuts where the bushes had slashed her. As she rubbed the stinging wounds, the pain suddenly stopped. When she raised her arm up for a closer look, her skin sewed itself up right before her eyes. She shook her head in disbelief. Her mouth hung open as she turned her arms in front of her. Within seconds the cuts had vanished, as if they were never there. *I could get used to this.* Her giggle echoed out into the open space.

She looked around for something to test her strength on, when her eyes rested on a familiar boulder. The one thing that could improve her spot was a nice place to sit. Bending down, she grabbed the boulder at its base and lifted it with ease. After scanning the ground for the perfect spot, she tossed it down, sending a loud boom thundering through the valley. "Oops!" Her fingers flew to her lips, but she couldn't help but grin.

Just as she stretched out on the rock, hands cushioning her head, the rain stopped. The angry clouds slunk away, revealing a pale evening light. Jada sighed. *Only a half hour till sunset.*

As the blue sky slowly changed to a muted pink and orange, she thought about her situation. She was a Nephilim, a descendant of a fallen angel. It still wasn't settling in. The whole thing felt like a never-ending dream—or nightmare. Now that she was thinking back on her life, a few more events made sense. One time Alex and Jen were over for dinner, and Alex sliced open her thumb cutting carrots. Jada remembered to this day that Alex had acted really strangely. At first she didn't even move, she just stared at the bleeding wound. Then, when she realized Jen and Jada were watching her, she started to fluster and look for a paper towel. The next day Jada saw Alex and Jen again, and Alex's cut was completely healed. Deep down Jada had known something wasn't right but couldn't put her finger on it at the time. All along their moms had known what they were and never said a word.

When there was nothing left but a dim purple glow behind the mountains, Jada made her way down the hill, letting the moonlight guide her. Feeling adventurous, she took a different way back, unsure where it would end up. After trudging through thick mulch for twenty minutes, she found herself at the base of the Bishop Cemetery. Ordinarily, being at the cemetery at night would frighten her, but she felt no fear as she approached. She was nearly indestructible, after all; who could hurt her now?

Meandering among the headstones, breathing in the dank smell of mildewed leaves and fresh dirt, she read the names as she passed. *Julie Smith 1929–1950 Beloved Daughter, RIP. Jack Harrison 1918–1965 Husband, Father and Friend, you will be missed.*

Ahead, a faint yellow light flickered on the face of a large tombstone. She tiptoed toward it, trying not to make a sound, but dead leaves crunched under her shoes, giving her away. She scanned the area but saw no one.

A few yards away she squatted down and eyed the dark stone. A bouquet of fresh roses had been placed at its base. She squinted but couldn't read the name through the dancing candlelight shadows. She was about to step closer when something moved to her right. A tremor ran up her body. She turned to defend herself, but it was too late. Thick fingers clamped onto her shoulders and a black shape hovered above her.

She threw her fists at her attacker, but they just bounced off like she'd punched a rubber ball. *What's happening? I should be stronger than anybody! I need to get out of here.* With all her strength, she heaved her body down, slipping out of her attacker's grip. But just as she turned to run, a calloused hand caught her wrist, jerking her back.

"What do you want?" She closed her eyes and shrank back, preparing for a blow.

"Jada, it's all right It's just me." The familiar voice made her heart jump. He released her and stepped out of the shadows.

Nathan.

"You scared me to death!" she screamed and then took a step back.

"I'm sorry. I didn't mean to." He put up his hands. "What are you doing in a cemetery at night?"

"That's none of your business." Her voice dripped with anger. An artic wind funneled through the graves, raising goose bumps on Jada's arms.

Nathan's eyes suddenly changed. The wall he had up, the caution, the distance. It all melted away in an instant. It was like she was looking at a different person. His shoulders slumped with relief but his eyes were laced with hurt. He shoved his hands into his jeans pockets and sighed. "So . . . your mom told you."

"Yes, she told me." Her voice shook. "Told me that you are supposed to kill me! So the time we spent together was all a lie. You were just getting close to me . . . so that you could . . ." She turned and wiped the corners of her eyes, trying to hide her tears. She wouldn't give him the satisfaction of knowing he'd hurt her.

He reached for her. "Jada, let me explain."

"There is nothing to explain." She picked up a boulder and threw it at him. It hit him in the chest and shattered to pieces. Wobbling on one foot, he nearly fell, but then regained his balance. A playful grin lit up his face. Then

170

she remembered—he had powers too, from Azael. Up in the forest, the bullet had bounced off his arm, unable to penetrate him. She pictured the thin red line of torn flesh on his bicep and smiled. He did bleed, though. He wasn't immortal.

Her eyes narrowed. "Well, I will just have to get more creative." She took off running and heard his steps close behind her. That pulsating power she'd felt earlier drummed through her body. As she ran, she heaved jagged rocks and tree branches over her shoulder, but he caught each one and tossed it aside.

"Jada, please, I'm not going to hurt you."

"Leave me alone!" She weaved between the graves, trying to lose him. Each time she looked back, he was farther behind her. She was faster than he was. With her mind, she lifted everything that wasn't stuck in the ground behind her, blocking his sight.

After grabbing an ax wedged in the dirt, she leveraged off a wheelbarrow and jumped to the top of a tomb. The roof shook when she landed, but she quickly steadied it. Somebody important must be in there to rate being laid to rest in such style. She slunk down, waiting for Nathan to pass so she could ambush him, but when he ran up, he leaped up in one fluid move.

"Yeah, I can do that too." He smirked.

She held up the ax, her chest tightening. The way his silver eyes gazed over her was making her feel weak. She was still falling for his manipulative ways. She had to get away from him.

"What are you going to do with that?" He crossed his

arms over his chest.

"Whatever I have to."

He took a step toward her, and she swung the ax, missing him by an inch.

"You can't hurt me, Jada."

"Why? You're part human at least, aren't you?" she spat. "Actually, never mind, you can't be. You have no heart."

His lips formed a tight line, and he looked away. "Jada, stop . . . please."

"No." She heaved the ax behind her then onto the top of the building. Shards of wood shot out like firecrackers as the roof caved in. Dropping the ax, she did a backflip off the roof just in time to see Nathan fall through it. When he had disappeared in the rubble, she ducked behind an oversized bush. Grunts inched closer to her, and then footsteps passed her and kept going. She paused for a moment, making sure he was still running and wasn't onto her. When she didn't hear his steps anymore, she let out a long breath and made her way back to the front of the cemetery.

"Jada!"

She ignored his calls and kept walking, tears now flowing freely down her face.

"Just hear me out!"

She saw the grave with the candles again and rushed up to it, kneeling down to see the name.

Millie Aron 1969–1999.

Nathan's heavy breathing sounded behind her, and she swung around and slapped him as hard as she could. Her hand curled up in agony as she let out a silent scream. His face was as hard as iron.

"Your powers don't work on me, Jada." He grabbed her hand before she could pull away and examined it. She let out a soft cry as he gently pressed on the swollen skin.

"You may have a sprain, but nothing's broken."

She yanked her hand away. "It doesn't matter. It will heal itself." She started to walk away but stopped.

"You lied to me. I can't believe I was such a fool."

A few seconds passed before he responded.

"You're right. But . . ."

Her shoulders curled forward at the blow. She realized a small part of her was holding out hope that her mom was wrong about Nathan. But that hope was gone. She spun around, determined to hurt him somehow, but stopped when she saw him. He wasn't on the offense. In fact he looked vulnerable. He was running his hands through his hair and had a sad look in his eyes. "But I fell in love with you."

Jada's mouth parted slightly, releasing a quick breath.

Love.

But then she scanned his face, and hate penetrated the backs of her eyes. This was cruel, even for him. Why go this far? Was it necessary to kill her body and her soul?

He knelt down and pushed the roses to the side of the headstone. The orange candlelight cast half-circle shadows under his eyes. "And I've tried to fight it, but I can't. That's why I'm here. The only person who would understand is my mom. If only she were still alive." His head slumped between his hands. Under his half-open lids, a shiny film appeared.

Jada looked down at the grave and then back at Nathan, her arms slack at her sides.

"You should know, we are only supposed to kill you if you abuse your powers—hurt people. It's our family code." He stood, and his face became hard, all traces of vulnerability gone.

Jada's blood felt like it had turned to ice. Her eyebrows formed a thick crease in her forehead. "Oh, well, that makes it all better."

"Jada—" He straightened and took a step toward her.

She put her hand up. "Don't. I can't trust you. I don't want anything to do with you."

Nathan looked at her, his eyes as black as the sky.

"Don't speak to me or come anywhere near me." She walked backward until she was sure he wouldn't chase after her. Then she sprinted home and didn't look back.

Before she could close the door, Lilah had her arms around her so tightly Jada coughed out her breath. As they embraced, the stale air of the heater burned Jada's nose.

Lilah looked her over, running her hands over her face and arms. "Where were you? I've been looking for you all over town. I was so worried."

Lilah took her arm and led her into the living room. After kicking off her shoes, Jada plopped onto the couch. "I know, Mom, I'm sorry. I just needed to be alone." She studied the room. It looked like a tornado had come through it. Nothing was left standing. "Is the house all right?"

Lilah smiled wearily. "Don't worry about the house. Your eyes are red. Have you been crying?"

Jada pulled her sleeves over her wrists. "I saw Nathan at the cemetery."

"What?" Lilah's eyes popped open. "Why were you at the cemetery? What happened? Did he attack you?"

"Mom!" Jada snapped. "No, he didn't attack me, okay?"

Jumping up, Lilah grabbed the broom and dustpan from the closet and started erratically sweeping the floor. "Well, I don't like it, not one bit." She stopped and pointed at Jada with the dustpan. "I *told* you to stay away from that boy."

Jada rolled her eyes. Her mom was acting insane. Wasn't it enough that she had to deal with being some ancient evil Nephilim and having her heart torn in two?

Chunks of glass clanked together as Lilah started sweeping again. "You can't go near him. Ever again. In fact, I think you should stay home from school until we can guarantee you're safe."

"What? No." Jada scoffed. "I'm not going to stay locked up in this house like some prisoner. Besides, Nathan said he's only supposed to kill me if I abuse my powers."

The broom handle started to bend under Lilah's grip. "You'll do what I say, young lady."

Biting down on her lip, Jada locked eyes with her mom. Anger started to bubble in her stomach like a hot spring. This was her mom's fault, and she wouldn't be punished for it. If Lilah had told her years ago, she would have been more prepared. More prepared to deal with her abilities and . . . Nathan.

"I'm *not* staying home," she said through clenched teeth and stomped to her room.

CHAPTER 17

Nathan's house came into view as his Chevy pickup dipped up and down the bumpy dirt driveway. When the headlights passed over the log cabin and lit up Seth's silhouette standing on the deck, he grumbled. He was sick of his brother hounding him about Jada. Seth didn't know anything about her. He was just blindly following his duty without stopping to think about it. After killing the engine, Nathan stepped out of the truck and waved away a cloud of golden dust. The thick smell of the wood-burning stove hovered in the night air. He strode up the steps, taking two at a time, and reached for the door handle without acknowledging Seth.

"I know what you've been doing," Seth announced.

Nathan stopped and let out an annoyed sigh. Gripping the door handle tighter, he contemplated continuing to ignore his younger brother. Finally, he released the door and turned to confront him. He shoved his hands in his sweatshirt pockets and lifted his head. "And what would that be?"

"I saw you at the park . . . with *her.*" Seth's voice dripped with disdain. "And then I saw you again tonight at the cemetery."

Nathan jutted his chin out. "You've been following me?"

Two female deer clopped up their driveway, chomping on shrubs that lined the border. A fawn trotted close behind.

"You've fallen for her. The *Nephilim.*" Seth hawked and spat over the steps.

In one stride, Nathan was within an inch of Seth's face, the muscles flaring in his arms. "I told you to stay out of it. Don't go anywhere near her, do you understand?"

Seth cracked his neck, his eyelids becoming lazy. "I told Dad."

"You did what?" Nathan's voice roared into the night. All three deer raised their heads and leaped into the bushes.

"You're useless to us now. She's got you in her snare."

The door screeched open. "Nathan, come inside."

His dad's dark blue eyes pierced through him. The door closed and his heavy footsteps went deeper into the house.

Nathan punched the door, leaving a fist-size hole, before storming in after him.

In the kitchen, Holdan flipped a steak on an iron skillet. The smell made Nathan's stomach growl, but he was too angry to think about food.

"What?" Nathan leaned in the door frame glaring at his father's back.

"Your brother told me what you've been doing. He's convinced you're falling for this girl. Is it true?"

Shifting his weight, Nathan looked down. "Yes, it's true."

Holdan flipped off the stove and pushed the skillet aside,

the steak still sizzling. "Sit down, Son."

Nathan yanked out the dining table chair farthest from his dad and sat just as Seth strode in and anchored himself against the kitchen counter. The dim kitchen light made the creases on Holdan's face look deeper than normal.

He rolled up the sleeves of his flannel shirt. "You don't know this girl."

"*You* don't know her!" Nathan shot back.

In his worst nightmare, Nathan couldn't imagine the look that came over his father's face. As Holdan studied him, everywhere his blue eyes grazed felt like they were slicing through his flesh. Then his mouth curled up in utter revulsion. "Son, she's fooled you. She's a master at seducing and tricking men, and she will tear this town apart if you don't stop her."

"You're wrong." Nathan broke away from his father's stare.

"Now, you look at me." He set his hands down on the table and leaned down to Nathan's face, his eyebrows forming deep ridges in his leathery forehead.

"You will not turn your back on this family and this town. You will do your duty. Do you understand me, boy?"

Nathan bit down on his tongue until he tasted blood.

Holdan slammed his fist down on the table. "I said do you understand me?"

Nathan's eyes rose slowly and burned into his father's. "Yes . . . I understand."

"Good. Now get out of here. I can't stand the sight of you."

Nathan burst out of the chair, sending it tumbling to the

floor. He stomped out, his pulse pounding between his ears. His dad's words burrowed deep in the pit of his stomach, tearing at it like a hungry wolverine. What had he just agreed to? Hurting Jada? What the hell was he going to do now?

Moments later, the front door banged shut and Nathan's truck rumbled and sped off. Holdan returned to the stove and sliced off a chunk of the steak, shoving the tender meat in his mouth.

"Do you think he'll do it?" Seth asked.

Holdan tossed his fork back on the skillet and walked to the window, crossing his arms over his chest.

"Yes. Yes, I do."

Jada sat in her car in the school parking lot, watching the kids arrive and make their way to class. Lilah had tried to stop her from going to school again this morning, but she just ignored her. She was going to live her life. She looked down at herself. Last night, after her argument with Lilah, she had gone out and bought new clothes. They fit her new figure perfectly. Today she wore a deep purple crewneck with a black scarf and some dark blue boot-cut jeans. Even though the dark colors would help to hide her body, Jada knew her classmates would still notice.

She thought about Nathan briefly but pressed her feelings deep into her mind where she hoped they would never resurface. Last night, she'd decided the only way to get through this alive was to focus on feeling angry. Pain only made her vulnerable. When Nathan had said he loved her, she'd felt the wall up around her heart start to crack, and that was dangerous. It could cost her life.

He doesn't love you. He is just a good liar.

Taking in a deep breath, she lifted herself out of the car, swung her backpack over her shoulder and headed toward the main building.

When she entered the halls, one by one, people started to look at her. She scoffed. This was all she needed to get noticed and be treated like she existed, a few more curves? She tried to meet their gazes and smile, but then they started to whisper, not knowing that she could hear them. When she heard what boys were saying, her jaw dropped. She looked away, and her face flushed with heat. And the girls, they were almost worse.

She totally stuffed her bra. How desperate.

Did she get hip implants over the weekend? Does she think that actually looks good?

That outfit looks stupid. Does she own a mirror?

Jada winced. She'd never done a thing to these girls, didn't even know them.

But then she realized they were jealous—jealous of *her*. It took her a few minutes to wrap her mind around the idea. No one had ever been jealous of her before.

When she saw Jen and Sam standing outside her history classroom, relief washed over her. They returned her smile and waved.

Jada closed the gap between them and Jen's eyes grew wide. "So that's what you were hiding under those baggy clothes yesterday."

Jada bit her bottom lip. "So it's that bad, huh?"

"No," Jen shrieked. "Actually, you look amazing! It's just a shock because you were so skinny before."

Jada cocked an eyebrow. "Gee, thanks."

"I mean, you're still skinny. You just have some hips now and some . . ." She giggled as she looked at Jada's chest. Jada couldn't help but laugh too but stopped when she looked at Sam. Sam had an irritated look on her face as she looked Jada up and down.

"What is it?" Tugging on her shirt, Jada looked down at herself, wondering what Sam was thinking.

"Oh, nothing." Sam flashed a strained smile.

A pinprick of pain stabbed Jada's heart. Why was Sam acting so strange? She seemed mad.

Jen ducked her head, trying to get Jada's attention. "No blue eyes today?"

"No, I have to wear contacts at school. There's no way I could explain my eyes changing color."

Jen nodded. "Well, you really do look great."

"Thanks Jen."

"I think this is pretty cool." Jen's eyes sparkled.

"Yeah, well, you won't be getting the nightmares." Jada fidgeted with her bottom lip.

Jen shifted her bag to her other shoulder. "I almost forgot that part. What are they like?"

A football flew by Jada's head, followed by three lacrosse players. After flinching from the noise, Jada forced her senses to focus. "It's graphic. I don't really want to talk about it."

Jen grabbed her and gave her a long hug. "It's okay. I

understand."

"Well, we should go to class." Samantha turned and strode into the classroom.

Jen and Jada shared a confused look.

"What's her problem?" Jen asked.

Jada shrugged, feeling rejection spread in her chest.

"Whatever. I'll see you at lunch." Jen half smiled then slipped inside the classroom next door.

Thankfully, the morning went by fast. She hadn't done any homework last night, so she had to quickly finish it during class, which left her no time to see if anyone was looking at her. And she focused on the lecture, tuning out all the horrible things people were saying. By lunch she was starting to think being attractive wasn't all it was cracked up to be. Girls hated you and boys just wanted to get in your pants.

Carrying her lunch over to Sam and Jen, Jada spotted Lori Messing sauntering toward their table from the opposite direction. When they arrived to the table at the same time, Jada grunted under her breath and sat next to Sam.

"Did you guys go get a homecoming dress?" Holding her cheerleading bag in one hand, Lori addressed Samantha and Jen, completely ignoring Jada.

Sam's face lit up. "Yes, a strapless baby doll, black lace on top with a white mesh skirt. Fits perfectly."

Lori nodded with wide, excited eyes. "Nice! I bought a purple empire waist with spaghetti straps."

"Oh, I saw that one." Jen set her fork down. "So cute."

Lori turned lazy eyes to Jada, who had been trying—

unsuccessfully—to space out during their conversation. "I would ask you which dress you bought, but I guess you didn't buy one at all, did you?"

At first, the usual sinking feeling of humiliation and defeat crawled down Jada's body. But then, every nasty word Lori had said to her since junior high scrolled behind her eyes like credits to the movie of her life. A warm circle grew on her shin, and she remembered Lori kicking her in PE. Suddenly, a fuming irritation exploded in her chest, quenching all semblance of humiliation. She lifted her head slowly and sat completely still, glaring at her.

"What? What are you going to do?" Lori mocked, waving her hand.

A seething anger paralyzed Jada, anger even more intense than she felt for Nathan yesterday. It boiled to the edge of her stomach, threatening to burst out.

Today, Jada had had enough of Lori's abuse. Today, she would finally stick up for herself. She was about to speak, but before she could open her mouth, Lori's head suddenly twitched.

"Are you all right?" Sam asked.

When her head jerked again, Lori reached up and dug into her scalp. She yanked her hand out, breaking off a few blonde strands. A maggot squirmed in her finger. Jen's hand flew to her mouth, and Sam shrieked and slid her chair back.

Holding the milky white worm in front of her, Lori released a blood-curdling scream. Silence flowed over the cafeteria in a wave. Practically in unison, everyone stood, gaping at their table. Wailing, Lori furiously scratched through her hair, sending maggots flying to the floor.

"Help me!" she screamed through tears.

But everyone kept backing away as more and more maggots bounced off the linoleum floor. The cafeteria door flew open crashing against the wall. Two teachers and a nurse ran in, stopping shy of Lori's flailing body. They hesitated but then quickly grabbed her arms and carried her out of the room. A tense silence remained for a full minute before hysterical conversations erupted, thundering into the walls.

Sam and Jen quickly got their stuff and yanked Jada from her seat, pulling her through the door that led outside.

When the doors closed behind them, Sam flipped around. "Was that you?"

The stiff chill in the air brought Jada back to her senses. She placed her palm on her forehead, her eyes moving rapidly back and forth. "I—I don't know. I was mad at her for her snide comment, but I wasn't thinking about maggots."

Sam took a step toward Jada, pointing at her. "It had to be you. How else could maggots randomly appear in her hair? Why would you do that?"

Jada started. "Why would I do that? How about because she's a bitch, Sam?"

"Whatever." Sam rolled her eyes.

Despite the cool wind gliding up Jada's skin, she tugged her sweater away from her chest, suddenly feeling hot. "She is to me, and you know it. And you know what?" She leaned on one leg and tilted her head." It would be nice if you stuck up for me once in a while. We're supposedly best friends."

At that, Sam huffed and stormed back into the cafeteria without a word.

Turning to Jada, Jen slumped. "I'm sorry, Jada, you're right. We shouldn't stand for her treating you that way."

Jada nodded. At least Jen was on her side. She let her gaze fall on the chipped metal door to the cafeteria. How could Sam be so blind to how Lori treated her?

"But did you really do that?" Jen's eyes lit up.

Jada gave her a mock frown before letting the corners of her lips lift up into a satisfied grin. "I guess I did."

"You enjoyed that, didn't you?" Jen lightly punched her on the shoulder.

"A little . . . I guess." Jada shrugged.

"All right," Jen winked. "I'm going back inside to meet up with Logan. You want to come?"

Jada shook her head. "I just need to be alone for a minute."

Jen left, leaving Jada outside for the rest of lunch. After brushing off a pile of leaves and dirt from a bench, she sat down, draping her backpack next to her. Was it possible she'd put the maggots in Lori's hair? Maybe her anger had triggered her powers? Resting her leg up on the bench, she turned around and looked through the windows into the cafeteria. There were two janitors sweeping up the maggots that had fallen on the floor. For a split second, she felt bad for Lori, but then a warm current sizzled from the top of her head down to her toes, and she smiled. Lori deserved it. All these years, she had taken her abuse. But no more.

After looking to her left and right to make sure nobody

was watching, Jada lifted her hand. A large rock followed her movement, rising in the air. Her fingers jerked into a claw, and the rock shattered into dust. The current coursed through her a second time, and she smiled again. Yes, Lori would regret the way she had treated her all these years.

CHAPTER 18

On her way home Jada received a text from her mom telling her to come to the flower shop. She groaned, tired from school and anxious to get home, but turned her car around anyway and headed back toward Main Street. What could Lilah possibly want that couldn't wait until tonight?

The familiar door chime rang when she walked in, followed by the sweet smell of a dozen different flowers.

"Mom, I'm here!" she yelled.

Lilah popped out from behind an oversized gardenia plant, adorned with elbow-length yellow rubber gloves, holding a pair of shears. "Come up here."

Lilah was using her authoritative 'mom' voice. Jada sighed and strode up to the front desk, knowing this wasn't going to be fun.

"I need help with a delivery. Can you grab that bouquet over there?" Lilah nodded to a red rose bouquet standing in a vase of water.

Jada eyed the bouquet. "Uh, sure but . . . where's your assistant?"

"I let her off early today." Grabbing a cardboard box, Lilah started gently packing in smaller bouquets and boutonnieres. There must be a wedding tonight.

Jada raised her hands in annoyance. "Why did you do that when you have a delivery?"

Lilah pulled off her gloves and leaned onto the counter. "Steph called me at lunch. Sam told her about what happened to Lori Messing in the cafeteria."

A wave of exhaustion numbed Jada's body, and she slumped against the wall. "Mom, I didn't—I mean, I don't—you can't prove I did that! I wasn't even thinking about maggots."

"Honey, there is no other explanation. Your emotions can affect your powers, and I know you don't like her." Lilah tilted her head down and raised a suspicious eyebrow.

Jada looked up at the florescent lights and didn't say a word. She was tired of her mom not taking her side when it came to Lori. It was true, she hated Lori, but she hadn't put the maggots there on purpose. What was the big deal anyway? Lori wasn't hurt. And maybe she'd learn a lesson for once.

"Either way"—Lilah straightened and grabbed the last boutonniere off the counter—"I think you should start working here part-time. You need something to do, to keep your mind busy. Working really helped me stay on track when I first changed."

Jada crossed her arms over her chest and rolled her eyes. "C'mon, Mom, that isn't fair. You're punishing me for something you can't even prove I did. Besides, I only have one year left of not working. Can't I just enjoy it?"

Lilah chewed on her lip and examined her.

Too bad she couldn't read her mom's thoughts. Uncrossing her arms, Jada went up to the counter and gave her most innocent look. "I promise I will try extra hard to control myself, okay?"

Lilah rubbed her lips together. "Fine—but one more screw up"—she pointed at Jada—"and you are working after school—got it?" Lilah grabbed a crate of cut roses and disappeared behind swinging double doors. "Now go home and study," she yelled from the back room.

The chime rang again on Jada's way out. Her ears felt hot as she slammed her car door behind her. First her mom had tried to make her stay home from school, and now this. She didn't like this new disciplinarian Lilah. Until now they had been more like friends than mother and daughter. *How can she treat me this way? There is no way I'm going to work. I have the rest of my life to do that.*

Still steaming when she got home, she threw her backpack on the floor of her room and plopped into her desk chair. Outside, a flood of voices rose to her window. Rolling her chair back, she pulled her curtain aside to find Derek and three other lacrosse players walking by. For some reason, Derek bumping into her on the first day of school came to her mind. Her eyebrows furrowed as she watched them. She cracked her window open an inch and listened. They were talking about the lacrosse game tomorrow. In the midst of their conversation, another voice rang in her head. She recognized it immediately. Edana.

Her senses heightened, and like a hawk watching its prey from above, she zeroed in on Derek and his friends. She heard their shoes hitting the cement, their jeans rustling against their legs, their breaths rumbling in their throats. Tiny sparks of anger flickered in her chest, and her breathing slowed into a shallow rhythm.

Suddenly, she shook her head and jerked her chair back. What was she doing? Rubbing her forehead, she willed Edana's disturbing words out of her head. *No, I'm not going to hurt them.*

She rolled back to her desk and took in a deep breath. She needed to get out of the house, relax. She'd never been to a lacrosse game, but maybe it was exactly what she needed to get her mind off things. Leaning down, she dug through her backpack for her phone.

"Sam, it's me. Hey, are you and Jen going to the lacrosse game tomorrow?"

"Yeah, why?" Sam's tone held the same annoyed tone that it had earlier when they met in the hall.

"I want to go."

"But you've never gone. Why now?"

Jada tucked her feet under her knees and rocked the chair. "I just want to get out more. Haven't you been telling me to do that all these years?" The line was quiet except for a Rihanna song playing softly in the background.

"Fine, whatever. Jen and I will pick you up at six." Sam hung up.

Jada threw her phone on the bed and brushed off Sam's lack of enthusiasm for her coming tomorrow. She was going to her first lacrosse game, and she was going to have a good time.

Sam's car horn beeped twice, and Jada headed out of her room. "Mom, I'm going to the game with Sam and Jen,"

she yelled down the hall before closing the front door.

Jen stepped out and pulled the seat forward to let Jada in the back. "What made you want to come to the game?" Jen asked as Sam pulled out of the driveway. "I thought you hated these things."

"I did, but I figured I should go to one at least just to see what it's like. I mean, how I can I hate it if I've never been to one?"

"That's what we've been telling you all along." Jen turned around and peeked over her sunglasses. "And you picked a good game to go to. We're playing Pacific Heights. We lost to them in the semifinals last year, and I think our guys are still pissed off about it. It'll be fun."

The sky over the playing field was a solid indigo blue with no clouds in sight. It looked menacing, but at least it wouldn't rain. The lacrosse players strutted onto the field, and the crowd erupted into a roar. Sitting between Jen and Sam on the cold metal bench, Jada winced as the sound battered her eardrums.

In front of them to the left, a swell of wind blew up a familiar mass of blonde curls. Lori turned around briefly and locked eyes with Jada. Lori tried to keep up her usual smug face, but Jada could see the slightest hint of defeat in her eyes. Jada looked away, then made herself meet Lori's gaze, feeling a little bad about what she'd done.

With a loud chirp of the whistle, the players scattered. Jada watched eagerly, trying to learn the rules of the game. In less than five minutes, Union High scored, sending the crowd into a fit of cheers. Sam stood and whistled through her thumb and middle finger, her other hand spread seductively on her hip. The high pitched sound scraped on her brain like nails on a chalkboard, and Jada plugged her ears. As if synchronized, every guys' eyes were on Sam in an instant.

Jada realized she would never be able to behave like Sam, even with her new curvier body. She just didn't have it in her. Sam sat back down, glowing from the attention.

The game started up again, quieting the chatter. As Jada followed the ball, Edana's voice sounded in her head again. She blinked and flicked her hand over her forehead. She didn't want to deal with her right now; she was just starting to relax. Union High scored and she jumped up, clapping and cheering. When she sat back down, Edana's voice quieted and slipped behind her mind. The first quarter ended and the players settled onto the bench, dumping water onto their faces. The score was 2–0. Union High was in the lead.

Ryan and Andrew strolled up next to them, and Sam perked up. Then, as usual, they acknowledged only Sam and Jen. Jada felt the muscles in her jaw tighten. Suddenly, everything went quiet. Lifting her head, she watched the four of them talk. She could see their lips moving but couldn't hear them. Only her heartbeat thumped in her ears . . . and a whisper.

They'll never change, Jada. You don't exist to them.

Ryan laughed, bringing Jada back. She watched him. As he raised a cup of soda to his mouth, Jada shook the ground beneath him. His cup crashed against his chest and brown sticky liquid spread down his shirt and pants. Jen and Sam chuckled while he furiously wiped the growing stain. Face red as an apple, he bolted up the stairs and out of sight.

Andrew jutted his thumb in Ryan's direction. "What a dumbass." And they all laughed.

Jada smirked. Her blood was hot now. Andrew left and the players took their places on the field for the second quarter. The whistle blew and Union High had the ball. Leaning her head back, she fought a grin as she gazed around to see if anyone was watching her. Trying to look as casual as possible, she focused on the grass under the ball. Then, like a hundred little fingers, the blades of grass carried the ball to the other team's possession.

After the shock wore off, the other team's player bolted for the goal and scored. A communal groan floated on the cool breeze. Edana's laugh echoed between her ears then faded away. For as long as she could remember, these guys had ignored her, treating her like she was less than human. The joke was on them, because now, she was *more* than human.

The game continued with Jada getting more and more creative. First, she tripped several of Union High's players, and then she sunk the goalie's feet in the dirt like it was quicksand, letting the ball fly by him.

With each mistake the crowd grew angrier, shouting accusations that the players were sabotaging the game. Jada had to cover her mouth to hide her ear-to-ear grin.

The third quarter ended too quickly for Jada, but not soon enough for the players. Jada heard them talking among themselves about forfeiting. She hoped that wasn't allowed. She wasn't quite done.

"What's going on today?" Sam raised her eyebrows.

"Everyone's a klutz."

Jada tuned out Sam and Jen's conversation and replayed the pranks in her mind. Just last week, she was a helpless nobody, but now she was powerful and in control.

And she liked it.

The game ended with a humiliating defeat of 2–15. Jada hoped the other team appreciated her efforts. After Sam and Jen dropped her off, she wiggled into bed and watched the candlelight dance on the ceiling. Her muscles relaxed, and she felt her mind clear.

She was nearly asleep when her phone vibrated on her nightstand. Groaning, she grabbed it and held it up to her face. The caller ID read *blocked*.

After a brief hesitation, she answered. "Hello?"

"Jada, it's me."

Jada's lips pursed at Nathan's familiar voice.

"What do you want?" she hissed.

"I'm outside. I want to talk to you."

Her chest tightened. "Why would I want to talk to you?"

"If you don't come out, I'm coming in, and I don't think you want that."

Jada grunted, hung up the phone and threw on a sweatshirt. He was right. She didn't want him in here. He could hurt her or her mom.

Outside, the moon was tucked behind a long silvery cloud, casting her front yard in a thick darkness. Behind the tree, a black shape moved. She walked toward it.

The streetlight flickered on, bouncing yellow light off Nathan's face.

"If my mom sees you, she'll flip. What do you want?"

His sweet smell filled her nose, reminding her of better times. She took a step back.

He locked eyes with hers. "I know what you were doing today."

"What does that mean?" Her muscles screamed for a fight.

"At the game."

Her eyes narrowed. "You were there? Watching me?"

"Yes, and maybe you would've noticed me too if you hadn't been so busy using your powers on people."

Jada clenched her fists inside her sweatshirt pocket. "So what, you came to tell me you know what I was doing? And now you are going to kill me because I tripped a few lacrosse players?"

Thick blue veins popped out on Nathan's arms. "I came to tell you that you aren't that person. You don't hurt people like that. It isn't you."

A pang of guilt sliced through her. She swallowed hard, fighting the feeling.

"What do you know? You think you know me after two weeks?" She took in long breaths, trying to release the pressure building in her head. "Maybe it *is* me. Ever thought of that? Maybe who I was with you was a lie, just like *you*." Her bottom lip quivered with the last words.

There was no mistaking the pain in his eyes.

Good. Now he can feel what I'm feeling.

"Is that all?" she spat.

He paused, locking eyes with her, then turned and walked away.

CHAPTER 19

"Why are we out here? We're going to get skin cancer." Sam lifted her hand and shielded her eyes. Jada had texted Jen and Sam that she wanted to eat outside today. She could really use some fresh air.

"You can't get skin cancer from sitting in the sun for thirty minutes." Jada lifted her face and closed her eyes. The warmth soaked into her skin, giving her temporary relief from the tightness that had settled in her chest ever since she saw Nathan last night. Feeling her left contact lens go askew, she wiggled it back into place and then turned to Sam. "What's going on with you today? You're kind of cranky."

Sam set her hand on the table and looked down at her uneaten salad. "I'm fine," She replied coolly.

"Are you worried about your eighteenth birthday? It's coming up quick, only a few weeks away." Jen smiled.

Sam rolled her eyes. "No, it's not that. Just drop it, okay?"

"All right, Sam jeez, calm down." Jen looked away, trying to hide the hurt expression on her face.

A cluster of blue and white skirts circled the corner of the main building. Sticking out of the top was a familiar round of buzzed dirty blonde hair. Jason made a cone with his hand and placed it over his lips. "Jadaaaa"

He whispered into one of the cheerleaders' ears before landing at their table. Sam perked up, her face fitted into a sultry smile. He plopped down next to Jada and flashed them a strip of straight white teeth. Jada ignored him and kept eating her sandwich.

He turned to her, his hot breath on her face. He clunked his elbow on the table. "Your party was awesome on Saturday."

"I'm so glad you had a good time," Sam said loudly. "I planned the whole thing."

Jason gave Sam a cursory glance before returning his attention to Jada. "Saw you at the game last night."

Jada nodded and stared at her sandwich, hoping he would get the hint.

Jen looked up. "Speaking of, you're in a strangely good mood despite the loss last night."

Jason shrugged. "I didn't make any mistakes."

Jada kicked herself internally. That's right, she hadn't done anything to him and she disliked him the most."

"Hey . . . you look *different*." He leaned back and looked Jada up and down. "I don't know what it is, but you look good." He winked.

"Thanks," Jada muttered. The sting of nausea churned in her stomach. He scooted closer to her and wrapped his arm around her waist.

She flinched and pulled away. "What are you doing?"

"Go to homecoming with me." He pulled her back. A bitter taste rose up Jada's throat. "Thanks Jason, but no."

Jason's face contorted in confusion and then went blank. He crossed his arms over his chest. Jada lifted her eyebrows. "Did you hear me?"

His lips curled into a half grin. "Oh, I get it. You're joking, right?"

"No, I'm not. I do not want to go to homecoming with you." Jada's voice was louder this time.

He laughed and looked at Jen and Sam. Then he ran his hand up her back and rested it over her shoulders. Her body twitched.

"I'm serious, Jason. Now get your hands off of me!" She shoved him with her forearm and jumped up.

His eyes filled with anger. He stood and faced her, his hands forming rigid balls and then releasing.

"No one says no to me," he growled.

"Well, I just did," she retorted. "Now please just leave me alone."

"Just go away, Jason," Jen yelled.

Jason ignored Jen and kept his eyes on Jada. He took a step in her direction. "No, I won't leave until you say yes."

Her fingernails dug into her palms.

He chuckled. "What are you going to do, hit me?"

She lifted her fists slightly, "if I have to."

Just as he took another step toward her an image flickered in her mind. It was Jason standing before her like he was now, except blood trickled down his face and his eyes were empty and black. She gasped, but the image was gone as fast as it had come. Her throat started to constrict, and she stumbled backward. "No, no!"

Jason's face crinkled, and he looked at Jen and Sam.

"What's her problem?"

"Just get lost." Sam glared at him.

"Whatever. I don't want to go homecoming with some crazy . . ." His voice faded as he stomped down the cement stairs back to where the lacrosse team was playing tag football.

"I've got to go." Jada grabbed her backpack and took off.

After bursting into the locker room, she threw on her Union High sweats and hurried out to the field to do her warm up run for PE. She needed to burn some energy, get the image of Jason's bloody face out of her mind. Her eyes suddenly stung. Edana had put that image there. She was sure of it. She was always on the cusp of her mind, ready to pounce at any moment. Would she ever stop? Nathan had told her last night that what she'd done at the lacrosse game wasn't her. Had Edana put her up to it? Jada rubbed her temples and took off running. The lines of where she ended and Edana began were starting to blur.

Halfway across the oval track she was passing every person, even the guys, but didn't care. Suddenly, her skin crawled as she remembered the feel of Jason's hand on her back. Who did he think he was, touching her and demanding she go to homecoming with him? She ran harder.

At the end of the track she slowed to a stop just as Lori Messing walked by her, bumping her in the shoulder. Jada turned around to find the all-too-familiar haughty face looking back at her. Apparently, she was over the whole maggot incident and back to her usual self.

Jada pressed down her feelings and turned away. She couldn't let Lori get to her. If she got angry again, she could lose control and hurt someone. But then she heard Lori whispering to herself.

"She's so ugly. I don't know why Sam hangs out with her."

Biting her bottom lip, Jada willed her body to keep walking.

Just let it go. She's not worth it.

Her legs felt like anvils as she trudged in the opposite direction. She wanted so badly to say something—do something.

While she waited for the soccer game to start, Jada's blood raced through her veins. Between Nathan, Jason and Lori she couldn't take any more abuse. She was going to snap.

The game started in a rush of players running toward the ball at the center of the field. Jada bolted at the ball, but the other team beat her, sending it down the field to her defenders. She groaned when the action remained at her goal, where she couldn't go as a forward. Finally, the opposing team scored, bringing the ball back up to the center to start the next play.

In one swift move, the center forward kicked the ball to her, and she was running. She spotted Lori and dribbled the ball to the left, trying to avoid her. As she approached, she could hear Lori whispering to herself that she was going to kick Jada even harder this time. Jada ground her teeth. When Lori came at her, she faked left then went right, passing her. Effortlessly, she weaved in between their last defenseman and scored.

The game continued in the same way for the rest of the class. With five minutes to go, she had scored seven goals, all by passing Lori. On the fourth goal, Lori's team had started grumbling at her and threatening to sit her out. Jada hadn't intended on humiliating Lori, but she had to admit, it felt good.

It was the last play, and she had the ball. As she raced toward the goal, a thick fog filled her head, and she felt like she was flying down the field. When Lori appeared in front of her, she felt her eyes dilate. Her foot pulled back and struck the ball. It flew at Lori and slammed into her face with a loud *crack*. Lori fell to her knees, cupping her face as a spray of blood shot out of her nose like an exploding champagne bottle.

A herd of students circled Lori, jaws agape. "Miss Bell, what on earth happened?" Mr. Jameson had his hand on Lori's back and was looking up at her, deep lines cutting into his forehead.

A splinter of remorse tried to pierce the fog in Jada's head, but was quickly snuffed. She looked down at Mr. Jameson and gave the same answer Lori gave him when she kicked her shin. "I don't know, Mr. Jameson. I was going for the ball. I guess I kicked it too hard."

Jada's heart pounded in her chest as she watched the school grow smaller in her side-view mirror. The fog in her mind was starting to clear when she turned her gaze to the road just in time to see Our Lady Church fly by on the right. She slammed on her brakes, and the tires screeched to a stop. An older lady walking a small white Pomeranian peered into Jada's car. Jada gave her a cordial wave before shifting her car into reverse and pulling back just enough so that she could turn into the church parking lot.

She ran up and flung the heavy doors open. A young priest was straightening some pamphlets on a table by the door. "Hello, miss, may I help you?" Hard lines fixed on his forehead and eyes concealed what could be an attractive face. Jada wondered what could have happened to him to make him look so bitter.

"Yes, is Father Steve here?"

His dark eyes narrowed before he returned to his pamphlets and pointed to the sanctuary. "In there."

"Thanks," she replied.

Father Steve was sitting in the front pew and had his head bowed in his hands. She could hear his prayer.

"Father, please speak through me tonight and help us raise enough money to help with Mrs. Adams's surgery."

Jada tiptoed toward him, feeling suddenly uncomfortable hearing his private prayer. She was just about to turn around when the wood floor moaned under her feet. Father Steve looked up.

"Miss B—I mean Jada, so nice to see you again." Other than dark circles under his eyes, he had the same warm smile.

"Hi, Father Steve. I hope I'm not disturbing you."

"Not at all. Come, sit." He slid aside and patted the spot next to him. She sat quickly and he smiled down at her. "How are you?"

"Fine."

He chuckled. "Fine is usually code for not fine."

Jada gave him a mock frown. "No, really. I've been good. This week's been better."

His usually carefree eyes suddenly became pensive. It felt like he was looking right through her. He shifted his weight so he was facing the front. "Hmmm."

"What's the matter?" Jada asked.

"Nothing, you just seem different."

A heavy silence settled between them. He flipped a pen between his fingers. Why had she come here?

Father Steve set his Bible on the pew with a thud and faced her. "Jada, you're a good person."

Jada started. That was out of the blue, and it sounded strikingly familiar to what Nathan had said to her. Did he know about Edana? "What do you mean? I mean, why are you telling me that?"

He locked gazes with her, and she felt his sky blue eyes piercing her again. She pulled her sleeves over her wrists and wrapped her arms around her chest.

"I'm just saying you have a good heart."

A comic strip of the last few days started to run through her mind, and a lump of guilt burrowed into her heart. She grunted and pinched her eyes shut, pressing the images away.

Suddenly, she leaped up out of the pew. "And how do you know that? You've only seen me twice now. Maybe I'm not a good person."

After Father Steve struggled to stand, he pointed at his heart. "I *know*, Jada."

A throbbing pressure inched up her neck. She thought her head was going to explode. She had to get out of here.

"You don't know what I am capable of," she sneered before she bolted out the door.

CHAPTER 20

Jada slammed her car door behind her and with shaking hands turned the key, releasing a *tsk-tsk* sound from the engine.

"Not now!" she yelled as she pressed on the key again and furiously pumped the gas pedal. This time it clicked three times and then went silent. Her head fell back against the seat, and she let out a pent-up breath. The ache in her eyes had become an unbearable burn, so she popped out the contact lenses and stuffed them into the ashtray. Jerking the car door open, she got out. Then she slammed it again and strode away from the church.

Droplets of water in the heavy fog tickled her face. Sparks of guilt rose through the anger for how she had treated Father Steve, but she forced them back down. He didn't know anything about her. Maybe she *wasn't* a good person. She took a sharp left, deciding to take the long way home through Main Street to give herself more time to calm down. As she trudged past the last row of houses, she let her attention fall on the families inside. Anything to keep her mind busy. Some were eating dinner, some were helping their kids do homework and others were watching TV. Her stare paused on a father scrubbing the top of a young girls head. Her red curls flopped around her little plump face, and she giggled. Jada felt her heart sink. Even though her dad wasn't a Nephilim, he would've known what to do. He could've helped her learn to deal with Edana.

She crossed the street, narrowly missing on oncoming car, and continued toward the main strip. When she turned the familiar corner, she was surprised to see most of the shops were closed. Other than a dim light cast from the grocery store and a small antique store, the street was black. She searched for the moon, but only a tiny white smile looked down at her. A young couple exited the antique store and gave Jada a superficial smile before getting in their car and driving off. In a split second, the air seemed to drop ten degrees. She kept going. A frozen breeze blew her hair back and whirled under her scarf, sending a shiver down her back. Feeling a slight uneasiness in her chest, she looked around. *What's there to be afraid of? No one can hurt me.* She rubbed her hands over her upper arms. *It's all right, I'm almost home.* From the corner of her eye, she saw three people exit the grocery store.

"Jada!" One of them called her name. She took a quick look and cursed under her breath.

"Oh come on, Jada, don't be like that."

"Leave me alone, Jason," she called back. "I'm serious."

She heard them cross the street and their footsteps quicken behind her. She walked faster, but they caught up to her. Jason circled in front of her and walked backward while Derek and Eddie framed her on either side. A sly grin spread on Jason's face.

"Why are you being so mean to me?" Jason asked, a sarcastic edge in his voice.

"I'm not. I just don't want to go to homecoming with you. In fact, I don't want to go to it at all, so it's nothing personal." She hoped that would sooth his ego and make him go away.

"That's just stupid. Every girl wants to go to homecoming."

Irritation bubbled in her chest. "I don't know what else to say, Jason. The answer is still no."

Jason's face knotted, and before Jada could react, he planted his feet, grabbed her shoulders and hurled her into an alley. She landed hard on her knees inches from an overflowing dumpster and let out a loud cry.

"What are you doing?" she shouted and looked up at him.

Eddie anxiously looked at Derek, who ignored him and grabbed his stomach releasing an obnoxious laugh.

Jason bent over her and tilted his head. "I think it might be time to teach you a lesson."

Jada felt a familiar electric current jabbing at her nerves. She closed her eyes and took deep breaths. *No, please no.*

"This isn't cool, Jay. Let's get out of here." Eddie's small voice bounced off the alley walls.

"Shut up!" Jason shot back. He grabbed Jada's waist, flipped her around and threw her against the wall. The solid cement cut into her back, knocking the wind out of her.

She choked in gusts of putrid air. "Jason, leave me alone. You don't know what you're getting into."

"Oh, yeah? What am I getting into?" He waved his

hands in mockery.

Jada's eyes burned. "I can't—control. I could hurt you."

He let out a long, arrogant laugh. "Hurt me? That's a good one, Jada. All right, I've had enough of your lip. Now let's see what you have under here." In one swift move, he lifted her shirt and slid his hands up until they cupped her breasts. "Nice!"

Anger imploded in her chest, like gasoline on a flame. She blinked and Edana's face looked back at her. Suddenly, three men picked up Edana and threw her against a tree. Blood trickled from the corners of her mouth. They ripped off her clothes, howling and snickering, then tied her arms behind the trunk. Jada snapped her eyes closed. She couldn't watch anymore. But the scene remained. One of the men slammed his fist deep into Edana's stomach. She choked and groaned before her head slumped to her chest. The other two men joined the beating, pounding and kicking Edana until she no longer looked human.

Jada ground her teeth, feeling the rage creeping up to the last inch of her mind. She opened her eyes. "Please, Jason, don't do this. You're going to get hurt."

His expression grew annoyed, and he groped her harder.

"I said stop." She pushed his hands away, careless of the force she exerted.

He flew back a few steps. He cracked his knuckles, the muscles twitching under the hem of his T-shirt, then jumped back with even more determination in his face. "Oooh, feisty. I like that."

Before she knew it, his hands were slithering over her body. When he reached down and started unbuttoning her jeans, her mind went black. It was over. There was nothing she could do.

"Get your hands off of me." Her smooth voice sounded foreign to her ears.

"And what are you going to do about it?" he grunted.

Deliberate and calm, she clamped her hands around his wrists and peeled his fingers off her.

His eyes grew wide. "Wow, you're stronger than you—" His bones crunched under Jada's grip. He drew in a quick breath then let out a deafening scream. Derek rushed over and threw himself on top of her, tugging at her unmovable arms. "What are you doing? Let him go!"

She rotated her head and smirked at Derek's terrified face. "All right."

Gracefully, she slid her fingers off his wrists. Jason fell back and let out a silent scream, his wounded hands flopping around like wet noodles.

"What have you done?" he cried.

"You haven't seen anything yet." She laughed and took a step forward, raising her arm. His body lifted into the air and flew back, slamming against the wall. She lowered her arm and he smacked face first onto the filthy ground, slabs of concrete crumbling onto his back.

"Jason!" Derek and Eddie fell to their knees and ripped the heavy chunks off him. Eddie looked at her imploringly. "Please, stop."

"Stop? You mean like I was asking him to do a few minutes ago? Sorry, Eddie, I'm not quite finished."

With one hand under each arm, Derek and Eddie hoisted Jason to his feet. A dark brown sludge was smeared on his cheek, and gray dust coated his hair. He raised his eyes and glowered at Jada. "You bitch!" he hissed.

Jada's fingers curled into rigid claws.

"You never learn," she spat through clenched teeth.

A large rock scraped the ground as it inched toward Jason. Derek and Eddie jerked their heads and watched it, their faces frozen in a look of shock.

"How are you doing that?" Derek's hoarse voice caught in his throat.

Jada half smiled. With a flick of her hand the rock flew up and smashed into Jason's skull, dropping him back to the ground. A few seconds passed before a stream of blood poured down the side of his head.

Eddie and Derek stood motionless, mouths hanging open. Jada sauntered over and bent down and cocked her head in the same manner Jason had done to her minutes before.

"Why so quiet? Nothing to say now?" she taunted.

"Get away from him," Derek growled.

"Fine." Jada shrugged her shoulders and stood. "I've got nothing more to say to him. He's all yours."

The few stars that were in the sky had disappeared, bathing the alley in blackness. A cat with matted gray fur, beaten up by the harshness of street life, strolled out from behind the dumpster, bringing the stench of rotting garbage with him. He trotted up to Jason and started licking his bloodied face.

"Get the hell out of here," Derek yelled and kicked at him. The cat hissed but only walked a few steps away before plopping down and looking between Jason and

Derek. His wry meows filled the alley.

Without taking their eyes off Jada, Derek and Eddie lifted Jason off the ground, slinging his arms over their shoulders. Jason's head swayed lifelessly against his chest. They slowly sidestepped out of the alley, keeping the front of their bodies toward Jada. She heard Eddie's soft sobs and the tips of Jason's shoes scraping the pavement as they dragged him down the street.

When they were out of sight, Jada headed home, smiling back at the moon.

CHAPTER 21

Jada's bedroom door opened with a *crack* and then her mattress dipped beside her. "Wake up, sweetie. It's almost six. I need to talk to you." Jada didn't have to see her mom's face to know something was wrong. She could hear it in her voice. She kept her eyes shut, pretending to be asleep. As far as she was concerned, nothing could be that important this early in the morning.

But Lilah persisted. "Jada, you need to get up. Something's happened." This time her voice shook.

"I'm awake." Jada faked a yawn and lazily peeked out under half-opened lids. "What is it?"

"Come to the living room," she said and left.

Jada sat up with a groan. As she twisted toward the edge of her bed, a faint tickle crawled on her back. What now? She reached around but didn't feel anything. She shrugged and stood, dragging her feet out of her room. A dim blue light flickered in the living room.

"Mom, what is it?" Jada asked, slumped in the doorway.

Without turning toward her, Lilah lifted the remote and turned up the volume on the TV. "Union High School student Jason States is in the hospital after two of his classmates called police near an alley on North Main Street.

He appears to have been attacked and suffered severe trauma to the head, among other injuries. He is in critical condition, and doctors say he is unlikely to survive."

An instant of shock, then like a movie on fast forward, it all came rushing through her mind. Father Steve, her broken car . . . Jason. Her stomach hollowed, and her hands started to tremble. Her back—now she remembered—Jason threw her against the cement wall. Then she remembered his slimy hands on her breasts. A shiver crawled up her spine.

Jason, no, no!

The room started to close in on her. She stumbled onto the back of chair in front of her.

"Sweetie, are you all right?" Lilah ran to her side holding the back of her hand to Jada's forehead. "You're pale, sit down. Is it Edana? Did you have a nightmare?"

Jada shook her head. "No, I just need some water."

Lilah guided Jada to the chair and then ran in the kitchen. Image after image flashed on the screen. A stretcher being pushed into an ambulance, the reporter walking down Main Street, pointing to where they found Jason. Jada's stomach felt like it had been hit with a cannonball. She gasped for air. Then two familiar faces covered in oxygen masks came on the screen.

Derek and Eddie. They saw everything. The camera zoomed in on their ashen faces and Derek's terrified eyes locked onto hers through the screen.

What have I done?

Headlights lit up the back of the curtains, and Jada jumped. It must be the police coming to get her. The car slowed to a stop, the engine sputtering into silence.

This was it. This was the end. Her life was over. Jason was going to die; the police were coming for her. She would go to jail for the rest of her life—or worse, she would be hanged and burned before the whole town just like Edana. Nathan would probably be right there with them, eager to string her up himself. Tears pooled in her eyes. She bit down on her lip until she tasted blood and willed them away. She would not let them see her cry.

Lilah returned with a cup of water, and the news reporter continued. "The classmates who reported the attack appear to be experiencing some form of shock and are unable to give a statement right now. They're receiving treatment and are not currently suspects. We will report back when we have more information on the status of this young man and if we learn the police have any suspects. If you have any information, please call 911 immediately."

In shock. That meant Derek and Eddie hadn't told the police about her yet. Jada went to the window and peeked out. The headlights were just her neighbor coming home. She expected to feel relief, but her heart just raced faster.

Lilah came up behind her and wrapped her arms around her shoulders. "Honey, I'm so sorry. He was in some of your classes, wasn't he?"

Jada cringed under her mom's touch. She rolled her shoulders, trying to relax her muscles. How long would it take to feel comfortable being touched again? "Yes." Her voice was raspy.

"How awful. Jason's poor parents."

They sat back on the couch, and when the pale light of

dawn started to creep through the window, Lilah turned off the TV.

"You got home late last night. Where were you?"

Jada buried her face in her hands. She didn't know what to say. She'd never lied to her mom, never. "I—was, I—can't deal with this right now, Mom," she snapped.

"Shhh, it's okay. We'll talk about it later." Lilah rubbed her back. "Well, I have to go to work. Are you going to be all right?"

"I'll be fine."

After her mom left, Jada sat on the couch for a long time. She couldn't get Jason's blood-soaked face out of her mind.

Finally, she pushed herself up. Her feet felt like heavy chains were shackled to them as she walked back to her room. She dressed in a pair of jeans and a T-shirt, combed her hair and dabbed on a little makeup.

At the front door she stopped. Her heart thumped so wildly, she thought it would tear through her chest. The police would find her, arrest her, probably today. As she took her last breaths of freedom, her childhood streamed through her mind. Once when she was four, her father was trying to teach her chutes and ladders in the living room. His eyes sparkled with laughter because every time she'd land on a chute and slide down, she would break out in tears. In the end, she won the game, but she knew now that he had let her win by jumping her piece forward when she wasn't looking. Fighting back tears again, she tried to get him out of her mind. It had been ten years since he left. Why had she been thinking about him lately?

Then in a flash, her father's image was replaced by Nathan's face. At first she felt anger when she looked into his eyes, but slowly the anger dissolved, and she felt herself longing for him. The comfort of his touch, his steel eyes tenderly looking down at her. But she would never feel that again.

She took one more look at her room and then strode out without looking back.

All the way to school, she tried to force herself to steer toward the police station. She couldn't do it.

If Eddie and Derek hadn't spoken to the police yet, Jada was certain the guilt written all over her face would give her away. But when she walked into class, no one gave her a second glance. Everyone was engaged in a flurry of conversations about what could've happened to Jason. Everything from a wild animal attack to a serial killer was discussed. She kept her head low as she walked back to where Samantha was sitting. Samantha's gloomy face met hers momentarily before she went back to a heated conversation with Lori.

Jada scrunched her face. Just when she thought she couldn't get any lower, Lori's two black eyes met hers. Jada had done that to her. She sat, crossed her arms on the desk and wedged her face in the crook of her elbow.

"Eddie and Derek were with him. The grocery store clerk said they left the store together. So they must have seen the whole thing." Lori's whisper flowed over Jada's shoulder. She sounded different, defeated.

"Apparently he's stable now," Sam added.

"What?" Jada snapped up. "He's not going to die?"

"No," Sam replied. "But he's in a coma, and they aren't sure if he will come out of it."

Adrenaline poured into Jada's chest and Sam's voice blurred into a wave of incomprehensible sounds.

He's not dead. Maybe there is still hope.

The classroom lights flickered on and off, cutting through her thoughts.

Mrs. Jackson dumped her briefcase on the floor then stood at the mantel and rubbed her eyes. "Settle down, class."

"As I'm sure you all know, Jason States is in the hospital. I just got out of a teacher's meeting, and as of ten minutes ago, he is stable but in a coma. They are still unsure if he will come out of it. Apparently he suffered some pretty severe blows to the head. Now the school is offering counseling to anyone who needs it. And some people might be pulled out of class to be interviewed by the police."

The class erupted into a roar.

"Calm down, everybody. If you are interviewed, it is just part of protocol. They have to rule out all suspects. If you knew Jason or saw him the day he was attacked, you will probably be questioned."

Jada had known this moment was coming. Her heart felt like an anaconda was coiled around it. She closed her eyes and focused on calming her rapid breathing. She knew she'd crumble under an interrogation by a police officer.

Maybe I should just turn myself in? But what if that sent

218

Edana into a rage? She could attack more people.

A hand rose to Jada's left. "I heard he was attacked by a mountain lion." Several students scoffed and offered their own opinions.

"I think it was a gang."

"Maybe it was a vampire. Why else would Derek and Eddie be so scared?"

"Class, stop. If you want to say something nice about Jason, we can spend the class doing that, but I don't want to drum up conspiracy theories about rogue animals or supernatural creatures okay? This isn't the latest Hollywood film."

Jada slunk low in her seat. This was going to be a long day.

By the time her last class before lunch ended, she was exhausted. She had suffered all the guilt she could take in one day. Each class was spent talking about what a great guy Jason was. In her third class, she'd started to get mad. Was Jason really a great guy? True, he didn't deserve what she did to him, but he'd tried to rape her. Maybe she should share *that* story. And then she felt guilty all over again for her thoughts.

At her locker, she stuffed her books into her bag. She couldn't take the looks on people's faces anymore. She was going home. When she grabbed her econ book, something fell out of it, landing on the floor. When she picked it up, her face flushed with heat. It was a picture of Nathan. She'd totally forgotten about it. On one of the rare occasions he was smiling, she had snapped the photo and printed it off. She had forgotten how perfect his face was and how his smile made her insides feel like Jell-O.

"What is that?" Sam's voice came from behind her.

She tore the photo up and threw it back in her locker before Sam could see. "Oh, nothing, just an old picture. Don't need it anymore." She flung away a tear from her left eye before turning to find Sam and Jen.

"Did your mom say anything about Jason?" Sam whispered to Jen. "She has to know something the news isn't reporting."

Jen looked around to make sure no one was eavesdropping on them. "She said there was a couple who left the antique store right before Jason walked out of the grocery store, and they saw a girl walking toward the alley where Jason was attacked."

Jada's blood felt like it had turned to dust.

"A girl." Sam's jaw dropped.

"Yup," Jen shrugged. "They doubt she's a suspect, but they just want to know who she is so they can talk to her, ask her if she saw anything suspicious."

"Are you feeling okay, Jada? You don't look so good." Jen reached up and pulled a strand of hair off of Jada's forehead.

"Y—yeah, I'm fine. This whole thing is just overwhelming. I'm going home."

Jen's eyebrows pressed together. "It's really scary."

Jada nodded but didn't make eye contact with them. They'd see right through her.

"Oh, there she is. Jada, wait!" Mrs. Jackson strode toward her, two men in suits trailing behind her. "Jada, this is Detective Morrison and Detective Brewster. They want to have a word with you."

Jada froze. They knew. "Wh—what for?"

Detective Morrison eyed her. He was tall and fit. Other than a few wrinkles around his cold blue eyes, he looked young. Detective Brewster was a few inches shorter, but the dark circles under his eyes made him look haggard. He must have gained a lot of weight recently because the spaces between the buttons on his shirt were stretched into small ovals.

"Just a few questions about Jason States, miss. Nothing to worry about." Detective Morrison held his hand out, motioning her toward the principal's office.

She glanced once more at Sam and Jen, who were wide-eyed and completely still. Jen silently mouthed, *it will be okay*. But it didn't make Jada feel any better. They didn't know what she had done.

As she followed the detectives, all the students' eyes were on her. She felt like she was walking down a prison corridor to the electric chair, not down the hall she had walked so many times. The detectives' faces were stoic as they ushered her inside one of the school's conference rooms.

They sat across from her and started turning pages in what appeared to be her school file. She tried to sit still, but her senses were on overdrive. Her hearing, which she had finally learned to control, picked up on every little sound. A fly darted in circles around Detective Brewster's head, sending waves of thunder in Jada's ears.

Detective Morrison started tapping a pen on the desk. The sound vibrated on Jada's nerves like a tuning fork.

"Miss Bell, the reason we called you in here is because you were seen arguing with the victim yesterday."

"Arguing? I don't recall that." Her voice shook as she wiped her clammy palms on her jeans.

"At lunch outside." Their eyes took in everything, seeming to even notice the beads of sweat forming on her brow.

Jada blinked rapidly. "Oh, yes. Sorry, I forgot about that. He, uh, asked me to the homecoming dance, and I told him no. He was persistent. I don't think he was used to hearing no." She let out a nervous laugh.

Detective Brewster crossed his arms over his chest. "Then what happened after that?"

Jada shook her head. "Nothing. He finally left, and I went to PE."

Detective Morrison nodded before shuffling through some paper. A loud tapping cut into the silence, catching everyone's attention. It took her a few seconds to realize it was her own foot rattling on the floor. Flashing them a nervous smile, she quickly crossed it over the other foot.

Detective Morrison leaned onto the table. "Miss Bell, where were you last night?"

"I was at home, with my mom." She hadn't meant to lie; it had just come out. Suddenly she remembered that her car was still at the church. A lump rose in her throat. Did they know? Were they just toying with her? She'd seen a few crime shows and knew the cops always tried to get a confession before they told the criminal they already had the evidence to arrest them.

"Do you know of anyone who might have a grudge

against Mr. States?"

"No. Not at all. He was one of the most popular guys in school."

"Okay, Miss Bell." Detective Morrison sighed and closed her file. "If you think of anything, please contact us."

She nodded, stood without looking at them, and bolted out. Luckily no one was in the hall to see her bent over the garbage can depositing her breakfast. Each second that had passed of that excruciating five minutes, she'd wanted to blurt out that she had done it. That she was the one they were looking for. But the words wouldn't come out. Each time she was about to say it, she pictured her mom's face and never seeing her again. She pictured the life she wanted dissolving into the wind.

Within ten minutes, she was back at home slumped on the edge of her bed. She'd closed her curtains, but the daylight still crept through. In the hall closet, she grabbed a spare blanket and went back in her room to drape it over her window. She hoped that the darkness would make her feel like she didn't exist, and maybe this whole mess with Jason would go away and somehow her life would return to normal.

It seemed to work for a few minutes, but then images flooded her mind, and this time she couldn't stop them. The maggots in Lori's hair, her broken nose, the lacrosse game, Jason. One by one she relived the events, but instead of pleasure in any of them, she felt ashamed. What had she become? Tears soaked her face and neck. Never in her life had she behaved this way. She was always a nice, caring person. And then, for the first time, it became painstakingly clear.

Edana.

Edana had come back through her to exact her revenge . . . to kill the whole town. Jada gasped, remembering the vision she had about Jason at lunch. She had seen exactly what she was going to do to him only hours later. This whole time Edana had been manipulating her. She knew Jada had been hurt and abused, and she used those feelings to control her. Jada's conscience had tried to warn her, but she'd ignored it. The whole time Edana knew what she was doing, building Jada up to kill. And she had won. A throbbing numbness filled Jada's body.

CHAPTER 22

A week went by, but Jada couldn't tell one day from the next. They intertwined in one long haze of misery. A heavy depression grew in her stomach like a cancer. She couldn't even look at herself in the mirror. Sam and Jen had asked her a million times what was wrong. At first she used her change as an excuse, made up stories of her mom grounding her, but by the last few days she didn't respond at all. Jen was acting strange too. She was barely eating and didn't say much anymore.

Sam spoke of nothing except changing. Every day she gave an update to Jada and Jen of how many days were left until her birthday.

When Jada got home that day, she was consumed with thoughts of Jason. She wanted to see him, but only family had access to his room. Plus, if she insisted, it might draw attention to her. She'd watched the news every night for an update, and every night they reported that he was the same. Every morning she'd resolved to turn herself in and even drove to the police station. But her legs would never get out of the car.

The following night, Jada woke up drenched in sweat. The same dream tormented her night after night. She was in the alley again, listening to that awful mangy cat wail while Jason's lifeless, bloodied eyes stared at her. And when she tried to run, the streets became a maze of alleys that always ended up back at Jason's body. She was torn between anger for what Jason had tried to do to her and remorse for what she had done to him.

When the sun finally rose, she felt like she had spent the night fighting a dragon. Her muscles were still tight from running in her dream. When she willed her limbs to move, they refused to budge, seeming to wedge even further into the mattress.

"I've got to go to school," she said to her legs as if they had a mind of their own. With all the strength she could muster, she heaved her torso up and slid to the end of the bed. When her image appeared in her mirror, she looked away and then sighed. Maybe it was time to face herself. She held her breath and slowly opened one eye, then the other. A zing of shame shocked her chest, but she kept her gaze. She had to get through this somehow. Turning her head from side to side, she was surprised to see that despite her insomnia, she looked well rested. Her skin no longer needed foundation, and her new naturally wavy hair bounced as if she had just gone to a salon.

One perk of being a Nephilim. She allowed herself a slight grin for the first time in a week.

When there were still no leads in Jason's attack, the mood at school became increasingly dark. While the first day the students were wild with theories about who attacked him and why, a week later they had become somber and even a little scared.

226

When Jada pulled into the parking lot, the front doors of the school stood open and the hall was packed with students.

She narrowed her eyes. *That's weird. Class starts in less than a minute. What's everyone doing?*

Right outside the main door, Jen was slumped against the wall and staring absently at the ground. Jada could tell she was upset just by the way her head hung against her shoulder.

Jada parked and headed toward her.

"Jen," she called as she closed the space between them. Jen's head whipped back, but she didn't return Jada's smile. Jada's posture deflated. She barely had the energy to keep herself going, let alone take care of Jen. She decided at least to try to push her own problems aside and be there for her friend.

"Are you all right?" Jada plopped onto a cement bench right next to Jen.

"Yeah, sorry. You just caught me off guard." As she returned her attention to the ground, she wiped a tear off her cheek.

Jada scooted closer to her and grabbed her arm. "Jen, are you crying? What happened?"

Jen sniffled and looked at her. A purple shadow circled her distant, glassy eyes. "Logan—" her lips pressed together and three small veins screamed in her forehead "—told me he never wanted to see me again."

"What?" Jada jumped up and planted herself in front of Jen. "I don't understand. Why?" She was practically yelling.

Jen waved her hand in the air. "He just said it's over, and I should move on. Seth was with him." Their eyes connected and a knowing passed between them.

Jen spun around and set her back against the wall. "Seth's told him about . . . us. That has to be it. I didn't do anything to deserve this!" Tears soaked her face, and she hiccupped.

Could Logan know who we really are?

"I'm so sorry Jen, but there has to be another reason. He's probably just tense about the Jason thing. You can't think of anything else you might have said to him to make him mad?" A thick knot rose in Jada's chest when she said Jason's name. She averted her face to hide the pain that she knew sat on her face like a mask. She pretended to pick some lint off of her jeans.

Jen shook her head and stared absently at the ground.

Jada pulled Jen into a tight hug and listened to her muffled tears. An overwhelming feeling of dread wrapped around her heart like a sheath of ice. *Maybe after I yelled at Nathan in the cemetery, he decided to rejoin Seth and his father and kill me after all. And now they've recruited Logan and are going to go after Jen and Sam too.*

She could handle whatever Nathan and Seth threw at her, but the thought of them hurting Jen or Sam made her blood boil. She knew there was no guarantee she could protect them before they changed.

"Just give it some time. It will pass." She released Jen and forced a smile. She couldn't believe Logan had done this. One moment he's going to propose, and the next he dumps her for no reason. What a jerk.

After grabbing her backpack, she nodded toward the door. "Why is everyone still in the halls?"

Jen fanned at her eyes. "Some kind of emergency assembly meeting in the theater. It starts in a few minutes."

"Well, we'd better go in and find a seat." Jada locked her arm in Jen's and guided her inside. In the auditorium they found three seats in the back. They looked around for Sam, but she was nowhere in sight.

A magnified tapping sound cut through the chatter in the room. "Testing, testing. Can you hear me?" A few students to Jada's right nodded to acknowledge the speaker.

"Mrs. Jackson will be out in a minute to address the school. Please keep your talking to a minimum. Thank you."

Puckering her lips, Jada blew out an exaggerated sigh just as Samantha entered the aisle and sidestepped toward her and Jen.

"Isn't it great not being in class?" Sam was a little too animated for the circumstances.

"Don't act so happy. It's probably about Jason. Maybe he's made a turn for the worse?" Jada scolded. Jason had to still be alive, had to. She wouldn't be able to take it if he died.

After sitting, Sam leaned forward, and her eyebrows bent down. "What's the matter, Jen?"

Jen bit her lip and stared at her hands. She clearly was about to burst into tears again, so Jada answered for her.

"Logan told her to never speak to him again."

Sam scoffed. "What? Why?"

Jen rubbed her temples. "I don't know." Just as the

words left her mouth, Logan walked by without giving her so much as a glance. She watched his every step with a desperate look on her face as he descended the walkway and took a seat between Nathan and Seth. Her moist eyes met Jada's for a split second before she bolted out of the theater.

"I can't believe it." Samantha's lips tightened into a straight line. "He can't do that to her. I'm going to go talk to that asshole." Sam sprang up, the bottom of her folding seat flipping back with a thud. But before Sam could reach the end of their aisle, Mrs. Jackson strode across the stage toward the microphone. Sam sat back down with a huff and crossed her arms over her chest, anger radiating from her eyes.

Jada studied Sam's profile, wondering if she would defend her like that when the time came. Jada hated to admit it, but she knew Sam well enough to know that she enjoyed fighting with guys more than she actually wanted to stick up for Jen. She loved to banter with them. But what would she do in a life-or-death situation? Once Sam changed, would she be on Jada's side? She assumed she knew her, but they hadn't really been in a situation where Sam really had to sacrifice herself.

"As you all know, we've had a tragedy . . ." Mrs. Jackson's mouth was still moving, but Jada couldn't hear what she was saying. A jolt of adrenaline shot through her. Her ears honed in on an approaching rumbling outside.

A truck . . . moving fast . . . headed this way!

Jada started to scream but she was drowned out when the truck slammed through the theater wall. Jada expected the crash to be moving in slow motion like she had seen so many times in the movies. Instead, screaming students and chunks of debris flew by her with lighting speed. She rushed toward the truck but one still figure caught her eye, and she stopped. It was Lori Messing's petrified face.

Jada's eyes followed her line of sight to a spear of wood that was flying right at her. She knew what she had to do. In less than a second, she clamped onto Lori's arm and threw her out of the way. The wood slammed into Jada's thigh and knocked her to the floor.

Then, just as quick as the accident erupted, it was over, and all that was left was a massive cloud of brown dust hovering around the mangled truck. Jada lay on the floor, unmoving, and watched the theater lights glimmer off the flecks of dust as they slowly floated toward her. Shock settled in, leaving the room in an eerie silence. When someone screamed her name and several faces appeared above her, Jada winced.

"Jada, don't move." Mrs. Jackson's voice rang in her head. At least twenty pairs of wide eyes were looking down at her.

"What's wrong?" Jada pressed herself up on her elbows but several students gently pushed her back down. Then, in an instant, the room went black. Her eyes searched frantically for any sign of light. A stench filled the air, so strong she could taste it. She coughed.

That smell.

She recognized the putrid smell of the dumpster.

I'm in the alley again. No!

She closed her eyes, refusing to look down where she

knew Jason's body lay. *This is only a dream. Focus Jada.* If she looked into his lifeless eyes one more time, she wouldn't be able to go on. A faint laugh floated through the damp air, sending a shiver down Jada's spine.

"Jason?" Her eyes shot open and squinted at the spot where his body should be. Nothing was there.

"Jaaada . . ." Jason's taunting voice penetrated her from every direction.

"Jason! No, it can't be you. You're in a coma." She turned around, frantically searching the ominous darkness.

She was about to run when the outline of a gray figure coalesced in the blackness and slowly made its way toward her.

She backed up until her shoulder blades hit the alley wall. "Jason. No, it's not possible!"

"Anything's possible, Jada. You of all people should know that." His low voice slithered over her. A strong wind blew up a heap of garbage and leaves, taking the gray figure with it as it danced down the alley.

"Jason?" She mouthed his name.

Jada felt hands on her legs, then her arms, then her stomach. Prodding, groping hands. Panic exploded in her rib cage. First there were two, then four, then it felt like hundreds of hands were crawling over her like snakes. Her limbs scrambled for freedom, but the hands gripped her tighter. She blinked, and she was back in the theater—except the faces hovering above her weren't the concerned faces of her fellow students and teachers. They were all Jason's face leering down at her. A fire lit behind her eyes.

"Get off of me!" The same smooth voice that had come

out of her in the alley growled through her teeth. Jason's faces smiled back at her, and more hands grabbed onto her. She screamed, and her body leaped off the floor in one fluid move, sending bodies flying in all directions. Jason would never touch her again.

"Jada." Jada's head snapped to the left, and she was disarmed by Samantha's wide eyes.

"You're in the theater at school. There's been an accident. Everyone is just trying to help you. You're hurt." Sam's eyes moved right pointing to the crowd of onlookers. When Jada turned, she saw the confused and pained faces of her classmates and teachers again.

Mrs. Jackson stepped forward hesitantly, clearly afraid of the strength Jada had just displayed. "Jada, you have a piece of wood in your leg."

Jada's eyebrows pressed together, and she looked down at the foot-long splinter of wood sticking out of her thigh. She raised her knee for a better look. More blood oozed out of the wound, turning her already red-stained pants even darker. The crowd groaned, and someone retched behind her. Jada reached for the piece of wood to remove it, but Samantha slapped her hand away and bore stern eyes into her.

"I'm going to take you to the hospital," Samantha declared more to the surrounding people than to Jada. "So they can remove that and bandage you up so you don't get an infection." She nodded slowly, as though willing Jada to nod back.

Jada came to, realizing where she was. "Yes, the hospital."

The door of the truck crashed open, and a few students jumped.

Large black boots came wobbling out. "What the—" The man's knees buckled together, barely holding up his massive frame. A half-empty bottle of Jack Daniels was clenched tightly in his fist.

"Mr. States, are you all right?" Mrs. Jackson cautiously stepped between the large pieces of rubble while eyeing the wall. "Come inside, you could get hurt out there." She waved him toward her.

His swaying torso looked as if it was going to topple over at any moment.

"Mr. States, now."

Mr. States looked down at the ground for a few seconds before his feet clumsily plodded forward. His foot caught on a slab of concrete, thrusting him in the air. Just in time, Mrs. Jackson and a student caught him under his arms and dragged him to a chair. Jada's chest sank as she watched the dejected face of Jason's father. He stumbled into the theater chair and start wailing uncontrollably. "Jason! Where's Jason?"

A deep, throbbing ache settled around the splinter embedded in Jada's flesh. She turned away and leaned next to Sam's ear. "Get me out of here."

CHAPTER 23

Distant ambulance sirens glided on the gentle breeze as Jada and Sam exited the main building.

They stopped at edge of the parking lot, and Sam drummed her fingers on her hips. "Jeez, Jada, you almost pulled that wood right out and let the whole school see your leg heal itself."

"Yeah, I didn't realize where I was. I was having a dream. I was back in the—" Jada's voice cracked.

"Back in the what?" Sam eyed her suspiciously.

"Nowhere. I mean, I was having a dream about Edana." She hoped Sam didn't hear the fear in her voice, hoped she believed her answer. Thankfully, Sam had lost interest and was looking off into the distance.

"Well, better get this out." After bracing herself, Jada grabbed the splintered wood and yanked it out, sending a spray of blood on the sidewalk.

Sam's face puckered in disgust. "Did that hurt?"

Jada's face crunched, and she let out a low whimper.

"Guess that's a yes." Samantha chuckled. After letting out a grunt, Jada laughed with her. It was the first time she'd even smiled since that night with Jason. It felt good, but wrong somehow.

Sam's posture suddenly stiffened.

"What is it?" Jada flipped around.

Condescending hazel eyes greeted them. "Hello, Jada, Samantha."

"Seth," Jada hissed. "What do you want?"

A smirk twitched on the corners of his lips as he crossed his arms over his chest. "Just came by to say hello."

"Well, as you can see, this isn't really a good time for a friendly conversation," Sam shot back, tilting her head.

He cocked an eyebrow. "Who said anything about friendly?"

"Did you come to kill me?" Jada defiantly locked eyes with his. Many times in the past week, she'd considered the possibility that she would die soon. But she hoped not at the hands of Seth.

His eyes turned into shiny black marbles as he peered back at her. He uncrossed his arms and cracked his knuckles. The school doors swung open and two guys jumped on skateboards. Jada turned away so they wouldn't see her healed leg. They stopped at a glossy black Charger, and one lit up a cigarette.

Seth rolled his eyes at them. "Not yet, but it's just a matter of time before you really hurt someone. And when you do, you will get what you've deserved all along."

Apparently, he completely missed Jada saving Lori, or he chose to ignore it, twisting the truth into whatever he needed it to be to fuel his rage.

Jada huffed. "Seems like it doesn't matter what I do, your mind is set."

Seth's chest shook as he laughed. "Yeah, guess you're

right."

"So why wait?" Jada challenged. She wasn't sure what she was doing. She was just tired of living with the guilt of Jason, tired of waiting to see if Nathan and Seth were going to make a move. She knew she was being stupid and impulsive but couldn't stop herself.

He was silent for a moment while he glared between Jada and Sam. "Just need to get a few things in order. You've proved to be a challenge. You're stronger than I expected, and you're fast."

He must be talking about when Jada saw Nathan in the cemetery. She'd fought him off and outran him. So Nathan had told Seth everything he knew about her and returned to his original plan. She chastised herself for the prickle of pain in her heart. Why was she surprised? She should be over him by now, but she wasn't. For the past week she'd managed to not so much as look at Nathan, and it was working. As long as she didn't see him or hear his name, she was fine. If she let him in her life again, it would cloud her judgment and get her killed. He couldn't be trusted.

At the far end of the main building, a group of students poured out, led by the head coach of the football team. The school must be evacuating because of the accident. Even at a distance Jada could see the clear outline of Nathan's form. Standing a foot higher than everyone else, he was impossible to miss. After scanning the parking lot, his gaze stopped on her, and without hesitation he trudged in their direction. Jada immediately turned away. He had a power over her even at a distance. She closed her eyes and rubbed her chest, trying somehow to make the pain go away.

Sam saw him too and wrapped her fingers around Jada's elbow, pulling her a step back. "Well, it's been fun, Seth, but we need to get going." She smirked.

Seth's eyes narrowed, and he pointed at Jada. "I'll be seeing you."

"I'll be waiting," she spat back.

When Nathan was a few yards away, Sam tugged at her arm harder, and they ran to Sam's car. Jada could feel the heat of Nathan's eyes on her back like a roaring fire. Something deep in her gut pulled her toward him. She desperately wanted to see him. She clamped her teeth down hard. Where had her anger for him gone? It was easier to deal with than this crazy, fiery desire. Her feet tried to turn around, but she forced them forward. She couldn't let his knowing gray eyes and the comforting smell of his skin disarm her. She had to remember that the second she showed weakness, he would attack her.

They jumped inside Sam's white Acura and sped by Nathan and Seth and out of the parking lot.

Jada watched them out the rear window. "Whoa, slow down. No one is chasing us, Sam."

She clicked her seatbelt on and gripped the edges of the seat as Sam darted through the neighborhood toward Jada's house. A squirrel hopped across the street, barely evading Sam's tires. Shouts from angry neighbors chased after them, and Jada slid down in her seat, hoping they wouldn't see her.

Sam's chin was low and she was breathing heavy like a bull about to charge. "I can't wait to change so I can take out that asshole!"

Jada sat back up. "Sam, you can't hurt him. Didn't you hear what my mom said? Whatever powers you get won't work against the Arons." She waved her hand in the air. "Trust me, I've tried."

"What do you mean you've *tried*?" Sam's lips pursed together. Jada rubbed her forehead and internally kicked herself for not being more careful with what she said. She was really bad at this whole secret thing.

"What is going on, Jada? I swear, lately you've been hiding something from me. What do you mean you've tried?" She pulled into Jada's driveway and thrust the gearshift into park, jerking the car forward.

Jada tapped her fingers on the door and watched a horde of cars go by in the side mirror. Students were probably thrilled to be able to leave school early. Their excited shouts rose and faded as they passed. She didn't want to tell Sam about what had happened with Nathan in the cemetery. It was possible Sam still liked him, even though he was supposed to kill her. Knowing her, she'd think that was exciting. If she found out that Nathan actually liked Jada instead, she would be insane with jealousy. The last thing she needed right now was to be in a fight with Sam.

"It's nothing Sam, I don't even know why I said that."

Sam shook her head and let out a long breath. "Okay, Jada . . . whatever." She was clearly getting tired of Jada's answers. Somehow Sam could always tell Jada was lying. She must not be very good at it.

Jada looked down at her hands. "I'm going to stay home for a few days. I have to make it look like I'm hurt. Will you call me if anything happens at school?"

Sam nodded and hit the unlock button, signaling to Jada that the conversation was over. Jada sat still and stared at Sam's stiff profile, willing her to look at her. If there was ever a time in her life when she needed her best friend, it was now. She needed just one look from her that said "I'm with you." But Sam fixed her hard eyes forward, slid on her sunglasses and shifted the car into reverse.

"All right, Sam, I'll talk to you later."

Just as Jada's feet hit the driveway, the car started rolling back. She leaped out of the way but had to chase after the car to close the door. Irritation puckered in her chest, and she threw up her hands in a what-was-that gesture. She couldn't tell if Sam saw her through her sunglasses, but she made no reply before speeding out of sight.

Once inside, she shed her torn, bloody jeans, pulled on some cotton shorts and heaved herself onto the couch. Jada hated lying to Sam, but there was no way she could tell her about her feelings for Nathan and certainly not about Jason. She didn't want to drag Sam into her mess.

She wished that just this once Sam would accept that Jada couldn't tell her everything. But she knew that was a lofty hope. Sam was the type of person who had to be in the know. She called it keeping an edge. She even threw a fit once when Jada told Jen something before telling her.

And today, the look in Sam's eyes . . . The muscles in Jada's face flickered. It was time to accept that her and Sam's friendship was changing. Jada wasn't so sure anymore that Sam was truly her friend. Sam had gotten mad at Jada's birthday when Nathan was talking to her. She didn't defend her against Lori, and she's been acting weird ever since Jada changed.

Jealous, Jada realized. She was jealous because Jason asked her out and Nathan liked her. Maybe even that Edana chose her. It wasn't fair. Ever since they were born she'd been in Sam's shadow, and now that she'd stepped out and started to become her own person and receive a little attention, Sam was pissed.

Gradually, her racing thoughts went quiet and her eyes became heavy with exhaustion. After a passive attempt to fight sleep, she gave in and pulled down the fleece blanket that was folded on top of the couch. She draped if over her body and closed her eyes.

Almost instantly she started dreaming. She was at school looking at her brown eyes in her locker mirror. She was back to her old self. She smiled, but suddenly her body moved on its own toward a guy who had his back to her. As she approached, he turned his head, revealing Nathan's strong jawline. She tried to stop, but her body kept its pace, being pushed toward him by an unseen force. When she was within inches of him, he turned around and gave her a warm smile. She relaxed. His hands rose, and he cupped her face as he had done before, and he started talking. His lips moved, but Jada couldn't hear a word he was saying. But it didn't matter. His eyes said all she needed to know. She looked into the dark gray and swam into the warmth that washed over her body.

He grabbed her hand and pulled her down the hall. When they entered the theater, Jada's shoulders went rigid, and she shook her head. Nathan kept smiling and didn't slow his pace. She looked around, terrified of what she would see. But everything looked normal. The wall that Jason's dad crashed into was intact and the students were safe.

Nathan pulled her into him and wrapped his large arm around her waist, lifting her against him. Her heart fluttered at his touch, and she rested her cheek on his solid chest. She could stay here forever.

Her eyes were lazily opening and closing when she saw a flash of black. Alarm rose in her stomach. She lifted her head and squinted. Yes, there in the first row of seats, a head of shiny black hair. The girl stood and turned. Her own image glared at her, but it was the new her, the one with blue eyes. She gasped and looked back at Nathan, but she didn't find a gentle, affectionate face. His eyes had become dark and the muscles in his jaw angry. He released her, a look of disgust on his face. Her heart felt like he had sliced it with a knife. From the corner of her eye, she saw movement. Her head jerked, and she saw her other self. The theater was dripping with blood. Everyone was dead. She fell to her knees as blue-eyed Jada sauntered toward her, her blood drenched palms opened out.

"No," Jada pleaded, her voice raspy.

She turned to look back at Nathan, but he was gone. Then, she hit the floor with a *smack,* and her eyes shot open. She was back in her living room. The dream had felt so real. Nathan's touch, his warm smile. It had felt so good. Then the gruesome scene, and Nathan's rejection. She took a few deep breaths.

It was just a dream. It wasn't real.

But she couldn't shake the image of the hundreds of dead bodies and Nathan's disgusted face. It had been tattooed on her mind.

A loud ringing filled the room, and Jada jumped. She pushed herself up and found her phone in the front pocket of her backpack. The caller ID said Mom Cell. She muted the ring and watched her mom's picture until it disappeared, sending the call to voicemail. She didn't have the energy to talk to her. By now the school had called Lilah and told her about the accident. She knew it was cruel to not pick up the phone and tell Lilah she was okay, but she just couldn't deal with her mom's excessive worrying right now.

Jada looked down at her bare leg and rubbed the place where the wound had been. Her skin was soft and smooth as if nothing had ever happened. She used her sleeve to wipe the beads of sweat that had formed on her forehead and leaned back against the edge of the couch. She couldn't take this anymore. She would never be able to sleep or lead a normal life again. Edana's visions of killing people would haunt her for the rest of her life. She couldn't trust herself. After what she'd done to Jason, she had vowed to never hurt another person again. But she had already almost broken that vow. When Edana had made her see Jason's face in the theater, she had nearly hurt someone again.

Her lip quivered. In just a few days her life had been flipped upside down. She was moving along in a simple, and then in one moment, she had turned into a Nephilim, been teased with love only to get it taken away, and— depending on whether Jason recovered—possibly killed someone. She was starting to think maybe it would have been better if Nathan had killed her. The town would be safe, her mom wouldn't have to worry about her anymore and she wouldn't have to remember what it felt like to be in Nathan's arms.

"No!" she yelled, slamming her fists on the carpet. "I can't give up. I have to fight this." She had to communicate with Edana somehow, get her to leave her alone. Edana was the one who was influencing her, forcing her to hurt people.

But how can I get through to her? Then it hit her. It had to work, she had no other options. Pushing herself up, she pulled on some jeans and a hoodie, grabbed her backpack and ran out the door.

CHAPTER 24

After locking the front door, Jada flipped around and slumped against it. Her car was still at the church, so she'd have to walk. A frigid wind coming in from the mountains was at odds with the thrum of determination sweltering under her skin. Moving off of the front steps, she fingered the items in her backpack, trying to locate her phone. She pulled it out, searched for the number to her mom's cell to let her know where she was going, then stopped. Lilah would think it was too dangerous to go to Edana's grave. It was better not to tell her. Jada needed to talk with Edana somehow, to reason with her. And this was the only thing she could think of. She stuffed her phone back into her backpack and started walking toward the church. But how would she find out where Edana was buried? She doubted they'd buried her in a cemetery. There had to be some kind of news or something about her death, something archived. Crossing the street, she pulled the hood of her sweatshirt over her head and made her way to the library.

The automatic double doors invited her in with a strained moan. She strode in, and her gaze honed in on the classroom door in the back. Unease ping-ponged in her belly. The last time she was here, she'd run into Seth, and that was the last thing she needed right now. Keeping her head down, she navigated the stale lobby, making her way to the technology center. After taking one last survey of the room, she plopped down at an empty computer. Tapping her fingers on the desk, she waited for the library software to load. Although she liked the old interior of the library, she wished they would update their equipment. Finally, the little hourglass icon turned into an arrow, and she was in. Placing her forehead on her palm, she closed her eyes and mentally calculated when Edana would've lived. When she figured a general time frame, she typed it in the search window and waited.

About a hundred news articles came back, and she grunted. This was going to take longer than she thought. Jada wiggled deeper into the chair and rolled her neck, then started to scroll through the images. An hour later her eyelids were starting to get heavy as she scanned obituaries, town meeting announcements and wild animal sightings. She was about to call it a day when a faded black-and-white picture filled the screen. She sat up in a jolt. Even though her sight was impeccable, she had to squint to see the degenerated picture. Two men held a dark-haired woman by the arms. Jada could only see her profile, but she knew instantly it was Edana. A shiver prickled the back of her neck.

She read through the article and found what she needed. Edana was killed north of Bishop, up near North Fork Bishop Creek, and buried not far from there. There was no tombstone placed, and the area was considered damned.

Great, the grave will be really hard to find. And she

would definitely need her car.

Jada wrote down the information and skittered out of the library. She pulled out her phone again and scrolled down her contacts. After she hit send, an endless number of rings filled her ears. She was about to hang up when a woman's high-pitched voice came through the line. "Our Lady Church. This is Gail. How may I help you?"

"Hi, my name is Jada Bell, and I'm looking for Father Steve."

"Yes, miss, let me transfer you to his office phone."

"Thank you."

A few seconds passed before she heard Father Steve's friendly voice. "Jada, what a pleasure."

"Hi, Father Steve. Thank you for taking my call. I'm really sorry about the way I behaved the other day. I, well, I hope you can forgive me."

"Don't even mention it, Jada. All is forgiven."

Jada ran a hand through her hair, suddenly at a loss for words. Father Steve made her feel vulnerable, even just his voice.

"Are you there?"

Jada kicked some rocks on the pavement. "Yes, sorry. I was wondering if you could jumpstart my car. It died in the church parking lot the other day."

"Sure, I can do that. I'll meet you outside."

"Okay. Thanks, Father Steve." She hung up and started jogging toward the church. She'd find Edana's grave, reason with her, plead with her, do whatever it took to get her to leave her alone.

It seemed ludicrous, like something out of a sci-fi

movie, but the one thing Jada had learned in the past few days was that anything was possible. The world as she had known it was gone. Besides, she had no other ideas, so this had to work.

When she arrived, Father Steve was already outside talking to husky man under a large aspen. The man's features were drenched in shadow, but there was something familiar about him. His gestures, the planes of his face. She'd seen him before, she was sure of it. Instinctively, Jada moved behind her car and watched them. Splashes of silver in his dark brown hair told her he was at least in his forties, and his hard eyes revealed the gravity of his intent. She focused in on their conversation.

"Thanks, Father. I'll be in touch." Then the man shook Father Steve's hand and left.

When he was out of sight, she poked her head out from behind her car. Father Steve was leaning against an older black Porsche. She walked over to him.

His smile was forced, and he looked tired. "Did you walk here?"

"Yes. I didn't want to bug my mom at work for a ride." Under the ray of pale sun, two sprinkles of water tapped on her nose, and she looked up. The cloud above her dipped in the center, looking like it was ready to gush.

Father Steve looked up also. "It will rain soon," he said flatly. He was different, more serious. It had to be the conversation with that man, whoever he was.

"My car is right over here." She pointed, and they walked over to it. Jada opened her door, unlatched the hood, then went and stood next to Father Steve.

With his hand on the edge of the car, Father Steve squinted at Jada's engine. "So where you off to?"

Jada licked her lips, thinking of what she should say. Suddenly, she felt weak. Her breathing slowed, and exhaustion weighed down her limbs. She wanted to tell him, tell him everything. She needed some words of encouragement. Someone to tell her everything would work out. Leaning on one leg, she watched his pale fingers tug at the wires connected to her battery.

"I'm going up near North Fork Bishop Creek."

His forehead formed into a ripple of hills. "I see. Do you need to go tonight?"

She looked down and swayed. For some reason, she couldn't lie to him. And it wasn't just because he was a priest. She felt him watching her, and she slowly raised her head and met his soft blue eyes. They were pensive and had a knowing about them.

"Yes, I have to."

"Hmm, well, shouldn't go alone then. Storm's coming." He dropped the car's hood back down and brushed his hands together. "Tell you what. Why don't I take you up there in my car, and I'll jump yours when we get back."

Nervously wrapping a strand of hair around her finger, she contemplated what to do. He couldn't find out about her. He would never talk to her again, and she couldn't handle that. She didn't know why, but she needed him. She met his eyes. What felt like a warm blanket wrapped around her heart, and she felt her muscles go lax. It would be nice have Father Steve as moral support.

"Okay, when we get there, I'll only be a minute, so you

can wait in the car." She eyed him sheepishly, hoping he wouldn't ask her any more questions.

"Deal." He walked her to his Porsche, opened the door and held his hand out. She slid in and let him close the door behind her. A few seconds later he shuffled in and started the engine.

"Fancy." She smiled.

His eyes sparkled, reminding her of when she had first met him. "Thank you. Saved up for years to get her. She's the only woman in my life. Stella." He stroked the dashboard affectionately.

They drove off in silence toward Route 6, which led into the mountains. When Father Steve pulled out onto the windy mountain road, Jada held back a grin. Behind the wheel, he drove like a teenager in a hot rod.

She pulled the lever on the seat until it reclined, then she hugged herself. It was nice having him with her, even if he was in a strange mood.

"So . . . how's it going with Mr. Aron?"

Jada cracked open the window to let the dewy mountain air cool her face.

"That good huh?" His face showed no emotion.

Father Steve rubbed his knee and stretched out his leg in the tiny car. They fell into a comfortable silence as tiny droplets started to cluster on the windshield. The sprinkle turned into a downpour, bouncing off the hood like a swarm of crickets. Jada could almost feel Edana's anger bearing down on them as they approached her grave.

"Turn left here, then go all the way to the end," Jada said.

With a hard jerk Father Steve tugged on the wheel and darted the car left onto a barely visible dirt road. The car slowed and inched its way down the narrow path.

Jada knew this area vaguely. This was the northernmost entrance to the creek.

When they hit a dead end, Father Steve steered the Porsche into a small alcove and turned off the engine. He folded his arms over his chest and gave her a parental look. When Jada met his eyes, the sadness there stabbed her heart. She hadn't seen that look in a long time. Being around Father Steve was making her realize how much she missed her dad and that safe feeling she'd had every time he was around. She thought she was over him, but she had simply buried her feelings behind a wall of indifference. And now, that wall was starting to crack.

She blew out a long breath and looked out the window. Water streamed down the glass, making the tree branches look like slimy claws waiting for her to come out. She squared her shoulders and blinked back the emotion behind her eyes. The fact was her dad wasn't here. She had to do this alone.

"Okay, I'll be right back." When she opened the door, a spray of water dotted the old leather seat. She stuck her foot out and heaved herself over a murky puddle, shutting the door behind her. Hurrying around the car, she snuck into the woods, eager to get away from Father Steve's questioning eyes. Once she was sure she was out of his sight, she pulled out the piece of paper from the library. According to the directions, it should be just up ahead.

She maneuvered her way along a jagged path, pushing

away branches as she went. A thick mist cast the forest in a hazy greenish gray. The rain came down harder, pounding in her ears like ceremonial drums, edging her forward. Icy water dripped off the end of her pony tail and down her back.

As she went deeper into the forest, the flora lining the path gradually became brown until finally every plant for miles was dead. She couldn't keep her eyes off the decaying plants. They seemed to be screaming at her as the life was being sucked out of their roots. Her next step fell on air and her chest smacked into the mud. Pushing herself up to a sitting position, she glowered at the shallow hole cupping her foot.

She threw her hands up in the air, "Anything else?"

After letting out a long breath, she brushed as much mud she could get off her shirt and stood. Then, she saw it. A tombstone.

Tombstone? I thought the article said Edana's grave was unmarked?

She took a step closer. The stone had an engraving.

Edana, my beloved.

Beloved? Who wrote that? Suddenly, her stomach caved in like someone had punched her in the gut. Pressure rose up her chest and squeezed her lungs. Falling to all fours, she gasped in air. She tried to scream but her throat closed. Terror raced through her body like hot electricity. Edana was attacking her. Why had she come alone? After a minute, the pressure released and freezing air shocked her lungs. Then a darkness came over her, weighing down on her chest like an anvil.

"Edana . . ." She choked.

She took a tentative step forward, unsure what Edana would do. Back at home, she had felt confident that she should come, but now that she was here, all sense was telling her to get out.

"Edana, it's me, Jada." As the words left her mouth, a loud hissing rose to her ears. Mounds grew in the dirt, and she stumbled backward. When they peaked, thousands of insects poured from the tops like a volcano spewing lava. In an instant, they covered the ground, rippling toward her like angry waves.

"Edana, stop . . . please!" She raised her voice. "I only want to talk to you. Please leave me alone. I—I don't want to kill anybody." Jason's pale face forced its way into her mind, and she winced.

"I know. I've already almost—" she stopped, unable to say the truth out loud. "Please." She fell to her knees. "You have to forgive them."

Thunder erupted above her, and the ground started to rumble. A boulder wedged from its hole in the dirt and lurched straight for her. She jumped to the side, and it missed her by an inch. Closing her eyes, she tried to use her powers to steady the ground, but it just shook harder.

"Edana, please!" An overwhelming understanding came over her that this was a mistake. There was no stopping Edana. She would never give up her revenge. She would haunt Jada forever. A mixture of anger and sadness burned her chest. Orange light suddenly flickered on the ground, and she arched her head up. Flames licked at the tree above her. A loud *snap* cracked through the dense air, and a branch broke off and plunged toward her like a missile. She closed her eyes and threw her arms over her head.

Maybe this is for the best . . .

Her body shook as she waited for the wood to pierce her flesh and the fire to consume her. Suddenly, a strong wind slammed into her and the branch flew to the side, crashing into a tree. The flames were snuffed out, leaving a wisp of black smoke.

You really think I'm going to let you off that easy? I need you, my sweet Jada. Edana's laughter echoed in her head.

Bitter tears stung her eyes, and all her strength drained out of her. What replaced it was a darkness Jada couldn't have imagined in her worst nightmares. Her body was floating in an abyss. Black and cold and wet. Nothing and no one to hold on to. She cried until her eyes felt like sandpaper. Dragging herself to a push-up position, she lifted her torso and heaved herself to her feet. She wobbled in the sticky mud and gazed at Edana's tombstone.

She had underestimated Edana's determination and power. Coming here was a mistake.

Dimly she remembered Father Steve was waiting for her. Stumbling back down the path, she wondered what she would do now. Wondered whether there was anything she *could* do.

She slid into Father Steve's car and ignored his concerned face. He started the engine and steered the Porsche back to the main road. On the way down the mountain, Jada curled up into a ball and stared out the window. Every couple of minutes, Father Steve patted her on the back. The warmth of his touch gave her only temporary relief from the defeat sinking into her mind.

Back at the church, after he jumped her car, she thanked him and drove home. When she took off her dirty sweatshirt, she felt a light vibration. She searched through the pockets and pulled out her phone. It read: *1 Missed Call Samantha.*

She dialed Sam's number and heard her voice after one ring.

"Jada, something's happened, have you seen the news?" Sam's voice had an accusatory edge to it.

Jada's heart rate shot up. "No, I've been out. What is it?"

"They found a homeless man. He was in the alley when Jason was attacked. It was dark so he couldn't see the details of the person's face, but he said . . . it was a girl."

CHAPTER 25

Jada's stomach felt as if acid had been poured into it. She gripped the phone tighter and started to pace.

"What else did he say?" She hoped Sam wouldn't pick up on her shaky voice.

"He said that two other guys were definitely there, so they're interviewing Derek and Eddie again. They're claiming amnesia or PTSD or something like that. Oh, and the only thing the homeless man remembered about the girl was that she had long dark hair."

Jada went into the kitchen, grabbed a glass from the cabinet and filled it with water. She took three long gulps.

"Jada, are you there?"

"Yes, I'm here." She knew she should be filling the conversation with things like, "Wow, I wonder who it could be," or "I hope they catch her. Poor Jason." But she couldn't get the words out. And she knew her silence was giving her away.

"Jada, is there something you want to tell me?"

This was it. This was the moment in Sam and Jada's relationship that she dreaded. Should she tell Sam that she'd attacked Jason? Should she burden Sam with her dark secret? Her thoughts swirled in her head like a tornado.

Leaning her elbows on the kitchen counter, she rubbed her head. She didn't want to hide anymore. Even if no one found out, the guilt would eat away at her until there was nothing left of her. She really needed to get if off her chest.

Maybe Sam could help her, tell her what she should do.

After a few moments, Jada sighed. "Yes, I do have something to tell you."

"You did this to him, didn't you?" It was more of a statement than a question.

Jada hesitated, shifting the phone to her other ear. "Yes."

"Oh, my god, Jada! Why?"

"It was an accident," Jada blurted out.

"What does that mean?" Sam spat back.

Jada started pacing again and relayed the story to Sam. When she was finished, she swallowed down a hard lump in her throat. "Sam, I—I lost it. Edana came over me. I couldn't stop her—myself." Jada let her chin fall to her chest and anxiously waited for Sam's response. She really needed her to understand.

"I don't believe you."

Jada's body went stiff as adrenaline lit up her nerves. "What? How can you say that?"

"There is no way you would reject him. I was thinking the same thing he said at lunch, that you were just putting on a show. I mean no one has . . . *ever* asked you out, so why would you say no to him? Admit it. You're the one who came on to him, but he turned you down, didn't he, because he was annoyed at your pathetic display at lunch."

Jada's cheeks burned. A cracking sound filled her ear as

her hand clamped down on her phone. "I can't believe you, Sam."

"I can't believe *you*! You're the one who attacked someone just because you couldn't get what you wan—"

Jada hung up the phone and shoved it in her pocket. As she walked out the door, she dug her nails in her palm then took off running.

A vein jutted out of Seth's forehead like an angry serpent. He leaned forward, resting his elbows on his knees as scenes of the local news anchor interviewing a homeless man flashed across his dark eyes.

A girl attacked Jason. She did this. I should've gone with my instincts.

The front door opened and a heap of dead leaves flew in. Seth jumped up and stomped down the hall, bumping shoulders with Nathan as he passed him.

"What's your problem?" Nathan yelled. But Seth didn't stop.

Seth's tires screeched as he sped down the windy road. He needed to find out for sure because Holdan wouldn't make a move unless he had proof. Seth already knew in his gut it was true, but he would get the evidence.

Twenty minutes later, he pulled up to the curb a block away from the sheriff's station. The news lady said that Eddie and Derek were being interviewed here and should be released any minute. They were still claiming amnesia. They must be afraid of Jada. Well, *he* would give them something to be afraid of. He'd do whatever it took to cure them of their so-called *amnesia* and find out the truth.

A group of people poured from the sheriff's office and spread out like cockroaches. He spotted Derek and Eddie heading up the sidewalk. They were alone. He pulled his car out onto the street and slowly made his way toward them. He didn't want to draw any unnecessary attention to himself. When he reached them, he rolled down the passenger window.

"Hey, guys, need a ride?" He lifted the best friendly smile he could muster.

"Oh . . . hey, Seth, what are you doing here?" Derek set his forearms on the top of the door and leaned into the car. Eddie squatted down so that he was eye level with Seth.

"Just thought we could talk." Hot coals of rage seared his chest.

Seth could almost smell the fear oozing off Derek and Eddie. Jada must have done a number on them, maybe even threatened to kill them if they said anything.

Derek let out a nervous laugh. "Man, we're pretty talked out. Can we do this some other time?"

"Get in." Seth growled. Derek looked at Eddie and then back at the sheriff's station. "What are you going to do, call the cops on me if I don't?"

Seth drummed his fingers on the steering wheel and glared at Derek, daring him to say no again.

Without saying another word, Derek jerked the door open, let Eddie in the backseat, and then shuffled into the front.

"Careful with that door, man. This is a new car," Seth said before steering away from the curb. A few blocks away he parked the shiny Audi in an abandoned gas station, then turned the car off, covering them in darkness, and got out. When he reached the front of the car, he stopped, shoved his hands in his pockets, and scowled through the windshield. Derek shoved the door open and cursed as he stepped out. Eddie followed with his head down.

"All right Seth, we're here. Now what is it?"

"I want to know what happened to Jason." The moon slid out from behind the dilapidated building, slanting long jagged shadows over them.

Seth eyed Derek's hand shaking next to his leg. Derek quickly tucked it under his other arm. To Seth's surprise, Eddie stepped forward.

"We've already told the police everything we know. We don't remember anything." Eddie's Spanish accent was thicker than usual, which always happened when he was nervous.

"We blacked out or something."

Seth's eyes narrowed as he searched their faces. He pulled his hand out of his pocket and started cracking his knuckles one finger at a time.

"Bullshit."

"I swear Seth, we don't rememb—"

Seth clutched his hand around Eddie's neck and lifted him in the air.

"What are you doing?" Derek yelled.

Seth squeezed tighter. "I know you know something, and I'm not leaving until you tell me."

Derek took a step back and stole a glance at the sidewalk.

"Don't even think about it," Seth hissed.

Eddie's legs kicked furiously but were no match against Seth's solid body.

Derek lifted his hands "Okay, okay . . . I'll tell you. Just stop. Please."

Seth released him, and Eddie smacked the pavement, loose gravel crunching under him. He grunted and gasped for air.

Seth lifted his eyebrows "I'm waiting."

Derek helped Eddie up. "We were at the store buying some food, and uh, when we came out, Jason saw her. He just went up to her and started asking her out. She wasn't interested, so she—"

"She hit him in the head!" Seth's voice rumbled through the empty lot. "Tell me who it was."

Derek looked at Eddie then at the ground. "It was Jada Bell."

Tremors rose from Seth's clenched fists up his arms and down the rest of his body. He cracked his neck and strode to his car.

"Wait, there's more," Derek called after him.

"That's all I need to know," Seth bellowed before he started his engine and sped off.

The door to Nathan's room flew open and crashed into the back wall. "What the hell!" Nathan tore off his head phones and sat up in his desk chair.

"She did it." Seth could barely get the words out.

"Who did what?"

"She attacked him. Jada attacked Jason."

Nathan's eyes narrowed. "How do you know?"

"I just spoke with Derek and Eddie. They confirmed it."

Nathan stood and walked to the window. He set his hands on the sides of the window frame and stared out at the dark tree line in his backyard. The muscles in his back grew tight. He'd hoped when his brother stormed out earlier he was just in one of his usual bad moods. He'd hoped it had nothing to do with Jada.

"I don't believe it," Nathan said.

"Believe it. I just spoke with them twenty minutes ago. They looked terrified, which was probably why they were playing dumb with the cops. They're afraid she'll come after them." Seth stomped across the room, grabbed Nathan's shoulder and flipped him around. "I told you she was bad. She tried to kill him, Nathan."

Holdan appeared in the doorway, his arms crossed over his chest. "What's going on?"

"Jada was the one who attacked Jason States. It took a little persuasion, but Derek and Eddie admitted it to me." Seth turned to leave. "I'm going to get her."

Holdan stepped in front of him. "No. We aren't going to do anything rash. Your mind is clouded with anger. You need to be sharp to take her."

"But her powers are useless against me," Seth yelled.

Holdan put his hand on Seth's shoulder. "You're still mortal, Seth. She could kill you if you aren't careful."

Seth punched the wall. "I don't understand why we can't just burn her house down or walk up to her and set her on fire. We're just wasting time!"

Nathan started pacing the room, confusion and rage warring in his mind.

Holdan shook his head and clamped onto Seth's neck. "Stop being a fool! We can't just kill her in plain sight. Do you want to rot in prison the rest of your life? And in case your puny pea brain forgot,"—he squeezed Seth's neck a little tighter—"Edana almost got away from your great-great-grandfather. She was tearing out of her ropes when he lit her on fire. She was inches from escaping. We will not take that chance. We have to subdue her *quietly* and take her out of town."

Holdan released Seth. He stumbled back and rubbed the red fingerprints on his neck.

"Even *more* important," Holdan growled. "We aren't just fighting one Nephilim. There are four. We need to plan this out perfectly. *No* mistakes."

Seth huffed and pushed past Holdan. Moments later, grunts and crashing sounds echoed down the hall.

Holdan leaned against the door frame and took a cigar out of his shirt pocket. "I need you to lead your brother. He's impulsive and volatile. He's going to get himself killed."

Nathan looked his father the eye, his teeth grinding, and nodded before walking down the hall. He stopped at the living room, which looked like a tornado had run through it. Seth faced him, snorting like a bull about to charge.

Towering over him, Nathan glared into his brother's feral hazel eyes. "Get a grip on yourself. You're out of control."

Nathan turned and headed for the front door. "I'm going

out."

I can't believe Sam is doing this to me. She's supposed to be my best friend. How could she say that I attacked Jason on purpose? Jada ran as hard as she could, trying to escape her racing thoughts. It worked. Her mind focused on the searing in her lungs that was creeping up her throat. When she reached a secluded area of trees on the far end of town, her body crumpled onto the hard ground. Heaving, she dragged herself to a rock and sank her back into it. Sam would turn her in. She knew that now. And Jason. Jason would die. What was she going to do now? She was running out of time and out of options. She had to try to do something to help Jason, and quick. Suddenly, something shifted in the air. She sat up and looked around. Nothing. Something felt different, but she couldn't put her finger on it. She shrugged off the uncomfortable feeling and looked down at her thigh. Then her mind went clear.

Of course. Why didn't I think of this before?

The bit of hope gave her new energy. She jumped up and took off back into town. The hospital came into view, and she slowed to a fast walk. She passed a man in a wheelchair with a metal circle screwed into his forehead. She gave him a sympathetic smile and prepared herself for what Jason would look like. After she walked through the automatic doors into the lobby, she made her way to the public phone. A friend of hers from Junior High had been in the hospital once for a fractured tibia, so she knew all she had to do to find out Jason's room number was to dial zero. The operator gave her the information without any questions, and she let out a satisfied breath.

In the elevator, she was feeling confident. No one had recognized her, and she had managed to skirt around the security cameras. She should be able to get in and out undetected. A loud ding announced she'd reached her floor. Jada strolled out and turned the corner to find a blockade of thick double doors. The Rehab Trauma Center, where Jason's room was, required badge access. She waited until a nurse opened the door and sneaked in behind her. She walked in slowly. Six feet away, Jason's parents were standing at an admissions counter talking to a doctor. Her breath caught in her throat, and she slid down a corridor. Jada closed her eyes and focused in on the conversation.

"I'm so sorry, Mr. and Mrs. States, but Jason hasn't shown any improvement. He does have some brain activity, but it's not enough. He likely won't wake up from the coma. It might be time to consider . . ."

Mrs. States' sobs cut off the doctor's last words. Jada peeked around the corner just as Jason's dad walked his wife in the other direction. Their postures were slumped as they wobbled down the hall. Jada tried to shake the guilt tugging at her heart as she made her way through the ward looking for Jason's room. She had to stay strong.

When she found it, she hugged the door and focused on the sounds inside. All she could hear was the gurgling of a respirator and soft voices coming from the TV. She hoped no one else was in there. In front of her, a yellow gown draped over a cart. She stood up straight and tried to look calm despite the drumming of her heartbeat against her rib cage. If she looked like she knew what she was doing, she would draw less attention. Grabbing the gown, she shrugged into it and then rummaged through the contents of the drawers. After finding what she was looking for, she waited until the nurses had turned their attention away, and with one swoop, opened the door and ducked inside. Jason was alone. Relief swept over her.

When she walked to his bed, an unexpected flurry of emotions tore through her. His face was one large bruise, and his head was misshapen under a heap of bloodied bandages. The ventilator, taped around a hole in his throat, artificially filled and deflated his lungs with a jerky motion. He looked worse than he had in the alley right after it happened. She felt her body clamping up at the memory. *Focus, Jada.*

Holding her shoulders taut, she circled the foot of his bed and lifted the blanket off his arm. She grimaced and lowered the scalpel she had snatched from the cart outside. When it touched Jason's forearm, she stifled a shriek and jerked it back up. She suddenly felt lightheaded and took in a few deep breaths. *You can do this, Jada. You have to.*

Setting the scalpel on his arm again, she bit her bottom lip and dug the sharp metal into him. His skin tore like a piece of chicken, and she gagged. Dark red blood poured out as she clumsily grabbed some gauze and dabbed his wound.

Okay, almost done.

She clenched her fist and looked away, then lifted her arm and sliced into her own flesh. She held back a scream and turned back to her trembling arm. Blood drained out and soaked into Jason's wound. Her skin healed in an instant, so she cut herself again. After the third cut had healed, she stood and watched Jason's arm.

Heal. Please heal.

She waited, counting each of Jason's forced breaths. His face remained slack and lifeless. She looked at the clock. Only minutes had passed. The door squeaked, and a cart entered the room, followed by a petite nurse with a short crop of red hair. Jada scrambled to cover Jason's bloody arm with his blanket just as the nurse parked her cart on the other side of his bed.

"Oh, hi there. Are you a friend of Jason's?"

Jada forced a smile. "Yes. I was just coming to see how he's doing."

The nurse's wrinkled lips formed a compassionate frown, and she reached her gloved hand over and set it on Jada's. "I'm sorry, miss, but he isn't doing well. I'm afraid he may not make it."

"No. He has to make it!" Jada shouted.

The nurse jumped back. "Miss, we are doing everything we can."

Suddenly, the machine above Jason started beeping furiously, then one long beep filled the room. Dread pooled in Jada's stomach.

The nurse pressed an intercom button on the wall and yelled into the speaker. "He's flatlining. I need help in here." She pushed her cart out of the way and threw Jason's blanket off of him. "Hey, what's this?" She turned Jason's bloodied arm toward her.

Jada ran past her, nearly knocking her over. Once she

reached the front doors, she dumped her gown in the trash and ran as hard as she could. At the parking garage, she stopped and ducked behind the entryway. She took off her sweatshirt and turned it inside out. It was another color on the inside and would throw off the hospital security if they came looking for her.

In the dingy garage, her emotions spiraled out of control. *Not going to make it.*

The words repeated in her head. If Jason died, she wouldn't be able to go on. In the distance, she heard two security officers relaying her appearance on their radios. One was coming her way. She snuck farther inside the parking garage and collapsed in the darkest corner she could find. It was black, except for a slender stream of light piercing through a jagged hole in the wall.

Her chest got tighter and tighter as her body sank into the cold grimy cement. She'd done it. She'd done what Edana wanted. She'd killed someone. And as if that weren't enough, she'd lost her best friend and the only guy who had ever liked her. Any will she had left to go on drained out of her body. Resting her face against the damp wall, she thought about what Nathan and Seth would do to her. Beat and burn her to death. She hugged herself and watched people come and go. Some were sad coming to see their loved ones in the hospital, and some were happy as they left in one piece. A family of rats wiggled their noses at her and then continued on uninterested. Shadows slowly inched toward her as the sun curved around the gray sky. She felt herself getting sleepy and tucked deeper into the shadowed crevice.

Footsteps headed her way jolted her awake. She turned just as Nathan emerged from behind a car. His face was hard.

"How did you find me?" The dejection in her voice was unmistakable.

"I followed you," he replied flatly. Followed her. That must have been him in the woods causing the uncomfortable feeling that came over her. But the sound of his voice warmed her stomach. She loved him, and nothing could change that. Even if she died today, at least she had loved. Jada could see his knuckles turning white as he squeezed his fingers into his palm.

"Is it true?"

She broke his stare and turned around. "Yes."

Her head and shoulders became heavy and slid down the wall. She couldn't fight anymore. Edana was winning. She should let Nathan kill her. She buried her face in her hands. Seeing the anger and rejection in his eyes would hurt more than any amount of physical pain ever could. Time passed in slow motion. She could almost hear a clock ticking in her head, taunting her with the few seconds she had left to live.

"What are you waiting for?" Fear crept up her body. The longer he stood there, the more strength she lost.

"Why are you doing this?"

Through the slits between her fingers, Jada saw Nathan unwind his fists and take a step back. Jada wiped the tears off her cheeks and pulled herself back up against the wall. A cold gooey liquid seeped into her jeans, sending a chill down her legs.

"What happened with Jason?" The anger in his voice pierced her heart like an arrow. Was it even worth telling him? Would he believe her? Sam hadn't.

She was tired of talking about it, but she had to try with Nathan. She owed him that much. "He saw me, and he pushed me in the alley. He was mad that I wouldn't go out with him. After that he started to . . . grab me."

When Nathan gave no response, a pain she had never known was possible cut through her. He might as well have thrown her heart in a blender. Did he care at all that another guy had tried to touch her?

"Why didn't you just push him off of you? You're strong enough."

"I tried, but he kept coming back. And Edana, she's always there, filling my head with violent visions and thoughts. I snapped. I'm sorry, I'm so sorry. It was an accident."

His eyes were hot on her.

Sobs racked her limp body. "So now you know everything. I'm a Nephilim and a killer, just like Edana."

A gust of wind twirled a heap of garbage into a small cyclone. The sound masked any movement Nathan could make. For all she knew, he could be right in front of her ready to strike. She scooted to the side and under half-open lids, gazed out the hole in the wall at the indigo sky.

CHAPTER 26

What felt like moments later, voices penetrated the black void in her mind. A short stocky man unlocked the car next to her and helped an elderly lady inside. Darkness covered the sky, and the icy night air had frozen her bones. She must have been out for a while. She stood and whirled around. Nathan was gone. He hadn't killed her. But why?

A small glimmer of hope gave her legs the strength to stand. Seeing Nathan had made her want to live, even though she didn't deserve it. She wouldn't give up on Jason. No, the blood hadn't worked, but she could try again, or try something else.

Her phone vibrated, and Samantha's picture lit up the screen. Anger thickened in her chest. Sam had no right to talk to her the way she had earlier. She didn't know what Jada was going through.

"Sam . . . Hi."

"Hi. Just called to remind you our history group meets tonight at my house. You still coming?"

"Yes, but we also need to talk. Alone."

"Sure, we can talk before. Come a little early."

Sam's voice was friendly and held no animosity. Had she had a change of heart? Jada couldn't tell. But it didn't

271

matter; she needed to talk to Sam face-to-face, to tell her side of the story about what happened with Jason.

Hope laced with anxiety swirled in her stomach. "Okay, I'll be there."

The speedometer needle on Nathan's dashboard vibrated as it climbed past eighty. As he passed car after car on the winding two-lane road, his tires screeched in the dark night.

It was an accident. Jada's words repeated in his head. But was it? No. She was lying! She was manipulating him. But the thought of Jason's slimy hands on her made his muscles flare. If what she said was true, and Jason ever came out of his coma, Nathan would teach him a lesson. Was it true? Nathan slammed his fist on the steering wheel. He didn't know what to believe. He wanted desperately to believe her, but he wouldn't be played a fool.

In front of his house, he flipped off the headlights and thumped his head back against the headrest. Through the dusty glass on his side window, he studied his house. Dim orange light streamed out of the windows, highlighting pots of dead flowers. His mom had loved those flowers. If only she were still here, she would know what to do. Holdan appeared in the living room window and walked into the kitchen. Maybe his dad was right. Maybe Jada was a good liar. Maybe she was acting the victim to trick him because she knew how he felt about her. He shook his head at the idea as a fresh surge of anger heated his chest. After closing the door to his truck, he tromped up the dirt path and went inside. His feet dragged mud through the hall.

In the kitchen, Holdan and Seth sat stiffly at the table, the room unmistakably thick with tension. His dad's Remington rifle lay between them. "We've been waiting for you, Son. We have an opportunity, and we are going to take it."

Nathan set his jaw. "What's the opportunity?"

Holdan's face was hard and still. "We'll tell you on the way. Go get ready. We leave in ten minutes."

Nathan looked at his brother, then his dad. Both of them kept their eyes on him like he was prey.

The seconds passed like a ticking bomb, the tension in the room multiplying.

He stared out the kitchen window. The night seeped in through the corners like black mold. His home, where he had spent his entire life, suddenly felt different. Alien. The soft outline of Jada's face appeared in the dark glass, her crystal blue eyes locking with his. A warmth filled his stomach as he replayed the moments they had spent together. Then, the visions of her helping Emily and then saving Lori in the theater flashed in his mind. He looked at his dad and brother again and knew what he had to do. He felt his pulse throbbing in his neck.

"No."

Holdan stood and grabbed the rifle. "No, what?"

"I won't let you hurt Jada."

Seth stood and slammed his fist on the table. "I knew it! I knew you would betray us and take sides with that *Nephilim*."

"Son, you will not disobey me." A deep red crawled up Holdan's neck.

Arms flexed at his sides, Nathan took a step toward his father. "Not this time, Dad. You're wrong about this. You're wrong about her."

Holdan gripped the rifle tighter and cocked it.

Nathan took another step. "Really? You're going to shoot me?"

Holdan leveled the muzzle of the gun inches from Nathan's chest. "If I have to."

"You know bullets can't stop me," Nathan retorted.

"Titanium bullet's will."

Nathan ground his teeth as anger and disbelief battered his head. Purchasing titanium bullets was never part of the plan. Holdan must have done it secretly, knowing he might need to use them on him.

After Edana had almost gotten away, his ancestors knew they had to find something stronger than rope so that a Nephilim couldn't break through it. When titanium was manufactured in 1932, it was the perfect solution. Lightweight and nearly indestructible, it was also fireproof. As a boy, he'd been told stories of his family using titanium wire to subdue and kill Nephilims. At the time the stories felt harmless and far away. Now the reality hit him like a cannonball to his gut. Titanium was impervious to the strength of his ancestors as well, but never did he think his own father and brother would use it on him.

"Seth," Holdan jerked his head toward the hall. "Go get the wire."

Silence filled the room as Nathan glared at his father. Holdan shook his head, his face strained with emotion. "I needed you on this."

Seth returned moments later, wire in hand, and unwrapped a long piece. Hate poured from his eyes, and Nathan wondered how his little brother had become so bitter. When he was younger, he was silly and fun, always playing pranks on Nathan. Now his face bore the hard lines of someone twice his age. And without any remorse or second thoughts, he was going to kill someone. Kill Jada. But Nathan couldn't let that happen. He loved her no matter what.

Holdan glanced at Seth for a split second, which was all Nathan needed. He threw his fist up, knocking the rifle out of Holdan's hands, and rammed his shoulder into his chest. Holdan flew across the room and crashed onto the table. It cracked in two. Before Seth could react, Nathan shoved his forearms into his neck, pinning him against the wall.

"Let go of the titanium."

"Never," Seth spat.

Seth's eyes flickered to the right, but by the time Nathan turned, it was too late. The butt of the rifle closed in on him, smashing into his temple.

By the time Jada went home, changed and headed to Sam's house, she was running late. The other people in her group would be arriving already. Hopefully, Sam had enough sense not to out her in front of them. She would be exposing herself too.

Knocking on Sam's door, she looked around the familiar patio. She had spent countless hours here with Samantha and hoped to spend many more. She had to get Sam to change her mind and believe her about Jason.

The door swung open to Sam's smiling face. "Come in."

Jada hesitated. Something didn't feel right. Sam looked a little too happy to see her. Jada peeked inside, but nothing looked out of place. When she stepped over the threshold, her heart started to race.

Sam closed the door behind her, then locked the bolt and chain. She crossed her arms over her chest.

A nervous jolt shocked Jada's body. "Where is everybody?"

"Oh, I canceled the study group."

Jada narrowed her eyes and gulped down the fear that was scratching at her throat.

Why was she afraid? Sam couldn't hurt her even if she wanted to; she hadn't changed yet. Despite her uneasiness, she decided to get on with it.

"Sam, I just don't understand how you can think I hurt Jason on purpose," Jada whispered, looking around to make sure no one was there. "Do you even care that he tried to rape me?"

Sam rolled her eyes. "Give me a break, Jada. We both know he didn't do that. He could have any girl in school. Why would he need to force himself on someone, especially you?"

Another puncture to her chest consuming what little was left of her feelings. How much more could she take? "How can you say that? I thought we were friends."

"I was your friend until you starting attacking people."

Jada took a step toward Sam, a flood of anger washing away her pain. "I told you it was an accident."

"I doubt that," a familiar voice announced from behind her, sending a tremor down her back.

Seth.

She followed him with her eyes as he strode around her and stopped next to Samantha.

Jada glared at her. "*You* let him in."

"Well, he's the only one who can stop you, Jada. I had to do something." A malicious smile spread on her face.

For a few seconds, Jada stared into her best friend's eyes. A hate resided there she'd never seen before. What could she have done to deserve this?

"He won't stop with me, Sam. He'll come after you when you change. Did you think of that?"

Sam flipped her hand at Seth. "He won't. He only needs to kill you because you're the most powerful and you're dangerous."

There is was again, that flicker of jealousy in Sam's eyes. Even when Sam changed, Jada would still be more powerful, and Sam couldn't stand it.

All over her body, her muscles flexed as she took in Sam's betrayal and thought about their lives together. Part of her wanted to cry and reason with Sam. The other part wanted to scream at her, tell her she was a liar and a bitch. But she did neither. She forced her mind to forget about Sam for now and focus on Seth. He was here to capture her, and she would not give up without a fight.

"All right, enough talk." Seth lunged at her.

She sidestepped, barely avoiding him by an inch. She turned to the door, and fumbled with the lock. It clanked and turned right before Seth's fist slammed into it, welding the metal and wood into an impenetrable mess. Jada turned to run to the back door, and Seth pitched his massive body at her again.

She picked up a side table and threw it at him. It shattered into pieces, leaving slivers sticking out of his chest. Darting down the hall, she heard him grunt as he followed.

When she reached the kitchen, she grabbed the knives from the knife block and threw them at Seth. He dodged all of them, except for one, which sliced across his upper arm. A red circle grew on his white shirt.

"So you *are* human? I was starting to wonder." Jada sneered.

Seth's jaw muscles twitched and a deep growl rumbled in his throat. Then, in one swift move, he leaped over the kitchen island and was at her feet. She threw open the back door, and they tumbled onto the deck, smacking Jada's face on the hard wood.

"Let me go!" she wailed.

Seth wrapped his arms around her chest. "Not a chance. You're going to see Edana real soon."

She squirmed and jerked, but she couldn't break his hold. As Seth gripped tighter, squeezing the air out of her lungs, her head started to spin. Desperate for a miracle, she kicked at anything she could find. Finally, her foot caught on the leg of Sam's huge barbeque, and she hurled them off of the deck. They hit the ground with a loud thump, Jada crashing on top of Seth.

To her surprise, Seth's grip loosened, and his arms fell to the ground. Jumping up, she heaved a huge rock above her head and stood over him. The fall had knocked him out cold. A heap of broken bricks circled his head. Suddenly, her arms froze and the rock started sliding down her hands.

Kill him. Edana's voice wafted over her mind.

Kill him before he kills you.

She stared down at the guy who had made her life a living hell.

"No!" she yelled and forced her arms to throw the rock to the side. She'd never hurt another person again, no matter what that person did to her. After checking his pulse to make sure he was alive, she walked around the deck and headed to the backyard gate. Feeling someone watching her, she looked back at the house.

Behind the sliding glass door, Sam's dark eyes glared at her. Jada shook her head and looked away. Never in her wildest dreams would she have predicted that Sam would betray her like this. All these years she'd thought they were friends, best friends, but she'd been wrong.

As she walked to her car, worry for her mom put her thoughts about Sam to the side. Seth would never give up. Their lives would never return to normal. As much as she had tried to avoid it, they'd have to leave Bishop for good.

And she'd never see Nathan again. The thought made her heart shrink. Even if he didn't believe her, she still loved him.

Where was Nathan? Why wasn't he here helping his brother? But before she could even begin to figure it out, a sharp pain sliced through the back of her head and everything went black.

CHAPTER 27

Jada's eyes opened to patches of twilit sky peeking through froths of yellow aspens. The fresh smell of rain-soaked trees wisped in her nose, cooling her lungs. Without looking down, she could tell her feet were bare. Her toes were stiff with cold, and coarse dirt scraped at her heels. A thick rope dug into her shoulder, scratching her cheek. She was moving; being dragged. As her surroundings slowly came into focus, she turned her head. Where was she? A faint tingle on the back of her head made her remember. Someone had knocked her out in front of Sam's house. But who? Seth was out cold in Sam's backyard and . . .

Oh no, please don't let it be Nathan.

She arched her head back but was blinded by two glowing white circles. All she could see was two sets of broad shoulders, one with a rifle and a small bag slung over his back. She tried to plant her feet in the ground, but they were tied together. Her heel caught on a sharp rock, and she yelped. She stopped moving.

The two dark figures loomed above her, swaying a lantern inches from her face. "Awake so soon?"

Seth. But how?

"She heals fast." A deeper, hoarse voice floated over

her.

She squinted through the light. A thick gray goatee circled tight, angry lips. Eyes darker and more sinister than Seth's stared down at her. A spark of familiarity pricked her mind. Where had she seen him before? She searched her memory, running through the last month. At first the details of the scene were blurry, then sharp lines formed around them. In a parking lot, he was shaking hands with . . . Father Steve.

No! Not Father Steve. All this time, he was . . . he knew . . .

"I don't believe you've met my father." Seth smiled sardonically.

Jada let out a whimper. How could Father Steve do this to her? She had so few people she could trust. She'd let down her guard with him, when all along he'd been lying to her. Her body went limp and her eyes burned. She looked away, not wanting Seth to see her defeat.

Seth looked at his dad. "Looks like she's giving up."

Holdan bent down and grabbed her face. His fingers felt like sandpaper and smelled of stale smoke. He lifted her eyelids. "She's probably faking. We'll keep an eye on her." He stood, and they started dragging her again.

"Now don't get any ideas that your mom or any of the others will be coming to save you. They've been taken care of," Holdan said.

Seth chuckled and peered down at her over his shoulder. "Even Samantha. You should've seen the look on her face when we tied her up with the rest."

Anger zapped Jada's heart like a defibrillator. She

screamed and threw her arms and legs in the air. Sharp pain shot up her body, and her limbs wouldn't budge. She lifted her head and looked down at herself. A thin silvery wire coiled around her wrists and ankles, cutting red lines into her flesh.

"That's right, Jada, titanium. It's stronger even than you." Seth yanked on the wire, digging it deeper into Jada's wrists. She ground her teeth and tried to think through the pain.

"What are you going to do to my mom? I'm begging you, don't hurt her. She's never harmed anyone."

Her body stopped moving again, and suddenly she was lifted up and slammed into a tree. Her feet dangled above the ground. Strips of bark dug into her back. She winced and gasped in air.

Seth clenched his hand around Jada's throat. "Is that what you think?" He hissed, his hot breath on her cheek. "You think little mommy is so innocent? She—"

"Seth, stop!" Holdan yelled.

Seth's face turned almost purple and trembled with rage. He released Jada's neck and punched the tree. The *crack* boomed through the forest as loud as a shotgun. A flock of birds burst from the trees and squawked as they flew up into the sky. Jada tumbled onto massive, twisted roots stretching out from the tree like octopus arms.

Holdan set down the lantern, leaped over her and grabbed Seth by the shirt. "Calm down. You're losing control."

The tendons in Seth's neck spindled under his skin, and he ducked and rammed his shoulders into Holdan's gut, lifting him off the ground.

Jada squirmed away, biting down on her tongue to suppress a scream each time the wire twisted into her skin. Grunts and the sounds of ripping clothing flew over her head. Spotting a bush, she wiggled her way behind it and blew out slow, quiet breaths. She bit down on the wire around her hands and tried to work out the knots. The tangle loosened then tightened again, and she felt the sting of panic in her chest. She banged her wrists on a rock in frustration.

Then the rustling stopped, and she froze.

"Where'd she go?" Seth's voice echoed in the stillness.

"She couldn't have gone far. Go look over there."

Jada squeezed her eyes close and curled herself in a ball. Footsteps ran in the opposite direction. She was just about to peek behind her when a hand grabbed her arm and yanked her out of the bush. "There you are," Holdan snarled down at her.

Jada screamed as he pulled her to her feet.

Seth stomped toward them, his shirt torn and hanging off his chest. When he reached her, he whipped his hand back and slapped her across the face. Her head snapped to the side and dark circles bloomed in her vision. She blinked and sucked in air, trying to stay conscious.

Holdan released her, and she was on the ground again, not even feeling the fall. Burying her face in her dirty hands, she closed her eyes. Her body trembled as warm tears dripped onto her frozen fingers. Seconds felt like hours as she waited for what came next.

Then, suddenly, her eyes shot open, and her body felt as

light as a feather. Her mind cleared as the familiar ball of fire ignited in her stomach.

"Edana's coming over her," Holdan said. "This is too risky."

That was all she heard before she blacked out again.

Nathan awoke with his hands tied behind his back and cursed under his breath. He strained his hands against the wire, his muscles carving deep ridges in his neck and arms. When his wrists bounced back together, he yelled from the pit of his stomach. His head thudded on the wall behind him. He knew no one would hear him except his dad or brother, who'd tied him up in the first place. It didn't matter anyway. They were already gone, and the next house was miles away. By now they had Jada.

When Seth told him about Jason, he was furious. He felt like a fool for believing she was good. But he'd been wrong. He should have trusted his gut. He already knew what kind of person she was, that she could never hurt anyone on purpose. And looking into her eyes at the hospital had confirmed it. It was an accident, Jason had tried to—he couldn't even think the word. *Jason got what was coming to him. He is going to have to face me if he comes out of his coma.*

He shouted again and thrashed his body around, but knew it was no use. The titanium could hold him forever. His eyes stung. He loved her and now she would never know. If she wasn't dead already, she would be soon. Seth and Holdan would show no mercy.

No! He had to find a way to escape, even if it meant cutting his own arms to get out of the titanium. Looking around for a tool, anything he could use, he thought he heard something and paused. Was that? Yes it was. A door had closed at the other end of the house.

"I'm in here!" His voice bounced off the walls back at him. Holdan and Seth couldn't be back so soon could they? It had to be someone else. *Had* to be.

Jada awoke upright, tied to a tree. As she tried to free herself from the titanium wire, she could feel the cuts on her wrists close up and reopen. Her jeans were soaked with blood and sticking to her legs. She looked around. The lantern was snuffed and lying on its side next to the bag Holdan had been carrying. Mist crept toward her through the trees, and dead branches reached to the sky like they were clawing their way out of hell.

Footsteps sounded toward her, then Holdan and Seth marched out from the trees with bundles of branches wedged under their arms. They stopped in front of her, Holdan dumping his pile on the ground.

I told you this would happen, Jada. You should have killed them when you had the chance.

Edana's rage soared through her body like hot oil. Jada took a deep breath of the dank air and tried to focus. She couldn't let Edana take over.

"Where's Nathan?"

A muscle ticked in Seth's cheek. "Well, it turns out my big brother fell for your lies. He tried to stop us from killing you, so we were forced to subdue him."

A faint smile rose on Jada's face.

He believed me.

Amid the darkness and cold of this menacing place, her insides felt warm. He still loved her. He believed her.

Seth knelt down and methodically placed the branches at her feet. When he stood, his face was hard, as it had been the first day she'd seen him. It seemed so long ago, that day he and Nathan had walked into her history class. But it had been only a few weeks. She pictured herself and Sam giggling and following Nathan and Seth in the hall.

Her life had been so simple. Her biggest problem was being embarrassed after running into Nathan. In these few intense weeks, her life had completely changed. She had changed.

Even though she might die, she wouldn't go back. She wouldn't go back to the person she had been. That girl had been in denial of her own emotions and a prisoner of fear. Yes, since she changed, she'd made some bad choices and some huge mistakes, but she had stood up for herself. And most of all, she had allowed herself to love. Since junior high, she'd thought all boys were like Luke. They were only out to hurt and use her. But Nathan had shown her that she was wrong, and she wouldn't trade the moments she'd had with him for anything.

Her mind focused back to the present. They had 'subdued' Nathan. He might be hurt. "What have you done with him?"

"Nothing yet." Seth sneered.

Yet. Fury boiled in Jada's blood and jerked her body

against the wire. "You're a monster! You would hurt your own brother?" She gritted her teeth. "How do you sleep at night?"

For a split second, Seth's eyes glistened with sadness. A sadness that Jada could tell ran deep. But rage quickly disfigured his features again.

"Oh, I sleep. And I'll be sleeping even better once you are out of the picture." He waved his hand in a half-circle. "Recognize where we are?"

Jada looked around. In her nightmare when she'd seen a bloodied Edana tied to the tree. This was the same place.

Seth leaned in inches from her face, his nostrils flaring. "This is exactly where your great-great grandmother died. We thought you might appreciate that."

Seth nodded to his dad, and Holdan knelt down and wadded a handlful of sticks together. Pulling his bag to his side, he dug out a roll of twine and a small bottle of lighter fluid. He ripped off a piece of the twine with his teeth and tied the bundle of sticks together. Jada's stomach hollowed, and she turned her head over her shoulder, trying to see her hands.

Fists clenched, Seth stomped over to her. "Don't even think about it." His chest grazing hers, he pushed her foward and tightened the wire around her wrists. She winced, not from the pain, but from being so close to Seth. His scent wafted over her, and it smelled similar to Nathan. Her heart squeezed, and she tried to remember that this was Nathan's brother. There had to be something good in him.

Seth stepped back and Holdan handed him the makeshift torch. Ripping off the rest of his shirt, Seth crumpled it into a ball and doused it with the lighter fluid. The sharp smell burned the inside of Jada's nose. After stuffing his soaked T-shirt in the top of the torch, he shoved his hand in his pocket and pulled out a box of matches. He tossed the box aside and flicked the red tip of a match over the stubble on his jaw. It burst into an orange flame, then lit up his T-shirt like dead grass in a wildfire.

You can still kill them. . . .

"While you're dying," Seth sauntered back up to her, "picture your mom . . . Sam and Jen . . . all of their pretty little bodies turning into ash."

Nooo! A throbbing pressure exploded behind Jada's eyes, and her muscles rippled. Her head shot up, and she let out a blood-curdling scream. Hot, salty tears glided down her dirty face. The ground rumbled, and Seth and Holdan wobbled to keep their footing. Slowly lowering her head, she glared at them, her heavy breath turning to vapor.

Snapping her head to the left, she lifted up a rock, and it flew at Holdan. He flipped around and punched it, shattering it to pieces.

She flared her eyes, and the tree next to her cracked. Chunks of bark snapped off, slicing into the bushes, and with one final crack, the tree split. The massive trunk moaned as it plunged straight for Holdan and Seth. Holdan jumped out of the way, but Seth's foot slipped from under him, smacking his back onto the dirt. Anger and fear crept over his features as the tree closed in on him. His hands flew up to his face just as Holdan clamped onto his arm and yanked him out of the way. The trunk bounced off the ground, sending a quake under her feet.

Why are you toying with them? You can kill them!

Jada set her jaw. "I will not kill anyone, even them."

If she could just stop them, she wouldn't have to be like Edana. Even now, bound to a tree with unbreakable titanium wire, her pyre at her feet and the flame racing toward her, she clung to the one thing in her life she had control over. She would *not* be like Edana.

Suddenly, Seth leaped over the fallen tree, Holdan right behind him. Snarling, with the torch in hand, he bolted toward her. She took in a deep breath and lifted rocks, dirt and loose branches and swirled the heap in a tornado around them. Seth raised his hand to block his eyes as the debri pounded into him. His feet started to slide backward. He kept sliding, his shoes digging trenches in the dirt. His muscles softened and a look of defeat came over him. She was doing it. He was giving up! But then, he jutted out his jaw and sprinted through the twirling mass. With one final jump, he landed at her feet and smashed his fist into her temple.

Her head slumped to the side, and the tornado died as fast as it had started. In her blurred vision, Seth knelt and dipped the crackling torch to her feet.

CHAPTER 28

"How the hell!" Seth bellowed.

A gust of wind struck Jada in the face, jerking her eyes open. The torch flipped in the air like it was part of a circus act, not a malevolent tool being used to kill her. It landed inches from the wood pile at her feet. The flames hissed and flapped toward her. Holdan was on his hands and knees rubbing his head, and a sea of arms and legs tumbled in front of her. The mass rolled in the dirt and then Nathan vaulted up, holding Seth by the throat. He grunted and heaved Seth across the clearing. Seth slammed into a tree, his neck whiplashing backward. He stumbled out, leaving a gaping hole in the trunk, a dizzying pain covering his face. Nathan barged over to her, the slight tremble in his hands revealing what his hard face was trying to conceal. When he reached her, he started to tug at the wire. "I'm sorry I didn't believe you." His steely eyes were fierce but tender.

Jada's chest felt tight and warm. She smiled as tears wet her face again. She looked up, and Seth's hateful eyes flashed behind Nathan.

"Watch out!" she shrieked. Nathan turned, but it was too late. Seth's fist slammed an uppercut into his back. Nathan's knees sank into the ground. His face was still with pain. Seth stood over him, sweat dripping down his wide chest. "How can you take her side?"

Seth lifted his arm for another blow. With his elbow pointed at Nathan's neck, he plunged his arm down.

"Nathan," Jada screamed.

Faster than she'd seen anyone move, Nathan ducked, whirled around and blasted his fist into his brother's jaw. Seth spun around and slammed into Holdan, knocking them both on their backs.

Scorching heat crawled up Jada's legs. "The torch," she yelped.

Nathan jumped up and kicked it out of the way, but the branches at Jada's feet were already on fire. He tore at the wires, cutting deep slits in his own fingers. The flames cracked and spat as they consumed the brush, billowing clouds of smoke in Jada's face. Her eyes and nose burned and she turned her head away. When she couldn't hold her breath any longer, she drew in the suffocating black air, coughing it out instantly. The orange light below her glowed brighter as the flames started to sear the bottoms of her feet. Curling her toes up in agony, she tried to scream, but her throat was raw.

Suddenly, everything went quiet. She watched Nathan's ash-smeared face. A tinge of fear flickered in the deep lines of determination around his brows. His arms moved with ferocity, but Jada no longer felt her body. Blackness blurred the edges of her vision.

She tilted her head back and gazed at the soft outline of the moon in the inky sky.

"Jada!"

She heard her name, but she couldn't get to the voice. It was so far away. Hot, slick fingers grabbed her cheeks and pulled her face down. Nathan's eyes locked onto hers. *Stay with me*, she read on his lips. Below half-open lids, she watched him step back and clench his fists. The darkness felt good and easy. If she could just close her eyes, everything would be better.

Nathan planted his foot in the dirt and barreled toward her, shoulder first.

Boom! He crashed into the tree. The trunk snapped at the base in one clean line. Jada rolled her head toward Nathan. Every muscle in his body twisted as he pushed on the tree. His mouth was open, screaming, but the sound barely reached her ears. Then, her eyes rolled up; she was falling. Her body flew up into the wire, then slammed back into the tree as it plummeted into the ground. When cool, fresh air filled her lungs, her heart jolted into overdrive, pumping life back into her. Nathan appeared above her, and he grabbed her face. "I got the knots in the wires loose. Try to slip your hands out."

Her wrists moved freely in the wire. She tucked her thumbs in her palms and pulled her hands free.

Nathan helped her up, but when her feet hit the ground, she shrieked and stumbled into him. The smell of her burnt flesh nearly made her sick. Nathan swooped her up and dashed across the clearing. When they reached the lining to the woods, a gunshot exploded in the smoggy air. They stopped with a jerk.

"Step away, Son."

They turned to find Holdan pointing his rifle in the air,

white smoke spinning from the tip. Seth stood next to him, rubbing his chin. Nathan held his father's stare as he set Jada down and pushed her behind him.

"No."

Holdan's face contorted with anger and confusion. He shifted his stance. "Don't do this, Nathan."

"I love her, Dad."

Holdan's lips formed a thin line. He jerked the rifle off his shoulder down into his other hand and cocked it. "You're weak." He spat on the ground.

Jada lifted her chin to Nathan's ear. "The bullets can't hurt you, like in the clearing right?"

His shoulder stiffened under her palm, and he shook his head. "These ones can. They're made of the same material as the wire that tied you to the tree."

Defeat suffoated any trace of hope in Jada's mind. She looked at Nathan again. His face was wild but steady. Jada knew he would die for her if he had to. He would give up everything. The thought made her heart ache, but she couldn't live without him. Gripping Nathan's shirt, she leaned her forehead on his back. The skin on her feet was blackened and still smoking. The thought of the hot flames on her body again made her shudder, but she knew what she had to do. She took a deep breath and swallowed the fear seizing her nerves. Lifting her head, she squeezed his arm and stepped beside him.

"Nathan. I won't let you die for me." Her eyes became moist. "Let him take me."

He grabbed her by the shoulders and searched her eyes. "Never."

"I can't live without you, Nathan," she choked through the lump in her throat.

Nathan shook his head, his face twitching, as Jada slid her hands from his grasp.

"That's right. Let the Nephilim go, Nathan." Seth smirked.

Nathan snatched her hands back and pulled them to his chest. "No, I can't."

"Nathan," she whispered. "This is our only chance. If they kill you now, then it's over. I can beat them, somehow." She hoped he believed her words, hoped she did too. "Please."

She heard his teeth grinding and reached up and grazed her fingers down his face. She wished, just this once, her powers worked on him and she could force him to let her go.

She nodded.

Before he could respond, Jada tore herself from him and willed her legs forward. She had to do this. She wouldn't have another person's blood on her hands, least of all Nathan's.

Nathan jabbed his forefinger at his brother and dad. "I won't let you do this. I'll do whatever it takes to stop you."

Holdan sighed and kept his gun on Nathan. "That's right, sweetie, a few more steps. Don't even think about running. If you do, I'll shoot Nathan."

Holdan's words made her stomach churn. How could a father shoot his own son? What had she done to this family? Inches away from Seth's grasp, she could feel the satisfaction radiating off of him. He had won, and he was enjoying it.

She took in a deep breath for her last step, but then stopped just out of Seth's reach. The bushes rattled behind Holdan and pried open.

Jada's eyes widened, and she stepped back. Holdan began to swing the rifle around, but Father Steve jumped out and slammed a rock onto his head. Holdan fell the to the ground like a wet noodle. Before Seth could reach it, Father Steve snatched up the rifle and stepped back to Nathan and Jada. Breathing heavily, he kept the gun pointed at Holdan and Seth and made the sign of the cross over his chest.

"What are you doing, old man?" Holdan grunted. "Give me the gun now."

The priest shook his head. "I'm sorry, Holdan, but you're wrong about this."

Holdan shuffled to his feet, holding his hand to his head. "We talked about this. We *planned* this."

"No, *you* planned this, Holdan." Father Steve looked at Jada, the rigid lines around his eyes softening. "I could never hurt her."

Jada's heart missed a beat as she looked into his soft blue eyes.

"But she's a *Nephilim!*"

"She's not Edana, Holdan."

Seth's eyebrows pressed together. "What are you talking about? She attacked Jason States. And the last time I saw him, the doctors said he was a vegetable. They were talking to Jason's parents about pulling the plug."

Father Steve handed the gun to Nathan, his arms starting

to shake under the weight of it. "It was Edana who made her attack Jason. You all know that. And besides . . . guys?" He peeked over Seth's shoulder into the bushes.

Everyone followed Father Steve's line of sight. After a few seconds, Derek and Eddie stepped into the opening.

Father Steve motioned with the gun. "Now, boys, tell them what you told me."

Derek visibly swallowed and looked anxiously between Holdan and Seth. "Jason's come out of his coma. He's alive."

Alive. Jason's alive! But how? *Her blood.* Jada cupped her hands over her mouth and fell to her knees. It had worked. Her blood healed him. All the emotions pent up in the pit of her stomach came pouring out. Her body shuddered as all the pain and guilt racked her limbs.

Nathan bent down and helped her up, wrapping her in his arms. "Satisfied? Jason's alive."

"Bullshit," Seth jeered.

Eddie stepped beside Derek. "It's true. We just saw him. It's some kind of miracle, the doctor said."

The clearing grew silent.

"How do you know she won't let Edana hurt another person again? And for no reason? Jason was innocent." Holdan crossed his arms over his chest.

"That's not exactly true." Derek looked at Jada, guilt clouding his eyes.

"What is that supposed to mean?" Seth glared at him.

"Jason, he was," —he cleared his throat—"trying to rape her. She was just defending herself." Derek nodded as he spoke.

Seth stepped in front of Derek. "I don't believe that for a second."

"It's true!" Eddie shrieked. "He kept touching her, and she tried to tell him no, but he wouldn't stop."

Holdan studied Jada for what felt like an hour. She could see Nathan in his strong features. A sense of loss cooled her body. Holdan was probably like Nathan once, but hate for her had consumed his life. Holdan ran his hand through his hair. "Is this true?"

She paused, looking into his hard eyes. "Yes. But it's no excuse. I lost control. I made a mistake."

Nathan hugged her tighter.

Holdan looked down as if in thought, the hard lines in his face slowly dissolving. "Seth, let's go."

Without looking at them, he turned and made his way down the path. Seth stood for a moment, the muscles in his arms spasming. "This isn't over," he growled before tromping off after Holdan.

CHAPTER 29

"Oh, you must be Nathan. I wasn't expecting you." Lilah's hand clamped down on the doorknob. She stared at him a beat, then inched the door open and motioned him inside.

Nathan didn't move, hands secured behind his back. "Mrs. Bell, I'm sorry for showing up like this. I hope it's OK?"

They both looked up when Jada appeared from the hall and tucked her hand in the crook of her mom's arm. "It's all right, Mom. Remember what he did for me," she whispered.

Lilah's face visibly relaxed, and she nodded. "Come in."

Nathan smiled and Jada could tell he was trying to appear non-threatening. It didn't help when he stepped in and towered over them both.

"It's nice to finally meet you." He held out his hand.

Lilah shook it, a glint of hesitation lingering in her eyes. "Let's sit on the couch."

As they made their way to the living room, Jada saw Nathan wipe tiny beads of sweat from his brow. She looked down and smiled to herself. He was nervous.

Another knock sent Lilah back to the front door. "Are you expecting anyone else?" She yelled over her shoulder.

"Father Steve, what a pleasant surprise."

In the living room, Jada stood from the couch and shifted nervously. Last night when she saw Holdan and thought Father Steve was on his side, she was heartbroken. Over the past few weeks she had come to rely on Father Steve, letting him fill the void her father had left. She couldn't lose that again. She still wasn't ready to face why her dad had abandoned her, but at least she was thinking about it.

Walking into the living room, he offered her a tender smile. "I came to see how you were doing."

She met him at the entryway, and they both looked down. Father Steve cringed. "How are your feet?"

The bottoms of her feet had returned to their normal color but were scarred with a few jagged edges wrapping around her toes. Jada shook her head. "Fine. I mean they're healed. I don't think the scars will ever go away though."

Suddenly, he closed the gap between them and wrapped her in a hug. At first she tensed, but then her muscles relaxed under his grip. She felt the bite of tears behind her eyes.

When he released her, she grabbed his hand and guided him into the living room. Father Steve tipped his head to Nathan, who was sitting on the couch, and slowly lowered himself into the side chair. After skirting the coffee table, Jada plopped next to Nathan and tucked her feet under her legs.

While unraveling his scarf, Father Steve lowered his chin, his clear blue eyes gazing at Jada over the top of his glasses. "So, what's with the tears?"

Jada slid closer to Nathan. "I'm just still so happy you

came for me."

Father Steve leaned forward. "Jada, I would never let anyone hurt you."

She fiddled with a thread on her jeans. "But you know . . . what I am."

"Yes, your ancestry will always be a challenge for you. But you can choose who *you* are going to be."

She tried to let his words sink in. Edana was so strong. She hoped he was right and that she could control her own actions. "Can I ask you something?"

He thumped his hands on the armrests. "Shoot."

"How did you get involved with Nathan's dad?"

Father Steve let out a long breath, puckering his lips. "Holdan came to me a few years ago, asking about Edana and your family. He knew what his father had told him, but he wanted to know more. Because Edana was created by Azael, the fallen angel, he knew I would have more information about it. We spent many hours talking about nephilims—and you in particular, Jada."

Jada rubbed her forehead then lifted her hand. "But how do you know who Edana is? And . . . how did Holdan know that I was the one Edana chose?"

Nathan's arm tensed under her grasp, and she turned, lifting her eyebrows up. He cleared his throat and met her eyes. "Our grandfather had a vision of you on his deathbed. He prophesized that you would be the one."

She blinked and looked down. Even though Nathan had believed her, saved her, it still hurt to think about him learning how to kill her all those years. She rolled her shoulders to release the tension building there and looked over at Father Steve.

He was smiling and looked a million miles away. Then, like he had just awoken from a deep sleep, his glossy eyes came back to the present. "My grandfather's brother . . . knew Edana. In fact, he was in love with her." His words hung in the thick air.

Loved her.

Then Jada remembered the story Lilah and Stephanie had told her. Edana had one friend, Father David. He must have been the one who put up her tombstone.

Jada smiled wearily. For the first time, she thought of Edana as a person. A person with feelings, desires and hopes. A person whose life had been destroyed.

Father Steve tapped his fingers on his thigh. "As you know, priests aren't allowed to marry, so he was forced to bury his feelings. He tried to get over her, but he couldn't. Thoughts of her consumed him every day. When she was taken by the angel, he was devastated. He prayed for her every day."

Jada walked to the window and cracked it open. The cool smell of freshly wet asphalt danced on her face. "Did he say what she was like before she changed? Was she a good person?"

Father Steve met her at the window and pinched her chin, forcing her to make eye contact with him. "He said she was the kindest person he'd ever met."

After releasing her, he walked over to the fireplace mantel and stuffed his hands in his pockets. "She was a good person, Jada. She had just grown so bitter over the years, and when she was finally free—"

"The town turned on her. Her closest friends wouldn't even speak to her." Jada finished his sentence.

"Exactly." Father Steve let out a long breath.

"What happened to Father David after she died?" Lilah asked.

"He never recovered. He became a recluse, never leaving his house except for his duties at the church."

A silence settled in the room that was both sad yet at ease. Jada went back to the couch and wedged herself under Nathan's arm.

Father Steve wobbled back to his chair, wincing as he sat. "Well, back to the story. When Holdan caught you, he called me, asked me to come. I'd told him that I had done a few exorcisms. I guess he thought that I would help. In all our conversations, I never told him where I stood on you, Jada. He just assumed. Anyway, he told me too that Nathan was against the whole thing and was tied up at his house. So, knowing that I couldn't take Holdan and Seth alone, I went to find Nathan. When I found him, he told me about Derek and Eddie, so I went and got them so they could clear up what happened in the alley."

"I don't know what to say, Father Steve. Without you I would be—"

"Don't even think about that, Jada." Father Steve cut her off.

Lilah shook her head. "I still can't believe Samantha turned you over to Seth."

"I know. We've been friends since we were born. I—" Still in shock, she didn't know what else to say.

"It was kind of you not to say anything to Stephanie,"

Lilah said.

Jada shrugged. "Well, I guess I'm still hoping Sam will come to her senses and apologize. Then things can go back to the way they were."

"I don't think things could ever be the same between you two." Nathan squeezed her hand.

As much as she didn't want to admit it, she knew he was right. How could they ever go back to being friends when Sam had handed her over to Seth knowing he intended to kill her? Everything she thought she knew about her was a lie. She had to get used to that now. The old Sam was gone.

"Well, I'd better get going." Father Steve wiggled his way to the edge of the chair.

"So soon?" Jada turned up her lip.

"Yeah, this old man is tired. Haven't been up all night in, well, forty years." He chuckled. "But can you do me one favor?"

"Of course, Father Steve, anything."

"Just help an old man up. I think I pulled a muscle when I leapt for Holdan's rifle." A playful grin made his face glow. Jada stood and gently placed her hand under his upper arm, lifting him effortlessly.

"Ha! Guess I asked the right person." He winked. "Are you available on an on-call basis?"

Jada laughed, and she and Lilah walked him to the door. Lilah wrapped his hand between both of hers and began to tear up. Something unspoken passed between them.

He turned to Jada. "Now you let me know if you need anything, and I mean anything, you hear?

"I will. Thank you, Father Steve."

She reached forward and gave him a long hug, then watched him tread down the driveway to his car.

"Well, why don't I go and make us some breakfast." Lilah rubbed her hands together.

"Sounds good, Mom."

Jada watched her mom sashay into the kitchen and pull a frying pan off the pot rack. Seth's words had been haunting her all morning. *You think your mom is innocent?* She knew her mom could never hurt anyone, but the rage and conviction in Seth's voice had made her think twice.

"What are you doing? Come over here." Nathan lifted his sculpted arm to the top of the couch and patted the seat next to him with his other hand. Father Steve's presence seemed to have eased the tension between Nathan and Lilah.

Jada bit her bottom lip and felt her neck grow warm. Walking back into the living room, she took in all six foot two inches of him and her stomach pulsed. She slid next to him and a wisp of his woodsy skin mixed with faint cologne filled her nose. Nothing could ever smell better to her in the world. His face was gentle now that they were out of danger, but his eyes still as wild as the first day she met him. Secretly, she hoped they'd always look like that.

Lilah peeked around the kitchen archway. "And Nathan, I want to see more of you. We should get to know each other."

Nathan's lips formed his signature grin, making Jada's heart quicken. "Thank you, Mrs. Bell." He locked eyes with Jada. "I plan on being here a lot."

CHAPTER 30

"Do you really need to do this?" Lilah's worried eyes met hers in the mirror.

"Yes mom, you know I do." Jada wrapped the last strand of her fishtail braid and wound a hair tie around the tip. "Most of the seniors will be at Rusty's in a few hours. Sam changed last night. If she is going to do something, it's going to be there. You know how she likes an audience."

"We never wanted this for you girls," Lilah said as she rubbed a kink in her neck. "You're supposed to be protecting each other, not fighting."

"I know, Mom. It makes me sad too. Maybe Sam will come around."

There was another reason she was going that her mom and Nathan knew nothing about. Jason.

They didn't know what she did to save him. She hadn't seen him since he came out of his coma. After finding out he was alive, she was relieved, but the vestige of his attack left her feeling violated. There was a rumor going around that not only was he completely healed, he was feeling better than ever. Jada had spent many hours worrying what that meant. *Better than ever.* She had a nagging feeling that something wasn't right. And it was going to be bad, really bad. What had her blood done to him? Was he furious with her for what she did to him in the alley? She had put the whole incident behind her. Although she and Jason could never be friends, she hoped they could at least coexist civilly for the remainder of the school year.

The doorbell chimed from the front of the house.

Jada arched her head to the side. "That's Nathan. Do you mind letting him in? I need one more minute."

Somehow, she needed to calm the storm building in her belly. If Sam used her powers tonight or Jason was there to seek his revenge, she needed to be ready. One final long breath, and she headed out of her room.

Nathan turned as she slipped her arm into her brown leather jacket. The corner of her lips curled up as he strolled toward her. Every day he seemed to get more handsome. A fitted striped shirt spanned his broad chest with a small portion of the front tucked into dark blue jeans. He had his hair behind his ears, which she loved, and those hungry eyes of his. For the first time, she understood what the term weak in the knees meant. She was sure he had no idea how attractive he was.

"*Please* be careful, and call me if anything goes wrong." Lilah gave Nathan a stern look. "I'm counting on you to protect my baby girl."

Jada rolled her eyes.

"I will, Mrs. Bell."

As Nathan drove, Jada tried to smother the nervous energy jittering through her muscles. Despite her attempts to be prepared for whatever was thrown at her tonight, she had no idea what to expect, and it was eating her up inside.

When they pulled into the parking lot, she scanned the familiar entrance to Rusty's. The long brick wall outlined a dingy window, and an array of colors from the glowing beer signs illuminated the sidewalk. Andrew and Ryan were propped against the wall on the other side of the door laughing about something.

"Are you all right?"

Jada rubbed her arms. "Yeah, I'm fine. Let's just go in."

Nathan pulled the key out of the ignition, and they both got out. The air was cool and thick with exhaust. A shiny black Harley rolled by, the popping of the engine floating into the night. She winced, and then jerked her hand to Nathan's chest, stopping them both.

"Wait. Is Seth here?" She was so worried about Sam and Jason, she had forgotten about him. Did he still hate her? She had been afraid to ask Nathan.

Nathan's eybrows pressed together, and he looked down. "No, he took off last night and didn't come home. We don't know where he went."

His face was strained, and Jada knew he had suffered for taking her side. She was sure Holdan would disown him and kick him out any day now, and he would blame Nathan if anything happened to Seth. She side hugged him as they walked up to the door.

Inside, a gust of hot, sour air hit her in the face. The place was packed from wall to wall, and the music was blaring. The whole senior class must be here. A tap on her shoulder separated her from Nathan's grasp.

"Hi, Jada."

"Lori?"

Jada hadn't seen much of Lori in the past few weeks. Ever since that day in the theater, she had practically become a hermit. Jada felt bad for what she'd done to her, with the maggots in the cafeteria and breaking her nose in PE. She was still hurt from how Lori had treated her all these years, but it was no excuse for what she had done.

"Jada, I never thanked you for pulling me out of the way when Mr. States crashed into the theater."

Jada couldn't believe what she was hearing. "Oh—uh, you're welcome."

"And for what it's worth, I'm sorry for how I've treated you all these years." Lori fiddled with the handle of her purse. "The truth is I've been jealous, jealous that Samantha always liked you more than me."

Jada opened her mouth but nothing came out.

"It's okay, Jada. That's all I came to say. I'll see you later?"

Jada nodded. "Sure."

When Lori walked away, Jada clung to Nathan's arm as they zigzagged their way to bar. "Did what just happened, what I think just happened?"

Nathan laughed. "Yeah . . . I guess people can change."

"Nathan, where have you been? Haven't laid eyes on you for weeks," Jagger called out. Everyone called Logan's dad Jagger. Jada still didn't know what his real name was. In his early fifties, his hair was still as black as Logan's. He gave Nathan a sideways smile and plunked a bottled *Coors* on the oak counter. He gave the boys beer but never more than two a night. His lively golden eyes shifted to Jada. "What can I get you, missy?"

"Just a cranberry juice. Thanks."

"Comin' right up." Jagger threw a white towel over his shoulder and flipped around. Jada took the moment to study the room, subconsciously listening to the sounds of clanking glass and swooshing behind her. It was too packed to see everyone from this vantage point. They would have to walk all the way through.

Grabbing her cranberry juice, they headed to the back of the bar where the pool tables were. No Jen. No Sam.

And no Jason.

"Looks clear." Jada's stomach unclenched a little as they headed back to the front.

Nathan put his hand in the small of her back and led her to the dance floor where a slow song was playing.

"I know this has been hard for you." His soothing voice came through the music.

"What has?"

"Losing your friends."

She leaned her head against his chest as they swayed, and her throat started to tighten. "Yeah. I never thought it would end up like this."

She allowed her muscles to relax, melting into Nathan's arms during the next few slow songs. As long as she had him, she could get through anything, even losing her friends.

"Let's go outside," Nathan whispered. He guided her through the crowd and out the heavy side doors. The night was clear, white stars scattered across a velvet black sky. They lowered themselves onto a bench with a clear view of the front door. If Sam showed up and started anything, they could be inside within seconds.

Jada had grown to love the night. Perhaps it had something to do with being a Nephilim. Having Edana's darkness in her now, she felt more comfortable with the black sky looking down at her. For just a moment, she let herself relax.

"Jada." Nathan slid his hand behind her neck. "I love you."

Her body stiffened with anticipation, her heartbeat loud in her ears. A tingling in her upper thighs made her let out a quick breath. His lip curved up into a sly smile. He was completely aware of what he did to her.

She jabbed her forefinger in his ribs. "You're enjoying this, aren't you?"

"Sure am." His eyes sparkled with mischief as he gently pulled her face toward his. When his lips met hers, Jada felt a hot current run throug her. Never had she even dreamed of a feeling this good. Warm, decadent, exciting. And now she could have it whenever she wanted. As their lips entwined, his body flexed under her touch, and his grip tightened. She pulled away slightly and laughed.

He unbuttoned the top of his shirt. "You're enjoying this, aren't you?"

"Mmm-hmm" was all she could get out before he pulled her lips into his again.

EPILOGUE

Knock. Knock. "Jennifer?"

Jen plugged a silver earring through her ear. "Come in, Mom."

Her door opened, jingling the bells draped over the doorknob. Her mom had put them there. Something about burglars, hearing when someone is coming. Her mom was paranoid. Nothing ever happened in Bishop.

"Wow, look at you." Hand on her hip, Alex smiled.

Jen looked down and pressed on the lavender mini dress. All the seniors were going to Rusty's. She should be going with Logan, but he had dumped her weeks ago. And with no good reason. She felt the usual pain start to build behind her eyes. What if he didn't even say hi to her? What if he was there with another girl?

"Honey, I know you're sad about Logan, but you should still try to have fun. I know you don't want to hear it, but relationships rarely last past high school. You'll find someone new in college."

Jen balled her hands into fists. "I don't want anyone else. And just because it didn't work for you and Dad doesn't mean it won't for me!" Alex smiled but Jen could see she'd hurt her. She sighed and looked back at her mirror.

"Well, I hope you have fun, sweetie. I'm going out to have dinner with some co-workers. I'll see you tonight." Alex clicked the door closed. Jen brushed away a tear and crossed her room to the window. The glass was cold against her fingers. She hadn't intended to hurt her mom. Alex was just wrong, and she needed to stop telling her it was over with Logan.

The bells jingled again.

"Good you haven't left yet, I'm sorry—" Jen stopped as the dark figure filled her door frame.

"Who's there?" Jen's heels clicked on the hard wood as she stood. Her eyes grew wide as the figure lunged in and grabbed her throat.

She tugged on his thick fingers, but they squeezed tighter.

Red Midnight

Chains of Darkness
~Book 2~

Now Available!

Samantha was popular; she always got what she wanted. So when Nathan chose her best friend Jada over her, she vowed revenge. Now that Samantha has become a Nephilim, she has the power to get Jada out of the picture and Nathan back for good. Meanwhile, as she battles Nathan's brother Seth for the title of Bishop High's decathlon champion, she starts to feel things for him she never imagined possible.

When her friends abandon her and her social status crumbles, she wonders if any of it ever mattered. In a final desperate attempt to win Nathan back, she turns to Jada's enemy Jason for help. But she underestimates his power and how deep his hate runs.

Will Jada save her after all Sam has done? Or will Sam die alone?

A Note to Readers

Thank you for reading *The Golden Hour*! If you enjoyed this book, one of the best ways to help me to continue writing is to leave a review on Amazon.

Thank you!

CC

If you want to learn more about me or check when my next book is coming out check out my website at: www.ccharwood.com.

Made in the USA
San Bernardino, CA
07 April 2020